SOME LIKE IT WILD

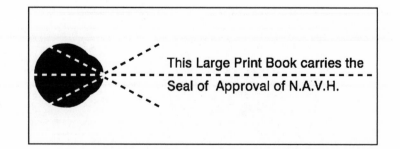

This Large Print Book carries the
Seal of Approval of N.A.V.H.

SOME LIKE IT WILD

TERESA MEDEIROS

THORNDIKE PRESS

A part of Gale, Cengage Learning

Detroit • New York • San Francisco • New Haven, Conn • Waterville, Maine • London

GALE
CENGAGE Learning™

Thorndike Press® Large Print Romance.
The text of this Large Print edition is unabridged.
Other aspects of the book may vary from the original edition.
Set in 16 pt. Plantin.
Printed on permanent paper.

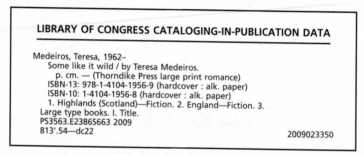

LIBRARY OF CONGRESS CATALOGING-IN-PUBLICATION DATA

Medeiros, Teresa, 1962–
    Some like it wild / by Teresa Medeiros.
      p. cm. — (Thorndike Press large print romance)
    ISBN-13: 978-1-4104-1956-9 (hardcover : alk. paper)
    ISBN-10: 1-4104-1956-8 (hardcover : alk. paper)
    1. Highlands (Scotland)—Fiction. 2. England—Fiction. 3. Large type books. I. Title.
PS3563.E2386S663 2009
813'.54—dc22   2009023350

Published in 2009 by arrangement with Avon Books, an imprint of HarperCollins Publishers.

Printed in the United States of America
1 2 3 4 5 6 7 13 12 11 10 09

To the memory of Eric Myers. You were the rarest of creatures — a natural athlete and a gorgeous geek who loved volleyball and *Star Wars* equally. Nobody imitated Christ more gracefully than you, dear friend. See you on the other side.

To Eric Medeiros — I'd always wanted a brother and then God gave me you, which means you should be careful what you ask for. Thanks for reading my books and letting me write at your house!

And for my darling Michael — my husband, my hero, and my heart. You make every day a grand adventure.

ACKNOWLEDGMENTS

Without my devoted readers, neither this book nor any other would be possible. I cherish your letters and e-mails and your bright, shining faces at my book signings. Thank you for opening your hearts to my characters and for making the story of my own life such a joyful one by allowing me to tell you the stories I've been given to tell. I treasure each and every one of you.

CHAPTER 1

The Scottish Highlands
1814

"I need a man," Pamela Darby proclaimed with the same matter-of-fact conviction she would have used to announce "I need a scrap of lace to mend my hem" or "I need a fresh turnip for tonight's stew."

From the coach seat opposite her, her half-sister Sophie glanced up from studying her worn copy of *La Belle Assemblée*. The periodical was two seasons out of date, but that didn't stop Sophie from sighing over its colorful fashion plates or poring over its recommendations for the rouge most likely to grace a young lady's cheek with a flattering hue.

"What I need — what *we* need," Pamela amended, "is not just any man, but some strapping Scots lad with more brawn than brains." She deepened her voice, faking a burr that would have done Bonnie Prince

Charlie proud. "A lad easily led by two canny lasses with more wits than he."

"And I'm guessing those lasses would be us?" Sophie ventured, cocking a knowing eyebrow. She winced and wiggled on the battered cushions as the coach shuddered and began to grind its way down another rocky trail that insulted their intelligence by calling itself a road. "Just how do you propose we find this handsome dullard? Should we ask the coachman to stop at the next village and post a broadsheet?"

Trusting that her sister would play along with her silly scheme, if only to pass the long hours on the road, Pamela bit her bottom lip. "Hmmm . . . that's not a bad idea. I hadn't considered a broadsheet. How about one that reads, 'WANTED: Thick-Witted, Thick-Necked Scotsman to Masquerade as Duke's Long Lost Heir.' Perhaps we could nail one up in the market square of each village we pass through."

"Just like that one we saw in the last village, warning us that there's a dangerous highwayman with a price on his head terrorizing these very roads — robbing travelers and ravishing innocent women?"

Sophie's mocking words brought Pamela's flight of fancy crashing down on the jagged rocks of reality. She remembered that broadsheet only too well. A crude sketch had accompanied it, depicting a masked man with a rugged jaw, a pistol in his hand and a ruthless light in his eyes. She had been drawn to it against her will, her fingertips lightly tracing the incongruous dimple set deep in his right cheek. She could not help wondering what would drive a man to defy both the law and God's commandments by stealing what he wanted instead of paying for it. When Sophie had approached, Pamela had quickly turned away from the broadsheet, afraid her sister might find an echo of her own growing desperation in the highwayman's steely gaze.

The memory of that gaze sent a faint shudder down her spine. She was painfully aware that two women traveling alone through these wild and rugged climes could easily become the target of more than just mild suspicion and disapproving glances. But they hadn't the means to employ maidservants to give them an air of respectability or outriders to protect the carriage they'd hired after disembarking from the public coach in Edinburgh. They would simply have to depend upon the elderly coachman and his ancient musket to defend both their lives and their virtue.

She forced an airy smile. "From what I've

11

heard about these Highland savages, they're more inclined to ravish their sheep than their women." She ran a hand over her reticule, deriving her own comfort from what she'd tucked away in the little silk purse.

Twirling one of her curls around her forefinger, Sophie sighed. "I still can't believe we've come all this way for naught. You heard that old crone in Strathspey. According to her, the duke's heir died nearly thirty years ago, when he was still a babe. Neither he nor his mother survived their first Highland winter."

"I can certainly understand why," Pamela muttered, tucking her hands deeper into her fur muff. She had been even more dismayed than Sophie to discover that the trail they'd been faithfully following for the past month had gone cold. Colder even than this god-forsaken country where the wind whipped right through you — even when the sun was shining. Colder than the icy drops of rain that began to pelt you the second you decided it was safe to put away your parasol. Colder than the dampness that sank deep into your bones, making you feel as if you'd never truly be warm again.

"Why don't we just forget all about the reward and go home?" Sophie suggested.

"A sound plan indeed . . . if we still had a home."

As a mist of sadness dimmed the sparkle in Sophie's light blue eyes, Pamela immediately regretted her sharp tone. Until six months ago, the Crown Theatre off of Drury Lane had been the only real home either one of them had ever known. They'd both been born backstage and pronounced 'very fine productions indeed' by their actress mother. But now the theater was gone, reduced to rubble and ash by the same tragic fire that had killed their mother and would have killed them as well had they not been sleeping in their nearby lodgings at the time. Pamela's throat tightened around a bitter and familiar ache. Her only comfort lay in knowing that their mother had never wanted to outlive her legendary beauty — or its devastating effect on her admirers.

A beauty that survived in the pale shimmer of her half-sister's curls. Curls trimmed in a fashionable bob that perfectly framed Sophie's heart-shaped face with its Cupid's bow of a mouth and enchantingly *retroussé* nose. It was whispered among the opera dancers that Sophie's father had been a wealthy French *comte* who had found their mother both *charmant* and *ravissant.* That he had lost his heart, only to return to France and lose his head before he could offer for their mother's hand.

Pamela was convinced her own father must have been sturdy English stock. How else to explain both hair and eyes that were a perfectly ordinary shade of brown? Her features were even in her oval face but hardly memorable, and the pleasing hint of plumpness in her cheeks would have looked equally at home on a Yorkshire dairymaid. She'd curves enough to tempt a man's eye, but nothing that would inspire him to prove his devotion by casting himself off of London Bridge into the icy-cold waters of the Thames, as one of their mother's more passionate lovers was rumored to have done.

Pamela regretted her careless words even more when Sophie lifted her pointed little chin, setting her jaw to hide its faint quiver. "The duke's reward isn't our last hope, you know. It is well within my power to provide for the both of us. The viscount's offer still stands."

Pamela scowled. "This isn't some overwrought gothic melodrama. I've no intention of selling my sister's virtue to the highest bidder just to keep a roof over my own head."

Sophie lifted one slender shoulder in a

14

shrug artfully designed to confirm her Gallic heritage. "You needn't be so provincial. *Maman* chose a life free from the conventions of society. Why shouldn't I?"

"Mama always had the stage. She sold herself for love, not money."

"Is it so impossible for a woman to have both?" Sophie asked wistfully.

"Oh, you might have them for a season in the viscount's arms. Until he tires of your charms, grows infatuated with some young opera dancer and decides to pass you on to one of his friends." Pamela reached across the gap between them and tenderly tucked a wayward curl behind Sophie's ear. "I'm not trying to be cruel, darling, but it's a very short path from mistress to whore. I've seen girls even younger and more beautiful than you plying their wares down on Fleet Street. I won't have you dying of the French pox before your nineteenth birthday."

"But the viscount swears that he adores me! That ever since he saw me in the chorus of *Pygmalion* when I was fifteen, he can think of nothing and no one else."

"Including his wife," Pamela said dryly.

Sophie's face fell at that stark reminder.

Pamela squeezed her gloved hand. "Don't give the blackguard another thought. If we can't collect the duke's reward, we'll simply give the stage another go."

Sophie's delicate nostrils flared in a glum snort. "Then we're destined to starve in the gutter."

While her sister ducked behind the periodical to mope, Pamela settled back among the cracked leather squabs with a sigh, all out of both cheer and convincing arguments. Unfortunately, their mother had been as impractical as she was beautiful. Upon discovering from the solicitor that she had left them nearly penniless, Pamela and Sophie had sought to make their fortunes in the only way they knew how — on the stage. But their one attempt to tread the boards had begun in triumph and ended in disaster.

Sophie's ethereal beauty had captivated the audience, generating gasps when she first floated onto the stage. But that spell had been broken the minute she opened her mouth and began to recite her lines in a delivery so wooden that one critic had suggested the manager should have nailed her into her coffin to prevent her from taking the stage. All their dreams of fame and fortune had died in a hail of rotting vegetables and shouted insults. They'd been forced to pack up their belongings that very night and flee the theater one step ahead of a howling mob.

They'd been running ever since. If they didn't find some way to plump up their purses before returning to London, their next stop wouldn't be the theater, but the workhouse.

Pamela gazed out the carriage window at the gathering gloom of twilight. There was much more at stake than even Sophie realized. But she couldn't bear to burden her sister with the ugly truth. Clouds drifted over the distant crests of the mountains like the ghosts of all her fears. Weary of facing them alone, she allowed the rocking of the coach and the growing weight of her eyelids to lull her into a restless doze.

Pamela awoke to the same sounds she'd heard in countless productions through the years — the crack of a pistol, followed by the bold cry of *"Stand and deliver!"*

"Did you 'member to light the flash pots, Soph?" she murmured without opening her eyes. "And don't f'get to bring down the curtain after the villain is vanquished."

She was sinking deeper into both the squabs and her dreams when a sharp claw bit into her shoulder and gave her a harsh shake. "Pamela! *Pamela, wake up!* We've been set upon by bandits!"

Pamela's eyes flew open to meet her sister's frantic gaze.

The carriage was no longer rocking, but had lurched to a shuddering halt. One of the horses let out a nervous whicker, which then subsided into ominous silence. Full dark had fallen while Pamela napped, and the window was veiled by a velvety-black curtain of night.

She sucked in a breath laced with raw panic. What if the coachman could no longer be relied upon to defend their virtue or their lives? What if he was lying in a limp heap in the middle of the road, a ragged hole blasted through his scrawny chest?

Swallowing her terror, she touched a finger to her lips, then clutched at Sophie's gloved hands. They huddled together, holding their collective breath to listen.

The silence seemed to swell and thicken. It was finally broken by the measured tread of footsteps moving around the side of the carriage. Perhaps it was simply the coachman coming to tell them that all was well, Pamela prayed. That the pistol report and the chilling cry had been nothing more than a prank played by village lads with more spirit than good sense.

But the muffled footfalls made a mockery of that cheerful thought. It took both grace and practice to be able to navigate such a road without disturbing a single rock. And anyone who had mastered that skill could just as easily slit a man's throat for his purse or creep into a woman's bedchamber in the dark of night to put his hand over her mouth and have his wicked way with her.

Since it seemed there was to be no escaping the inexorable approach of those footsteps, Pamela gave Sophie's hand one last reassuring squeeze, then slipped her hand out of her sister's grip and into her reticule. As her fingers curled around the solid weight of the object within, they ceased their trembling.

The footsteps also ceased, leaving in their wake a silence that was even more chilling.

Pamela drew Sophie behind her with her free arm, waiting for the carriage door to fly open, waiting for a ruthless arm to reach in and yank her out by her hair.

The carriage door slowly creaked open on its hinges. There was no sign of their attacker. There was nothing but a yawning maw of darkness that threatened to swallow them whole.

A voice came out of that darkness, laced with gravel and menace. "I know you're in there. I can hear you breathin'. Step out of the carriage with your hands raised or I'll blast you straight to hell."

Pamela could feel Sophie pressed to her back, trembling like a baby bird in the talons of some fearsome predator. It was the scent of her sister's fear that tightened her jaw and stiffened her spine. This faceless bully might be able to rob her of her life and her virtue, but there was one thing she'd always been able to lose without anyone else's help — her temper.

Ignoring the frantic clutch of Sophie's hands on the back of her skirt, she lurched forward and went spilling out of the carriage.

She tripped over the hem of her pelisse but quickly righted herself, straightening her crooked bonnet with a furious jerk. "For the love of God, sir, who writes your dialogue? I've never heard such atrocious tripe. 'Stand and deliver'? 'Step out of the carriage with your hands raised or I'll blast you straight to hell'? Why, you wouldn't last through one performance on Drury Lane! They'd bring the curtain down on your thick head before the end of Act One. Has it never occurred to you that you might make a more convincing villain if you didn't spout such horrendous drivel?"

As the angry ringing in Pamela's ears subsided, she realized she was standing nearly toe to toe with a faceless shadow. A faceless shadow that towered over her by more than a foot. The imposing expanse of his shoulders blocked out the light of the rising moon.

His silence was a weapon all its own, so effective that she nearly jumped out of her skin when he finally said, "What would you prefer, lass? Should I blast you to hell first and spout the drivel later? I fear it would be even less convincin' without an audience to appreciate it."

His mocking burr was as rough as burlap, yet soft as velvet. It was like having both the rose and the thorn dragged across her quivering flesh at the same time.

Pamela inched sideways, thinking to lure his attention away from Sophie and the carriage door. But she had cause to regret the motion when he shifted his own weight, inviting the moonlight to spill over the long, polished barrel of the pistol cradled in his hand. The weapon rested there as if he'd been born to wield it.

Too late, she remembered the poor coachman. She glanced toward the front of the carriage to find him sprawled in the road just as she had feared. A sharp cry of dismay escaped her. She lifted the hem of her skirts and took an involuntary step toward him.

The highwayman blocked her way, his silent grace more menacing than another man's shout. "He's not dead. He'll come 'round after a while with nothin' more than an achin' head and a story to tell his mates down at the tavern while they buy him a few pints."

As if to prove his words, the coachman stirred and uttered a weak groan. Pamela glanced at the coach box. His musket was still neatly sheathed in its holder. He'd never even had a chance to draw it.

Emboldened by relief, she glared up at their assailant. "What a fine profession you've chosen for yourself, sir! Assaulting old men and frightening helpless women."

He took a step forward, bringing them so close she could feel the heat radiating from his body through the fabric of his shirt. "You don't seem very frightened, lass. Or very helpless."

In truth, she was terrified. But she hid her terror behind a disgruntled sniff. "I've simply never been able to abide a bully."

"And what makes you think I chose this 'profession'?" His voice was a mocking caress that made the delicate hairs at her nape shiver with reaction. "What if it was thrust upon me by cruel fate?"

"We all have choices to make if we want

to be masters — or mistresses — of our own fate."

"And are you mistress of yours?"

His gently barbed words struck an unexpectedly tender target. After her mother's death, she had quickly discovered that without means or a male protector, a woman was at the mercy of this world. All she could do was sit back and watch her choices vanish one by one along with her dreams.

Even when her mother had been alive, Pamela had been subject to her mama's mercurial moods, her baby sister's needs and demands. She'd always been the one left to pick up the pieces of her mother's numerous broken hearts, scrimping and scheming to make sure the family didn't end up in the streets between productions when times were lean and her mother's lovers disappeared.

"Not at the moment," she admitted. "But then I'm not the one with the gun in my hand."

"What if you were? Would you be willin' to surrender it to the first man — or woman — who branded you a bully? Maybe I made my choice a long time ago, when I decided I didn't want to go hungry and barefoot while the English and their coffers grew fat on riches that rightly belonged to the Scots."

"But surely you must see that it's only a matter of time before you're brought to justice."

"When an Englishman robs a Scot of his land and his dignity, it's his God-given right. But when a Scot nabs an Englishman's purse, he's a dirty, thievin' criminal." The outlaw's snort came out of the darkness. "Where's the justice in that?"

Pamela brought her hands together in a round of dry applause. "Bravo, sir! I was wrong about you. Your passion adds a stirring note of conviction to your dialogue. If your weapon didn't happen to be pointed at my heart, I might even be tempted to cheer on your noble effort to relieve me of my purse."

He surprised her by slowly lowering the pistol to his side. Oddly enough, the gesture didn't make him look any less threatening. Her heart began to beat faster. Perhaps he'd decided to punish her for her scorn by strangling her with his bare hands.

She couldn't see his eyes, but she could still feel his gaze against her skin — as forceful as a touch. With all of his fine talk about the oppression of the Scots, she would have expected him to be wearing a kilt and carrying a shiny claymore or a set of bagpipes. But he was garbed all in black — the midnight shade of his shirt, breeches and boots making him nearly indistinguishable from the night.

She took an experimental step backward, then another. He followed, shadowing her every move. She continued to back away from him, wondering if there was some way to use their dangerous dance to her advantage. If she could lure him away from the carriage door, perhaps Sophie would be clever enough to slip out and run for help.

Or for her life.

Pamela stole a glance over her shoulder at the sweeping arms of the towering Caledonian pines bordering the rocky trail. There was only one sure way to distract him. One chance for Sophie to make her escape.

Knowing she might very well earn a pistol ball in the back for her efforts, Pamela spun around to run.

She had barely taken two steps when the highwayman seized her wrist and roughly jerked her around to face him. She stumbled over a rock and right into his broad, unyielding chest. She shook her hair out of her eyes and tipped back her head to glare at him, anger once again foolishly displacing her fear.

For the first time, the moonlight shone

full upon his face.

Pamela froze, all of her schemes for escape forgotten.

The narrow slits in his black leather half mask revealed eyes as luminous and silvery gray as the light of the moon. Pamela was close enough to count each of the thick lashes that framed their striking depths. His nose was strong but slightly crooked, as if he'd started more than his share of tavern brawls.

Although it was no struggle for him to subdue her with just one hand, he was breathing hard and his jaw was clenched as if he was doing battle with some enemy neither of them could see.

It was a rugged jaw with an unlikely dimple set deep in his right cheek. At the moment his mouth was set in a stern line, but it wasn't difficult for Pamela to imagine the devastating effect that dimple might have on a woman's heart should he smile.

Her breath caught in her throat. She was just as powerless to resist its charm as she had been when gazing upon the broadsheet in the village. Some might argue that the crudely drawn sketch could have been any one of a dozen men, but Pamela would have recognized its subject anywhere.

He held himself as still as a granite statue

as she lifted one trembling hand and lightly brushed her fingertips over his cheek. The broadsheet had been cool to the touch; his cheek was warm and rough with a day's growth of stubble.

His indrawn breath was both sharp and audible.

"I saw the broadsheet in the village," she confessed, lifting her gaze shyly to his eyes. "If they catch you, they have every intention of hanging you."

"Then perhaps it's time I stole somethin' worth bein' hanged for," he replied, his voice a husky rumble she felt all the way to the tips of her toes.

"Such as?" she whispered.

He lowered his gaze to her lips, giving her the answer she both feared and longed for.

His grip on her wrist gentled; the callused pad of his thumb caressed her fluttering pulse. He closed his eyes and lowered his mouth to hers, his lips no longer stern but soft and warm with invitation. They played over hers with a deliberate tenderness that was far more dangerous than force.

Pamela was well acquainted with the art of the stage kiss. How its purpose was to convey passion without actually provoking it. This was accomplished with the merest brushing of lips — neat and dry, with no communion of hearts or souls.

Which was why it came as such a shock when the highwayman boldly breached the seam of her lips with the rough, silky heat of his tongue. There was nothing neat or dry about his kiss. His tongue swirled over hers — tasting, teasing, tantalizing — urging her to take him deeper inside of her with each maddening pass of his mouth over hers. He smelled like freshly crushed pine needles and wood smoke and tasted of whisky and danger.

Too late, she realized she was no longer his prisoner. She had no recollection of him freeing her wrist, yet somehow both of her hands had ended up flattened against the muscular contours of his chest. Her palms measured each thundering beat of his heart as if it were her own.

Despite his threat, he hadn't yet committed a hanging offense. Her kiss was not stolen after all, but freely given. And given with such generosity and enthusiasm that no court of law in the land would dare to convict him.

He threaded his fingers through the thick coils of her hair, knocking her bonnet away until it was hanging down her back by its velvet ribbons and tilting her head back to allow him to take even more shocking liberties with her mouth.

In that moment, she forgot Sophie, forgot all about their doomed quest for the duke's heir, forgot they were only a few shillings away from utter ruin, forgot everything but the utter joy and madness of kissing a highwayman in the moonlight.

Until a shrill shriek pierced the pleasant roaring in her ears and a fluttery, pink object came crashing down on his head.

CHAPTER 2

In his twenty-nine years of life, Connor Kincaid had been shot twice, stabbed three times and nearly drowned in the rushing waters of a burn. He had survived a botched hanging and had both his nose and his ribs broken in brawls more times than he could count. But he could honestly say he'd never been assaulted by a shrieking virago wielding a parasol.

The assault might not have been so startling if he hadn't been rendered deaf, dumb and blind to everything but the intoxicating taste of the woman in his arms. The thick coils of her hair played through his callused fingers, trapping him in a web of silk. Her breathless sighs were like a song only he could hear. The eager press of her hands against his chest betrayed both innocence and hunger — tempting him to steal the one and satisfy the other. He was a kiss away from carrying her into the forest, laying her back on a bed of moss and doing just that when reality came crashing down on his head in the form of something frilly and pink.

Had his assailant been armed with a pistol instead of a parasol, she could have shot him in the back with equal ease. It would be no more than he deserved for being such a careless fool. He had learned long ago that fate was a heartless mistress, who would simply laugh in his face if he escaped the hangman's noose only to be shot dead for stealing a kiss.

"Unhand my sister, sirrah!" his attacker shrieked, her delicate arm rising and falling as she continued to beat him about the head and shoulders with her makeshift weapon.

Connor wheeled around and raised one arm to ward off the blows. Since the parasol was trimmed with feathers, it was like being attacked by a flock of bloodthirsty pink sparrows.

As she landed a savage blow to his right ear, Connor roared an oath and instinctively raised the pistol in his other hand.

The girl went stumbling backward, still clutching the parasol. Before he could gather his scrambled wits, the woman whose kiss could have cost him his life darted out from behind him and threw herself in front of his attacker so that his pistol was once again leveled at *her* heart. Her striking amber eyes had lost none of their defiance, but her entire body was trembling with reaction.

The sight of the two women cowering before him only sharpened the edge of his temper. He'd never had much of an appetite for bullying women, but when word had reached his ears that two Englishwomen draped in jewels and furs were traveling these roads without the protection of armed outriders, he had been unable to resist the temptation. He had planned to rob them and send them on their way, confident that they could easily coax their wealthy fathers, husbands or lovers into replacing what he took from them. But just a few seconds earlier he had been considering taking something that could never be replaced.

He glared right back at the woman for a moment, resenting her for making him feel like the villain he was, then slowly lowered the pistol, tucking it into the waist of his breeches.

" 'Unhand my sister, sirrah'?" he echoed. "And you dare to scold me for spoutin' drivel!" He flung a finger toward the wee blonde peeping over her shoulder. The girl's cornflower blue eyes were as round as saucers. "Who writes *her* dialogue?"

Before either of them could react, he stalked over and snatched the parasol from the blonde's hand. He slammed it down over his knee, snapping it neatly in two. As he flung the pieces into the forest the girl had the nerve to look crestfallen, as if he had just beheaded her favorite doll.

Shooting him an equally reproachful look, the brunette with the tart tongue and the honeyed lips gently took the girl by the shoulders. "How could you have been so foolish, Sophie? You could have gotten us both killed."

"I'm sorry, Pamela," the girl replied, wrinkling her pert nose at Connor, "but I wasn't about to just stand by and let some barbarian ravish my sister."

At Sophie's words, Pamela lowered her lashes and stole a look at the barbarian in question. He was watching their exchange, his arms folded over his chest. Oddly enough, his smoldering glare and the sulky set of his jaw only served to make him *more* attractive. She could hardly accuse him of attempting to ravish her when she had not only allowed his kiss, but welcomed it. If he had dragged her off into the woods and had his way with her, she would have had no one to blame but herself.

A damning mixture of dismay and shame flooded her. She'd always prided herself on her restraint where the male sex was concerned. What was to become of them if she had inherited their mother's weakness for a pretty face and a brawny shoulder?

"There was no need for you to risk your parasol or your life defending me. I was in no danger whatsoever," she lied, tearing her gaze away from his face with more difficulty than she cared to admit.

Sophie blinked up at her. "Well, I know you told me that most Highlanders were more inclined to ravish their sheep than their wom—"

Pamela clapped a hand over her sister's mouth. "You must have misunderstood me. I simply said they prefer women who are more . . . docile."

She stole another nervous glance at the Scotsman. His eyes didn't betray so much as a spark of amusement, but she could have sworn his dimple deepened.

"I was simply trying to distract the man so you could make your escape," she told Sophie before releasing her and turning stiffly to face the highwayman. "I can assure you, sir, that I am not in the habit of kissing strangers. Or highwaymen," she added as an afterthought.

His stony expression never wavered. "Oh, I believe you, lass."

She frowned. How did he know she wasn't in the habit of kissing? Was it because she was a dreadful kisser? Was he secretly horrified by her lack of restraint? Was she supposed to keep her lips pressed tightly together when he sought to part them with the silky heat of his tongue?

Determined to seize the remaining shreds of her dignity before they could completely unravel, she said, "I suppose it's a bit late for formal introductions, sir, but my name is Pamela Darby and this is my sister, Sophie."

Well-schooled by years of helping their mother practice stage cues, Sophie stepped forward and executed a flawless curtsy. As she straightened, she tossed back her buttery curls and gave her silky golden lashes an extra flutter. Sophie was just like their mother in that respect. She couldn't help preening in the presence of any male — even a villainous cutthroat. As an *enfant terrible,* she'd kept every man in the theater — from the loftiest actor to the lowliest stagehand — wrapped around her pudgy little pinkie.

Pamela sighed, waiting for the highwayman to succumb to her sister's spell. It had felled far mightier men than he. Pamela knew all of the signs — the leaden clumsiness of the limbs, the dazed look in the eye, the awkward stammering of the tongue. Once a man was blinded by the glamour of Sophie's beauty, Pamela knew that she would fade into the backdrop, no more substantial or interesting than a potted palm painted on a stretch of canvas.

To her surprise, the highwayman barely flicked a gaze in her sister's direction. His glittering eyes remained locked on her as he sketched them a bow that was surprisingly graceful given his imposing size. " 'Tis a pleasure to meet you and your bonny sister, Miss Darby. I'm the man who's goin' to relieve you of your valuables and be on my way."

As if to remind them all of the highwayman's nefarious goal, the coachman groaned and struggled to a sitting position on the edge of the road, blood trickling from a shallow cut above his eyebrow. Without batting an eyelash, the highwayman tugged the pistol from the waist of his breeches and swung the muzzle toward him. The grizzled old man's hands shot into the air.

"And that's where I'll thank you to keep them until I've finished my business with the ladies," the highwayman said smoothly.

Keenly aware that they now had an audience for their little drama — Or was it a farce? — Pamela relaxed her arm so that the reticule still dangling from her wrist would sink into the folds of her skirt.

As she watched the highwayman cow the coachman with little more than a look, her thoughts veered into oddly philosophical territory.

Who really determined a man's destiny? Must it always be an accident of birth? A spin on the fickle wheel of fate? Was it not possible for chance and opportunity to collide and forever alter a man's course in this life?

Pamela didn't even realize her lips had curved in a thoughtful smile until she caught Sophie's bewildered glance. She clapped a hand over her mouth, struggling to look suitably terrorized as the highwayman tugged a burlap bag from his belt and marched back over to her, tucking the pistol in its place.

"Why don't we start with that ermine tippet, lass?" he suggested, holding out his hand.

Pamela reluctantly unwound the fur scarf from her throat, shivering at the sharp bite of the night wind, and laid it across his palm. He ran his hand over it, an avaricious glint in his eye. But when he reached the end, a fat clump of fur clung to his fingers.

"What in the devil is this?" he demanded, glowering down at the offending stuff with palpable revulsion. "Rat?"

Pamela sniffed. "Of course not. I'll have you know it's prime Hertfordshire squirrel."

Still scowling, he gave the garment an experimental shake. Fur flew everywhere, including up Pamela's nose. She made no attempt to stifle her sneeze.

Tossing the rapidly balding stole over a nearby bush, he growled, "Let's have a look at those ruby earbobs, shall we?"

"If you insist," she replied, tugging the earbobs from her delicate lobes and surrendering them to his hand. The gemstones glowed like drops of fresh blood against his broad palm.

As he studied them, the appreciative gleam in his eyes slowly faded. He lifted his gaze to hers. "These are paste, aren't they? Nothin' but worthless paste."

She shrugged. "I suppose it's possible. Unscrupulous jewelers have been known to take advantage of their more naïve customers."

He did not wait for her to hand over the diamond brooch adorning the lapel of her pelisse. Closing the distance between them with one step, he tucked his hand beneath her collar to hold the fabric steady while he deftly unfastened the brooch's pin with his nimble fingers. She shivered as his warm knuckles lingered against the vulnerable skin of her throat. Their gazes met and held for the space of a ragged heartbeat before he secured his prize and stepped away.

He didn't waste a precious second ogling the brooch. He simply tucked it between his lips and dug his teeth into it before hurling it away in disgust. "What sort of dangerous game are you and your sister playin', Miss Darby?"

"One we're determined to win," she replied, her hand inching toward her reticule.

He studied her through narrowed eyes for a moment, then held out his hand. "Give me your drawers."

Pamela's own hand froze. Behind her, she heard Sophie gasp.

"Pardon me?" Pamela asked, eyeing him with fresh suspicion.

During their years in the theater, she'd encountered several actors who delighted in donning feminine garb and playing the female roles in the pantomime. But this strapping Highlander hardly seemed the sort to drape himself in ruffles and lace and prance across a stage warbling a suggestive ditty.

"You heard me, lass. Drop your drawers and hand them over."

She gave him a withering glare. "How could I deny such a romantic request? With that quicksilver tongue of yours, you must be quite irresistible to the ladies."

This time the deepening of his dimple was unmistakable. "Oh, I've other tricks for gettin' them off you, but I don't you think you want me to show you those." He cut his eyes toward Sophie. "At least not right now."

Gritting her teeth in exasperation, Pamela turned her back on him only to find the coachman gawping at her, his knobby hands still thrust into the air. Muttering beneath her breath, she faced the woods and reached beneath her skirts. She was determined to deny the larcenous scoundrel so much as a glimpse of stocking or well-turned ankle. After much struggle, she finally managed to extract herself from her drawers by clutching the trunk of a nearby alder and hopping up and down on each foot in turn.

She turned to hurl them at the highwayman. "There! I hope you're happy, you odious, insufferable boor!"

He caught them neatly with one hand, no longer bothering to hide his smirk. "And just when I feared your affections for me were wanin'.'"

She averted her eyes from him, heat rising in her cheeks. Despite the sheltering layers of pelisse, skirts, petticoat and stockings, she still felt woefully exposed. It was almost as if the chill night wind was deliberately whistling its way beneath her hem and between her clenched thighs.

She stole a sullen look at the highwayman. At least she didn't wear ridiculous scraps of French silk like her mother had. Her drawers were sturdy English wool — decent, practical, and dull . . . just like her.

As she watched him examine the worn garment with far more care than he had shown the stole or the brooch, curiosity overcame her annoyance. "What on earth are you doing?"

"A woman can lie in a thousand different ways with her lips and her eyes, but not with her undergarments." He ran his hand along a recently darned seam until he reached a frayed hem. When he finally lifted his eyes to her, they were darkened by a mixture of disbelief and contempt. "Why, you're *poor,* aren't you?"

Pamela recoiled. He had bitten off the word as if it were the most damning of accusations — far worse than being charged

41

with accosting two helpless women in the wilderness.

One would have thought that being pelted with rotten cabbages and wormy potatoes while fleeing an angry mob would have squashed the last of her pride. But as she met this man's condemning gaze, she felt her spine stiffen and her chin lift.

"My sister and I may have fallen on difficult circumstances since our mother's death. That doesn't mean we're destitute."

"Oh, no?" He balled up her drawers and tossed them into the underbrush, then began to stalk her, backing her up with each step. "Then why are you wrappin' yourselves in dead rodents and wearin' paste jewelry? Why have your drawers been darned so many times they're fit for little more than the rag bin?" He kept right on coming until she backed into a tree, leaving her with no way to escape him, no way to catch a breath that wasn't laced with his smoky, masculine scent. "And why did you venture onto these roads with only a pathetic old man to protect you?"

"Eh!" the coachman brayed in protest.

"Hush!" Pamela and the highwayman snapped in unison, still glaring at each other.

The driver subsided into a sullen pout.

The highwayman reached to tuck a

tumbled coil of hair behind her ear, his voice deepening and softening until it was all velvet and thistles again. "Have you any idea what could happen to a bonny pair of lassies out here with no man to protect them?"

Pamela was trying to decide if that was a warning or a threat when Sophie piped up. "They could be set upon by a wicked highwayman and have their drawers stolen?"

He ignored her, all of his attention still fixed on Pamela. "Why are you pretendin' to be rich, lass?"

Pamela could feel her temper rising again. "Because people treat you differently if they believe you have means. They're kinder and more helpful and don't look at you as if you're about to nick the silver. They don't mock the shabbiness of your bodice or whisper that your bonnet has been out of fashion for three seasons. Perhaps we didn't care to be scorned — or worse yet — *pitied* by a man who's probably never earned an honest day's wage in his life."

"Oh, I tried earnin' an honest day's wage once," he replied, his face hard. "But it didn't take much more than a day of strugglin' to survive on the pennies they paid me to learn that I didn't care for bein' cold and hungry and barefoot. That I'd rather take

43

what I wanted without the by-your-leave of some fat English overlord."

Although Pamela was loath to admit it, his defiant words stirred her blood, as did the ruthless glint in his eye. In that moment, there was something almost *noble* in his bearing.

Her hand slid into her reticule. Before she could regain her sanity or lose her nerve, she drew out a pretty little pearl-plated pistol and leveled it at his chest, raking back the hammer with her thumb. "I hate to interrupt another stirring speech about Scots' rights and the tyranny of the English, but I'm afraid it's *my* by-your-leave you'll be needing from this moment on."

CHAPTER 3

The coachman squeaked in shock as the pistol appeared in Pamela's hand. "Why, ye've all gone mad as March hares," he cried, "the whole lot o' you!" Before any of them could react, he sprang to his feet and went scrambling down the hillside, abandoning coach, musket, horses, and paying customers without so much as a backward glance.

"If you weren't pointin' that pistol at my heart, lass, I might be tempted to agree with him," Connor said, eyeing the woman holding him at gunpoint with newfound respect.

With its dainty size and pearl plating, the pistol looked more like a feminine trinket than a weapon capable of blasting a hole through his chest and putting an end to his misspent life.

"Pamela, what on earth are you doing?" her sister demanded, looking even more shocked than the coachman had. "Have you lost your wits?"

"Hush, Sophie. I know exactly what I'm doing."

Connor nodded toward the weapon in her hand. A hand that was remarkably steady, he noted with reluctant admiration. "Then I suppose you also know a weapon that size only holds one shot."

She smiled sweetly at him. "At this range one shot is all I would need. So why don't you be a gentleman and hand over your pistol?"

He smiled back at her, just as sweetly. "If you want it, you'll have to come get it."

Her smile faded. Eyeing him warily, she inched forward until she was just within reach of the muscular arms he'd folded over his chest. She crept closer, forced to look up at him through a tumbled skein of hair. Several sleek coils tinted a rich, warm mahogany had spilled down from their pins to frame her face.

It was a perfectly ordinary face — as oval as a cameo with a straight, slender nose, a generous rose of a mouth and full cheeks. But those eyes . . . they sparkled like amber gemstones beneath the arched wings of her brows — glowing with intelligence, good humor . . . and a tantalizing hint of mischief.

With those remarkable eyes still locked on

his, she reached for the weapon tucked into his belt. As the back of her hand brushed the taut planes of his belly through the folds of his shirt, she wavered. He cocked one eyebrow, challenging her to continue. She was so close he could smell the intoxicating scent of lilac water wafting from her hair.

"Careful, lass," he murmured. "We wouldn't want that thing to go off, now would we?"

He felt the tensed muscles in his abdomen twitch with reaction as she closed her free hand around the heavy grip of his pistol and smoothly slid the long barrel out of his breeches.

She slowly backed away from him. He studied her, intrigued by the meticulous care she took to keep the muzzle of his pistol pointed at the ground until she could get it tucked safely into the crimson sash of her pelisse.

"What now, lass?" he quipped. "Shall I hand over my drawers?"

"No, but I'll thank you to remove your mask."

Connor felt all traces of humor flee his face. "What if I told you that none of my victims has ever seen me without my mask . . . and lived to tell the tale?"

She looked taken aback, but only briefly.

Lifting her chin, she said coolly, "I'd accuse you of spouting overwrought drivel again."

Connor held her gaze for a long moment, then reached behind his head with an impatient motion and jerked loose the strings binding the crude half mask. The scrap of leather fell away, exposing his face to the moonlight and her avid gaze.

This time she crept closer as if she were helpless to do otherwise. He stood stiffly at attention as she circled him, her pistol still held at the ready.

Sophie edged closer as well, but her horrified gaze was fixed on her sister, not on him. "I know what you're thinking, Pamela, and you *can't* be serious. This man is little more than a barbarian. Why, he would never do!"

"Do what?" Connor snapped.

"Are you so sure about that, Sophie?" Pamela asked, her eyes glowing with fresh excitement, her ripe, rosy lips parted ever so slightly. "Just look at him! He must be close to the right age. He has broad shoulders. A savage yet noble brow. A hint of arrogance in his bearing. An unmistakable air of command."

"Rope scars on his throat," Sophie retorted. "A chipped front tooth. Hair that hasn't been trimmed — or possibly combed — in months. And a brutish demeanor." She

48

hugged the shoulder cape of her woolen cloak tighter around her shoulders, shivering. "If I'm not mistaken, he threatened to murder us both only minutes ago."

Scowling, Connor ran his tongue over the jagged chip in his front tooth, remembering the bleak night when he had earned it. He wasn't used to listening to two women argue his merits — or the lack of them — right in front of him. He was starting to feel like one of the savage African lions King James had once displayed in the yard at Stirling Castle for the amusement of his guests.

"You have to use your imagination, Sophie," Pamela was saying. "After all, what separates the brute from the gentleman? The fashionable cut of his coat and breeches? The smoothness of his jaw?" Pamela eyed the wind-tossed sweep of Connor's hair with a critical eye. "The clever way his freshly trimmed hair curls against his collar?" She reached up and boldly swiped a smudge of dirt from his jaw with her fingertips. "Why, if you polished him up in the bath, I wager he'd be as grand as any of the dandies at White's or Boodle's!"

"Are you volunteerin' for the task, lass? Because if you are, you can give me back my gun. I'll go with you freely."

Instead of slapping him for his impertinence, Pamela simply smiled fondly up at him.

"He has a price on his head," Sophie reminded her. "Just how do you intend to smuggle him out of Scotland?"

"You heard him. No one who can identify him has ever seen him without the mask."

"No one alive, that is," Sophie said glumly.

Connor could hardly believe what he was hearing. "Am I to understand you two lasses are plannin' to abduct me?"

Pamela nodded, looking endearingly contrite. "I'm afraid so. At least for now. Once I explain our plight, I'm sure you'll be only too happy to accompany us to London."

A helpless bark of laughter escaped Connor. He had managed to elude the clutches of the law for well over a decade and now here he was being kidnapped by two flibbertygibbeted Englishwomen. And all because he hadn't been able to resist stealing a kiss in the moonlight.

"Sophie, fetch a length of rope from the coachman's box," Pamela commanded.

Although Sophie's gamine face was still scrunched up in disapproval, she scrambled to obey her sister.

Connor shook his head in warning. "If you think I'm just goin' to stand here and let a wee bit of baggage like her tie me up . . ."

"Don't be ridiculous," Pamela said primly. "She's going to hold the pistol. *I'm* going to tie you up."

Her movements brisk and efficient, Pamela accepted the rope from Sophie's hands and surrendered the delicate pistol into her sister's keeping.

Connor snorted. "The lass can't weigh much over five stone soaking wet. I doubt she has the strength to pull the trigger."

"Not a chance I'd want to take," Pamela replied, disappearing behind him, rope in hand. "Unless you're a gambling man, that is. Sophie has always had the twitchy temperament of a cat. I wouldn't make any sudden movements if I were you."

"If you really wanted to put the fear of God in me, why didn't you just give her a parasol?" Connor muttered as Pamela captured both of his wrists in her small but sturdy hands and began to wrap the length of rope around them.

After securing her knot with a tidy jerk, she retrieved the elegant little pistol from her sister and pressed it against his ribs. She gave him a slight shove, urging his feet into motion. But after only a few steps, she was the first to falter.

She bit her bottom lip and peered down the darkened road. Apparently, now that she had him, she wasn't quite sure what to do with him. Connor had several suggestions, any one of which would probably earn him a well-deserved pistol clout to the back of the head.

As the wind rose, sighing mournfully through the branches of the pines and bringing with it the unmistakable scent of rain, she was finally forced to turn to him, her reluctance visible. "It's only a matter of time before the coachman returns and brings the authorities with him. Is there somewhere nearby we could go to pass the night? Some sort of cottage or shelter?"

Connor ducked his head to hide his smile behind a curtain of hair, hardly able to believe his good fortune. Perhaps fate wasn't such a heartless witch after all.

"I might know of such a place. But you'll need to fetch all your things. I've a horse waitin' in the trees over there big enough to carry you and your sister."

"What about you?" she asked.

"It's not far. I can walk."

"Walk? Or *run?*" She narrowed her eyes at him, struggling to look menacing. "I should hate to have to shoot you in the back, you know."

"Why would I want to run? Now that you've got me all trussed up, I'm hopin' the two of you will decide to have your way with me."

Her blush gave him a wicked thrill of satisfaction. "I think not," she said lightly. "As I told my sister, I've heard you High-landers prefer your females to be more doc-ile."

He leaned down, bringing his lips danger-ously close to her ear before whispering, "You heard wrong."

Apparently, *not far* was Scottish for "we might arrive by dawn if we don't perish from the cold first" with *big horse* being synonymous with "shaggy monster the size of a small dragon." Pamela wouldn't have been the least bit surprised if the massive ebony beast lumbering beneath her and Sophie had sprouted wings and began to breathe jets of fire from his flared nostrils. Although the creature seemed perfectly content to plod along at a demure pace, Pamela feared he was just biding his time, patiently waiting for his master's signal to buck both she and her sister over the near-est cliff.

An exhausted Sophie had already dozed off against Pamela's back and was snoring in her ear. Fortunately, the horse was also large enough to bear the two modest trunks they'd rescued from the coach. Trunks that contained the remainder of their earthly belongings. Securing the trunks to the horse's broad flanks had been no easy feat without the brawny Highlander's help, but they'd finally managed it.

Celebrated actor John Kemble might be able to afford to bring real horses and even the occasional elephant on stage over at the Royal Opera House, but Pamela's previous experience with horses had been limited to those of the stick variety. The beast seemed large and dangerous and unpredictable to her . . . much like the man leading them deeper into the forbidding shadows of the forest and farther away from civilization with each of his long, confident strides.

She scowled at his broad back. Although their lengthy trek had led them over some wild and rocky terrain, he might have been enjoying an afternoon stroll through the pastoral climes of Hyde Park. Judging from his casual saunter, he could probably walk all night without breaking a sweat — even while leading a horse with both hands bound behind his back. As they scaled a particularly daunting hill that had Pamela clinging to the beast's shaggy mane for dear life, he even had the temerity to break into a whistle. The cheery notes drifted back to her ears, borne by the brisk wind.

"What, pray you, is that tune, sir?" she finally called out, hoping to silence him.

"A wee ditty they call 'The Maiden and the Highwayman,' " he replied.

She snorted. "Given your people's dour dispositions and fondness for the romance of tragedy, I'm sure they pledged their eternal love to each other, then met some gruesome and bloody end."

"On the contrary. The highwayman seduced the maiden into his bed only to discover she was a lusty wench who couldn't get enough of him." He tossed her a roguish smile over his shoulder. "He robbed her of her maidenhead and she stole his heart."

Pamela was thankful her cheeks had already been rubbed raw by the wind so he wouldn't see her blush. He resumed both his pace and his cheerful whistling, bringing the tune to an end with a trilled flourish.

Just when she had given up any hope of them ever reaching their destination, the trees began to thin and the wind to roar. They emerged from the sheltering boughs of the pines onto a broad shelf of grassy meadow.

Pamela gasped, the breath snatched right out of her lungs by the greedy fingers of the wind and the unexpected sight before her.

She had served her entire life at the altar of make-believe without ever once imagining that such a place could exist in the real world.

It was as if the castle before them had risen out of the sea itself, flung heavenward on its island of stone by some mighty pagan god. Moonbeams slanted through the gusting clouds, painting its walls, turrets and towers in a glowing wash of silver. She blinked at the magnificent sight, wondering if she, like Sophie, had somehow dozed off and slipped into a dream.

But a dream wouldn't explain the gooseflesh rippling across her skin or the briny scent of the sea in the air. It was no longer just the roar of the wind she was hearing, but also the thunder of the waves hurling themselves against the jagged cliffs surrounding the castle.

She had expected the highwayman to lead them to some ramshackle barn or perhaps one of the many abandoned crofters' huts they had passed on their journey. She most certainly hadn't expected . . . *this.*

Sophie awoke with a start. Her snore deepened to a wheeze as she too caught sight of their destination. "Oh, my!" she whispered. "Perhaps he's not truly a robber at all, but a king of some sort."

"Don't be ridiculous," Pamela replied. "Scotland hasn't had its own king for two centuries. King George is his liege, just as he is ours."

"Then perhaps he's a prince. A robber prince," Sophie suggested, the note of awe in her voice undiminished.

Pamela shifted her troubled gaze from the castle to their host, wishing she hadn't been the one to point out that there *was* a regal quality to his bearing.

As he tugged on the reins to urge the horse forward, she saw the narrow, meandering bridge of land that connected the meadow to the castle for the first time. Far below, the wind whipped the sea into a swirling mass of whitecaps pierced by jutting rocks.

Letting out a moan, Sophie clutched at Pamela's waist and buried her face against her back. "Tell me when we arrive. If we do."

Given the battering force of the wind and the dizzying height of their perch, Pamela should have been equally fearful they were about to plunge to their deaths. But their mount started forward with brisk confidence, no less sure-footed than his master.

They were halfway to the castle when icy needles of rain began to spill from the sky.

Before Pamela could tug up her bonnet to cover her hair, both the rain and the cloud that had spawned it were gone, blown on their way by a chill gust of wind. Instead of cursing the mercurial weather as she might have done earlier, Pamela threw back her head and laughed aloud, feeling a strange exhilaration at the beauty and wildness of it all. It was as if they were riding straight into a fairy tale on the wings of a dragon.

As a second cloud passed over the moon, bathing the highwayman in shadow, her smile slowly faded. It still remained to be seen if their guide was prince or ogre.

The great chasm between castle and land should have formed a natural moat impenetrable to men and the brutality of their cannons. But as they passed beneath what must have once been the castle gatehouse, Pamela saw that it had failed miserably in its duty.

The highwayman drew their mount to a halt in the courtyard of the mighty fortress. The once gentle moonlight now seemed harsh and unforgiving, spilling without mercy over the shattered walls and heaps of crumbled stone. It seemed the fairy tale castle was only an illusion after all, no more real than a painted backdrop in a production of *King Lear*. As she surveyed the ruins of what must have once been one of the crown jewels of the eastern coast, the pang beneath Pamela's breastbone felt oddly like grief.

Even in its advanced state of decay, there was no denying the melancholy beauty of the place. Although some chambers and towers appeared to be intact, all that remained of the castle's chapel was a lone wall overlooking the sea, its stark silhouette standing guard over a crumbling white cross hewn from limestone. Moss had crept over every inch of exposed stone, softening the jagged edges with a thick veil of green.

A gaping window that must have once housed a bell was set high in the wall. Pamela could almost hear the ghostly echo of its pealing, calling those who were long dead to worship or battle.

With nothing but the endless indigo sweep of sky and sea beyond the wall, it was as if they'd reached the edge of the world itself.

"What is this place?" she asked, lowering her voice to a reverent whisper without realizing it.

The rich timbre of the highwayman's voice paid its own respects to any lingering ghosts. "This is where Clan MacFarlane made their last stand against the forces of

Cromwell's army over a hundred and fifty years ago. Rather than let the castle fall into the hands of their enemies, they blew it up themselves — set the charges and went marchin' off into the night, their bagpipes wailin' a final farewell."

As she gazed around them at the heaps of rubble and the shattered dreams they represented, Pamela wanted to weep at the tragic waste of it all. "Are you one of these Mac-Farlanes? Were they your clan?"

A cloud skittered across the moon, casting a fresh shadow over his face. "I'm afraid my grandfather lacked both the courage and the scruples of old Angus MacFarlane. He sold out our clan at Culloden for thirty pieces of English silver."

An involuntary shiver danced down Pamela's spine. She'd never heard the word *English* uttered with such icy contempt. Before she could consider digging her heels into the horse's sides and making a mad dash for freedom, the clouds parted to reveal the highwayman gazing up at her, his expression guarded.

"So here we are," he said. "All the comforts of home. I'd help you down but . . ." He shrugged his broad shoulders to remind her of his bound hands.

"That's all right. We can manage," Pamela

assured him, throwing one leg over the horse's neck and sliding to the ground.

She would have kept right on sliding until she landed on her bottom if the highwayman hadn't stepped forward to brace her with his weight. She hadn't taken into account how long they'd been riding or how unaccustomed she was to such exercise. She clutched at his shirt, her thigh muscles quivering like a pot of jam. His chest felt as sturdy as a rock beneath her trembling hands, reminding her of those dizzying moments back at the coach when she had clung to him while he sipped tenderly from her lips.

"Thank you," she murmured, keeping her eyes lowered. She quickly untangled her fingers from his shirt, telling herself it must be the near tumble that had left her so breathless. As she stepped away from him, the bitter wind whipped stinging strands of hair across her eyes. "It's no wonder you Scots are such a hale and hearty lot. If you weren't, you'd never survive this climate."

"Once you get a wee dram of Scot's whisky in your belly, you'll discover the wind is nothin' more than God's breath whisperin' against your cheek."

He watched through heavy-lidded eyes as she lifted her arms to Sophie, hoping to spare her sister a similar embarrassment.

As soon as Sophie was settled safely on her feet, she drew the little pistol out of her sash and leveled it at him, hoping to regain their only advantage. His pistol was safely secured in the horse's saddlebag. "If you would be so kind as to lead the way, sir."

" 'Twould be my pleasure, lass," he drawled, offering her a mocking bow before turning away and striding into the shadows.

As they fell into step behind him, Sophie slipped a hand into hers and whispered, "Are you certain we're not making a terrible mistake?"

"No," Pamela whispered back, her own courage faltering as they followed him down a grassy path that brought them closer to the churning sea with each step.

At first she thought he was going to lead them right over the edge of those towering cliffs. But he shifted direction at the last minute, guiding them beneath a stone arch to a set of flat, narrow stairs that seemed to disappear into the earth itself.

"Watch your step," he warned them. "I can't catch you if you fall."

Nor could he catch himself if he stumbled, Pamela realized, fighting a twinge of guilt. But as he disappeared into the murky gloom, his steps were as sure and steady as they'd been in the forest. She and Sophie exchanged a nervous glance before following. The roaring of the wind soon faded. As they descended deeper into the earth, they were enveloped by an oppressive hush broken only by the steady drip of water on stone and the shallow rasp of their own breathing.

Pamela was beginning to wonder if the steps led straight down to the bowels of hell itself when she spotted a thin sliver of light below. The highwayman paused, waiting for them to catch up.

He nodded toward the broad oak door set deep in the stone wall. "Would you mind doin' the honors?"

Pamela closed her icy fingers around the iron handle and gave the door a push. It swung open easily, inviting them inside.

She brushed past the highwayman without a second thought, unable to resist the seductive lure of warmth and light. The chamber was no rat-infested dungeon as she had feared, but simply a long-forgotten vault to a tower that no longer existed. A fire crackled on a stone hearth set against the opposite wall. Pamela breathed a sigh of relief. The long, low-ceilinged room was not only warm and dry, but also cozy and welcoming.

That is, until the air resounded with the echoing clicks of a dozen pistol hammers being drawn back at once.

One by one, the men holding those pistols emerged from the shadowy corners, their eyes gleaming with lust, their lips twisted into delighted leers.

The largest of those men wore a silver hoop in one ear and a leather vest hanging open over his sun-bronzed chest. He looked Pamela and Sophie up and down with a jovial familiarity that made Pamela's blood curdle with dread.

Firelight glinted off the gold tooth set in the front of his mouth as his meaty lips split in a grin. "Och, Connor, and what have ye brought us tonight?" he inquired of their guide. "Bawds or brides?"

CHAPTER 4

"Neither," Connor replied, shaking the length of rope from his wrists as if it were a silken ribbon and neatly plucking the pistol from Pamela's hand. "If you want bawds or brides on this night, you'll have to hunt them yourself."

Pamela gaped at him in disbelief.

He tucked her pistol into his breeches and tipped her jaw closed with one finger. "Don't blame yourself, lass. I once used the same skills to escape the hangman's noose and his knots were much better than yours."

Pamela began to sputter. She couldn't have said why she was so outraged that he had foiled her one pathetic attempt at a kidnapping by leading them straight into a trap, but she was. "Why, you — you —"

"Blackguard?" one of the men provided.

"Rapscallion?" offered another.

"Swivin', whoremongerin' son of a —"

"That's enough," Connor snapped. "I

doubt the young lady needs any help comin' up with a vile-enough insult for me."

Pamela snapped her mouth shut and folded her arms over her chest. "He's right. There's no need to waste your breath. There is no insult vile enough for the likes of him."

The giant who had perused her and her sister with such glassy-eyed lust chortled with glee, a cloud of copper braids bristling around his head. "Oh, she's a spirited one, isn't she? I do love a spirited lass. I'll give ye a jar o' whisky and a pouch o' tobacco for an hour alone with her."

Pamela instinctively edged closer to Connor, preferring the devil she knew to this leering ogre.

Connor snorted. "And just what do you plan to do with the remainin' fifty-seven minutes, Brodie?" When the rest of the men burst into raucous laughter, Connor included them in his glare. "I'll thank you all to get your tongues back in your mouths and your pistols back in your breeches. The lass belongs to me."

That bold claim silenced the men and sent a peculiar shiver rippling across Pamela's flesh. One by one, both the grins and the pistols disappeared.

"What about the wee one, then?" Brodie asked, his voice rising to a childish whine that seemed at odds with his impressive girth and the beefy slabs of muscle that composed his upper arms. "I've no doubt ye could handle the both o' them with yer hands still tied behind yer back, but there's no need to be greedy, is there?"

Connor's face went so still that Pamela feared he was actually considering the cretin's request. She curled her hands into claws, fully prepared to launch herself at the first man who dared to lay a finger on her sister — even if that man was Connor.

Especially if that man was Connor.

"What I'd like you to do, Brodie," he finally said, "is take the 'wee one' into the next room and fix her a nice cup of hot tea with a splash of whisky to warm up her blood." When Brodie's expression brightened, he narrowed his stormy gray eyes in warning. "The lass is a lady and I'll expect her to be treated as such."

Brodie's broad face fell. Connor reached to draw Sophie forward. She dragged her feet and cast Pamela a beseeching glance, her eyes huge and her beautiful face as pale as wax.

"She won't come to any harm," Connor murmured, his smoky voice dangerously close to Pamela's ear. "You have my word on it."

Pamela had no idea why she was so inclined to believe him. Especially when he wasn't offering her any similar promises.

For Sophie's sake, she managed to dredge up a comforting smile. "He's right, dear. You must be chilled to the bone. Why don't you go and have a hot cup of tea with the nice man?"

"What about you?" Sophie asked, shooting Connor a worried look.

Pamela held her breath, waiting for him to proclaim that she too was a lady and would be treated with all the tender regard due to such a delicate and refined creature.

As his stony silence stretched, she was forced to fill it with a burst of high-pitched laughter. "Don't you worry your pretty little head about me. This will give me and Mr. . . ." She slanted him a questioning look.

"Kincaid," he volunteered.

". . . me and Mr. Kincaid a chance to discuss our business in private."

One of the men nudged the fellow next to him, his stage whisper clearly audible throughout the room. "The lass'll be walkin' bow-legged for a fortnight after discussin' her *business* with our Connor."

His friend nodded in agreement. "Aye, there's some that say the hangman had to let the lad go after he realized he couldna hang him no better than he was already hung."

As several of the men snickered, Pamela bowed her head, wishing desperately that she could sink through the stone floor.

At Connor's curt signal, Brodie stepped forward and offered Sophie his burly arm. One would have thought he was about to escort her into supper at a private ball in Mayfair.

"So are ye married, lass?" he inquired of Sophie as she gingerly tucked her hand in the crook of his arm. When she shook her head, still eyeing him warily, he beamed down at her, his gold tooth winking in the firelight. "Would ye like to be?"

Pamela sighed. She had rescued her sister from the viscount's lascivious offer just so Sophie could receive her first legitimate proposal from a randy bandit with a silver hoop in his ear and a tattoo of a wriggling serpent on his upper arm.

Connor sent the other men fleeing from the room with little more than a look. Although they muttered beneath their breaths and scuffed the stone floor with their booted toes as they filed out, they didn't seem any more inclined to defy him than the coachman had been. Apparently he didn't even require a loaded pistol to impose his will on others.

Which didn't bode well for her own future, Pamela thought grimly.

A future that grew even darker when Connor bent to scoop up the length of rope she had used to bind him. When he came for her, she stood her ground, knowing it would only embarrass them both if she tried to flee. She held herself stiff as a plank as he wrapped one powerful hand around her upper arm and backed her toward the wooden chair nearest the hearth with a grip that warned it would brook no disobedience.

One minute she was standing on her own two feet; the next she was landing in the chair with an undignified *plop*. He looked even larger looming over her in the firelight. She had to tilt back her head just to shoot him a defiant glare.

As he studied her through narrowed eyes, his capable hands toyed with the rope, wrapping one end around his right fist, then taking up the slack with his left. Pamela swallowed back an icy lump of fear, waiting for him to whip the rope around her wrists — or more likely her throat. She was helpless to hide her start of surprise when he tossed it to the hearth.

"I don't really think we'll have need of that, do you?" he asked, his voice as gentle as if he was speaking to a child.

Pamela let out a shuddering breath, knowing he was right. Given his superior strength and size, she could fight him to her dying breath and still be utterly at his mercy.

"Especially not when I have this," he added, drawing her delicate pearl-plated pistol from the waist of his breeches.

As he held the weapon up to the firelight, turning it this way and that, Pamela couldn't quite take her eyes off of it. Or him.

He admired the pistol's gleaming beauty from all angles. " 'Tis hard to believe such a bonny wee thing could be an instrument of death, is it not?"

She held her tongue, afraid to let out so much as a squeak. If he had bound her to the chair hand and foot, she would have been no less paralyzed.

He leaned closer, covering her with his shadow. She gasped aloud at the cool kiss of the pistol's mouth against her temple.

His voice deepened to a husky whisper as he stroked the barrel down her cheek to the curve of her jaw. "It's so beautiful, yet so dangerous. Much like its mistress."

The barrel brushed her trembling lips so softly she might have imagined it, then glided slowly downward to the delicate hollow at the base of her throat. She closed her eyes, feeling her flesh betray her by heating beneath that steely caress.

Her eyes flew open as the barrel of the pistol continued its downward slide, nudging the lapel of her pelisse aside until the mouth of the pistol was resting against the soft swell of her breast, directly over her stuttering heart.

Connor looked her dead in the eye.

And pulled the trigger.

A bouquet of colorful feathers burst from the pistol's muzzle while the music box concealed within its grip lurched into a bright and tinkling tune. Pamela flinched and let out a muffled shriek, her nerves completely undone by his wicked game.

Connor leaned back and blew across the mouth of the gun, ruffling the plume of feathers. His gray eyes sparkled with devilish amusement.

Pamela glared up at him, her heart still on the verge of pounding its way out of her chest. "How long have you known?"

"I began to suspect it was nothin' more than a toy when you were so squeamish about pointin' my own pistol at me."

"And if you had been wrong?"

He shrugged. "We wouldn't be havin' this conversation, now, would we?" As if unable to resist the temptation, he tickled her beneath her chin with the plume of feathers like a doting uncle trying to coax a smile from a surly baby.

Infuriated by his cavalier attitude, she smacked the gun out of his hand. It went skittering across the floor and struck the stone wall, its last tinkling note dying on an off-key whine.

"If you knew the gun was only a prop, then why did you allow yourself to be taken captive?"

He grinned. "I was still holdin' out hope you and your sister might ravish me."

The reappearance of his dimple only made her feel more peevish. "Why? Did your favorite sheep run away?"

The dimple vanished. He folded his brawny arms over his chest, deliberately deepening his burr. "Oh, we only dally with the livestock when we canna find a willin' woman."

"Or an unwilling one?" she snapped, regretting the words the instant they left her lips.

Their gazes collided and held until the smoldering heap of logs on the fire collapsed in a cascade of fiery sparks. Pamela was the first to look away.

When she finally spoke, her voice was low but steady. "Set my sister free. She doesn't deserve to be punished for my folly. See her to safety and I won't fight you. I'll . . . I'll . . ." — she swallowed and closed her eyes — "I'll do whatever pleases you."

Connor gazed down at Pamela's averted face, his wayward imagination providing lurid images of all the things she could do that might please him. A faint blush graced her cheek. She was an English rose, never meant to bloom in the stony soil of this wild and brutal land. And here he stood with the power to crush her tender petals — and her prickly pride — in his fist. The realization should have made him feel strong, invincible. Instead, he felt dirty and dangerous. Like a man who would tear a flower from the dirt just so he could watch it wither in his hand.

"That's a noble offer indeed, lass. And a very temptin' one as well. But I've no intention of throwin' your wee lamb of a sister — or you — to that pack of wolves in the next room."

He had to admire her nerve as she mustered up the courage to look him in the eye. "What about the wolf in this room?"

The wolf in this room had spent too many years paying for his pleasures with stolen coins and was starved for a morsel of something tender.

Afraid she would catch a glimpse of that hunger in his eyes, Connor dropped to one knee at her feet and began to unlace one of her kid half boots.

"What are you doing?" Pamela demanded of her captor, half afraid he would answer.

But he held his tongue and all she could do was watch helplessly as he tugged off her boot and set it aside. He rested the sole of her foot against his muscled thigh, the firelight picking out the streaks of honey in the warm maple sugar hue of his hair.

Her stockings were in even more shameful condition than her drawers had been. Her little toe was peeping out of the shattered silk, rosy with mortification.

As he tugged off her other boot, then encircled one of her slender ankles with his hand, she could feel her cheeks growing equally pink. Men weren't even supposed to see ankles, much less touch them. That's why so many of them delighted in coming to the theater, where they could gawk at the scantily clad opera dancers to their heart's content.

Pamela hadn't realized how cold and numb her feet were until Connor began to briskly massage the feeling back into them. Heat seemed to radiate from his touch, penetrating the threadbare silk of her stockings. As he pressed the broad pad of his thumb into the sole of her foot, she had to bite her bottom lip to keep from betraying herself with a moan.

He stole a glance at her face, a knowing smile playing around his lips. "You English never take the dangers of the Highlands to heart," he said as he began to subject her other foot to the same irresistible torture. "You may think your feet are just a wee bit chilled, but add the damp to the cold and before you know it, you've lost a toe or two."

Pamela sank deeper into the chair, her eyes drifting out of focus as the tension oozed out of her body and into his capable hands. If he kept stroking his thumb down the center of her foot in that provocative manner, she was going to be in danger of losing more than just a toe.

Her eyes snapped into focus. She sat up with a jerk, going as stiff as a marionette. It had happened again. She had succumbed to the lure of the sensual just as her mother would have done.

Yanking her feet out of his grasp, she tucked them beneath the hem of her skirts. "I'd rather lose a toe or two to the cold than have them nibbled off by a wolf."

Amused by Pamela's wary scowl, Connor rose and began to circle her chair. "And I'd rather be branded a wolf than a wolf in sheep's clothin'. Especially one wearin' fake furs, fake jewels and carryin' fake pistols. Is there anythin' real about you, Miss Pamela Darby?" He reached down to rub a shiny coil of her hair between his fingers, wishing he could forget how warm and real her mouth had felt beneath his when she had opened it to welcome his kiss. "Or is that even your name?"

"Of course it's my name! Our mother was the great stage actress Marianne Darby. Perhaps you've heard of her?"

She looked so hopeful that Connor bit back his sarcastic retort and instead said gently, "I'm afraid I haven't had many chances to attend the theater of late. You mentioned earlier that your mother had passed on, but where is *Mr.* Darby? Why hasn't your father locked you and your sister away in an attic or a convent . . . or perhaps an asylum?"

"There is no Mr. Darby," she informed him. "Unless you count my mother's father, and he died when she was still a babe."

Her matter-of-fact confession only served to remind Connor that he had once been blessed with two parents who adored him. "So after your mother died, you decided to journey to the Highlands and kidnap the first highwayman who crossed your path."

"Need I remind you, sir, that *you* were the one who accosted us," she said with an exasperated sniff. "We came here searching for a man, not a highwayman. And not just any man, but the heir to a vast fortune."

Connor dragged a second chair around to face her and sank into it. *Now* she had his attention. "How vast?"

"His father is one of the wealthiest noblemen in all of England. And one of the most powerful. The Duke of Warrick can command a dozen households of servants, a fleet of trading ships and most of the members of Parliament with nothing more than the snap of his fingers." She boldly snapped her own fingers beneath his nose to illustrate her point. "But none of his wealth or power has been able to win him the one prize he desires above all others — the return of the son who went missing nearly thirty years ago."

Connor frowned. "What happened to the lad? Did he run away? Was he kidnapped for ransom?"

"Neither. Apparently, when he was younger, the duke had a bit of a roving eye. Most pampered ladies are content to look the other way when their husbands stray, but not his duchess." An admiring glow warmed Pamela's amber eyes. "After she found the duke's mistress in their bed during a ball, she bundled up their newborn babe and ran away with him."

Connor's voice reflected his incredulity. "And the duke's been searching for the lad for nearly thirty years?"

"I believe he lost hope a long time ago, but he's recently redoubled his efforts."

"Why now, after all this time?"

"Because he's dying," Pamela said flatly. "His health has been declining for several years now, and according to gossip he has only months — if not weeks — to live. I'm convinced that's what prompted him to offer the reward."

"Reward?" Connor edged his chair even closer to hers. He knew all about rewards. There was a rather hefty one on his own head right now. He also knew a reward on a man's head didn't mean he was worth anything.

Pamela leaned forward in her chair, her eyes sparkling with excitement. "The duke is offering ten thousand pounds to anyone who can bring him proof that his son is still alive."

Connor let out a low-pitched whistle. "With a prize like that at stake, I gather you and your sister aren't the only ones out searchin' for the lad."

"That may be true, but we were the only ones searching in the right place."

"How can you be so sure of that?"

She tilted her head to study him. "I'd be a fool to trust a man like you, wouldn't I?"

"Aye," he agreed solemnly. "That you would."

She studied him for a few seconds longer, then shook her head. "I don't suppose any of it matters now that we've learned the truth."

Connor had believed his interest had reached its peak when the words *vast fortune* and *reward* had been introduced into the conversation. But he was wrong. As Pamela slipped a hand into the bodice of her pelisse, rooting around between the generous swell of her breasts, he sat up straighter in the chair, feeling the rest of his body snap to attention with equal fascination. He was on the verge of offering her his eager assistance when she finally drew forth a folded scrap of foolscap, yellowed with age.

She laid the paper in her lap, handling it with the utmost of care. "For almost thirty years, everyone has believed the duchess took the baby and fled to France, which is why all of the searches have been centered there." She tapped the paper with one neatly trimmed fingernail. "This document proves otherwise."

"What is it?"

"A letter the duchess penned the night before she ran away. A letter addressed to her dear childhood friend — a woman she could no longer acknowledge in polite society without fear of damaging her own reputation but who had always been her most faithful and treasured confidante — one Marianne Darby."

Pamela's amber eyes grew misty as she tenderly stroked the crumbling wax seal that had once shielded the letter from prying eyes. "This is the only document proving the duchess had no intention of ever boarding that ship for France. She confessed to my mother she booked that passage to France to deliberately mislead her husband, all the while planning to seek asylum with her maternal grandfather — a man who had once been a powerful laird in the Highlands of Scotland but —"

"— who had lost everything to the English," Connor finished for her. Too many stories had the exact same ending. Including his own. He nodded toward the letter. "How did you come by it? Did you find it among your mother's things after she died?"

Pamela's face hardened. "Her belongings

were all destroyed in the fire that killed her. The letter was presented to us by her solicitor upon her death." The corner of Pamela's mouth quirked in a rueful smile. "Unfortunately, it was all she left us."

"And your mother never received any other letters from this grand lady? Not even a note sayin' she'd arrived safely at her grandfather's house?"

"Not another word from her for all these years." Pamela shook her head sadly. "But now we know why. According to an old woman Sophie and I found in Strathspey, they never made it that far. It was a harsh winter and both she and the babe died of a fever somewhere near Balquhidder."

They were both silent for several minutes.

"Wouldn't this duke be equally grateful for proof of his son's fate?" Connor finally asked. "At least the poor man could die in peace, knowin' his search was over."

Pamela gave him a glum look. "Have you ever heard the old proverb about shooting the messenger? The duke has quite a fearsome reputation, and I'm afraid if we brought him ill tidings, he would be more inclined to have us tossed into Newgate, never to see the light of day again." Still clutching the duchess's letter, she rose from her chair and paced a few feet away before turning to face him. "That's why I thought that perhaps it would be far more charitable — and more profitable — to give him exactly what he's been looking for."

Her expression was so hopeful, so very winsome, that Connor could not resist asking, "And just what would that be?"

She smiled at him with all of the beguiling tenderness of a lover. "Why, you, of course!"

CHAPTER 5

As Connor sprang to his feet, Pamela took a step backward, thinking it might be wise to stay out of his reach until he'd had time to fully digest her words.

He glared at her accusingly. "So that's your game, is it, lass? You're thinkin' to set me up as an imposter so that when the truth comes out, *I'll* be the one rottin' away in Newgate while you and your precious sister make off with the reward." He raked a hand through his hair, dragging the windswept strands out of his face. "Why, I should have shot you when I had the chance!"

Pamela took another nervous step backward, thankful there were no firearms in the immediate vicinity. At least not genuine ones. "Now, Mr. Kincaid, there's no need for histrionics. Or gunplay. It would be a harmless-enough ruse. Why, we'd be fulfilling the dream of a dying man!"

Connor shook his head, visibly torn between disgust and admiration. "And they call *me* ruthless! You must have ice flowin' through your heart. If you even have one, that is."

Her conscience more stung by his words than she cared to admit, Pamela waved the letter at him. "I'll have you know that this is the same man who took another woman into his wife's bed while she was entertaining guests downstairs. The same man who vowed she would never again lay eyes on her own child if she dared to create a scandal over his affair. As far as I'm concerned, we'd be doing the scoundrel a far greater kindness than he deserves."

"What would you have done?"

"Pardon?"

"What would you have done if you'd found your husband in your bed with his mistress? Would you have taken the child and fled?"

"Probably," she replied with a sullen sniff. "After I shot the wretch through his miserable cheating heart."

Connor surprised her by bursting into laughter. She had anticipated the devastation his smile might wreak on a woman's heart, but the rich, warm timbre of his laughter proved to be even more hazardous. Especially since she suspected he wasn't a man who laughed often or with such hearty abandon.

"Bloodthirstiness becomes you, Miss Darby. It makes your cheeks pink and your eyes sparkle." Connor dragged his chair around backward and straddled it, then shoved back his sleeves to reveal well-muscled forearms dusted with hair the color of maple sugar. Pamela tried not to gawk as he folded those imposing arms over the top rung of the chair's ladder back. "Why do you need me? If your mother was a celebrated actress, you must still have friends in the theater. Why don't you just trot back to London and hire an actor for your masquerade?"

Scowling, Pamela shook her head. "Actors are a greedy and ambitious lot. You can't trust them."

"Unlike highwaymen," Connor pointed out, his voice gentle with sarcasm.

"Is there no such thing as honor among thieves?"

He snorted. "Not among any of the thieves I've met. Most of them would slit their grandmothers' throats for a jar of whisky and a used pair of boots."

"Including you?"

"I don't have a grandmother. So tell me, lass, just what do *you* hope to gain from this balmy scheme of yours?"

She clasped her hands beneath her breastbone and offered him a benevolent smile. "The joy of reuniting a dying father with the man he believes to be his long lost son."

Connor cocked one eyebrow, inviting her to tell him another lie.

She sighed, feeling her smile fade. His gaze was entirely too sharp. It was going to take every acting trick she'd ever learned from her mother to shield her secret from him. "Is it so unthinkable that I might just want the reward? You've seen my sister, Mr. Kincaid. I'm sure you can imagine the challenges of being responsible for such a ravishing young creature."

"She's comely enough, I suppose, if you fancy the type." His frank gaze skated lower, deliberately lingering on her generous hips and the swell of her bosom before returning to her face. "I happen to prefer a lass with a wee bit more meat on her bones."

Although Pamela knew she should probably scold him for his insolence, she felt a perverse little thrill of pleasure. Hoping to hide it, she paced a few steps toward the hearth as she spoke. "If Sophie had a father or an uncle to look after her, her beauty would be a blessing. But in our circumstances, it's nothing but a curse. I already have one married viscount desperate to seduce her. If we return to London even poorer and more helpless than when we left, I'm afraid he'll try something even more nefarious."

"Would you like me to kill him for you?"

Pamela jerked her head around to meet his steady gray gaze. She would have laughed, but she wasn't entirely sure he had made the offer in jest.

She cleared her throat. "I'm hoping that won't be necessary. With the reward I could provide a dowry for Sophie and find her a decent husband — not a nobleman of course, but some nice young man in trade. Or perhaps a second son in the militia or the clergy."

"What about you? What's to become of you once you have your sister safely tucked away in some pious vicar's bed?"

Connor's blunt question unsettled her. "I haven't really thought about it. I suppose I could purchase a small cottage with the remaining money and retire to the country or the seaside."

"To do what? Bake shortbread and collect cats? 'Tis a bit tame for a lass like you, don't you think? Especially after a career of kid-nappin' bandits and swindlin' wealthy gentlemen out of their inheritances." One corner of his mouth quirked upward in a lazy smile. "You might just decide a life of crime suits you."

She gave him an icy look.

"What are you really after, lass?" He tilted his head to the side, studying her through narrowed eyes. "You just don't strike me as the sort who would make off with what doesn't rightly belong to her."

"Why, Mr. Kincaid," she said lightly, "you of all people should understand the irresistible temptation of ill-gotten gain."

"You're forgettin' one thing, Miss Darby. A man who lies, steals and cheats for a livin' can usually tell when someone else is lyin'."

Pamela swallowed but his frank gaze made it impossible to keep choking back the truth. Lifting her chin to meet his gaze squarely, she said, "You're absolutely right. I'm not a thief by nature but by necessity. I do desperately need the means to protect my sister, but I'm also after the monster who murdered my mother."

CHAPTER 6

Now that the dam was broken, the words came pouring out of Pamela in a steady stream. "Sophie doesn't know. She *can't* know. It would break her heart. But my mother's death was no accident. Someone set the fire that killed her. And when her solicitor gave us this letter — the one he'd been protecting for all these years at my mother's request, I knew why. Because —"

"— someone wanted to destroy the letter and anyone who might have known about it," Connor finished for her. "Someone wanted to make sure the duke's heir was never found." He scowled at her, haunted by a grim image of what might have happened had she and her sister been in the theater when that fire was set. "Once you knew, why didn't you go straight to the law?"

"I'm the illegitimate daughter of an actress, Mr. Kincaid. What was I supposed to do? March up to the nearest constable and accuse someone in the duke's household of burning my mother alive? Why, they would have laughed in my face and thrown me into Newgate! Or Bedlam!"

"So you decided to take matters into your own hands."

She nodded. "And what better way to foil this murderer's plot and lure him out of hiding than to show up on the duke's doorstep with the man's long lost heir in tow?"

Connor shook his head, torn between disbelief and admiration. " 'Tis a crafty plan, lass. And it might even have worked if the duke's heir had been long lost instead of long dead."

"Which is why I need you to help me resurrect him."

Pamela crumpled her mother's fragile letter in her white-knuckled fist, her gaze both fierce and pleading. It had been a long time since a woman had looked at him like that.

A lifetime.

Connor's voice came out far brusquer than he intended. "Last I heard, there was only one fellow who could raise the dead. And he came to a very bad end at the hands of the law." He shook his head with genuine regret. "I'm truly sorry about your mother, lass, but my services are not for hire. I can't help you."

Pamela's lips tightened. "If you won't help me, then why don't you help yourself? Have you thought about what *you* would stand to gain?"

"What? Another date with the hangman? One I won't be able to wiggle my way out of this time?"

As Pamela took one step toward him, then another, he sat up straight in the chair. Her voice softened, hypnotizing him with a beguiling note of huskiness he hadn't noticed before. "What about wealth and power beyond your wildest imaginings? What about never having another door slammed in your face but being welcomed into the drawing rooms of noblemen and the palaces of kings? What about having your opinion lauded and your approval courted by everyone you meet? You could have respectability, admiration" — she dared to draw within his reach, leaning close enough to whisper in his ear — "and all the willing women you care to woo."

Connor surged to his feet, his hand shooting out to seize her wrist. She tried to twist away from him, but he bent her arm up between them, drawing her roughly against his chest. The lush lips that had courted him so boldly only seconds ago were now trembling just a few inches away from his.

He gazed down into her eyes, noticing for the first time how thick and dark her spiky lashes were. "It sounds like you're tryin' to trap me in a cage, lass. A gilded one, but a cage all the same. At least if I die swingin' at the end of a hangman's noose here in these mountains, I'll still be free."

He allowed his gaze to linger on her lips for a dangerous moment before releasing her wrist and turning his back on her.

He was striding toward the door, eager for a breath of fresh air to drive the enticing scent of lilac from his nostrils, when she said, "There's one more thing you stand to gain."

He didn't slow or turn around. "And what would that be?"

"Revenge."

Connor stopped and slowly turned on his heel to face her.

This time she was wise enough to keep her distance. "You can't honestly believe I've already forgotten all of your impassioned speeches about the oppression of your people by the English. If you agree to play this role for me, you'll still be a thief. You'll simply be stealing an Englishman's birthright just as Jacob stole Esau's. It will be your ultimate joke on your enemies."

Connor studied her through narrowed eyes. However lovely and clever she might be, she was still one of those enemies.

But she was also offering him a way to take a life without staining his hands with a single drop of blood. A way to take revenge on the ruthless redcoat bastards who had murdered his parents and the wealthy landowners who had sent them. And he would still be doing what he'd always done best — robbing the English.

His time was running out. He had left behind his ancestral lands and his clansmen almost five years ago, hoping to make a better life for himself. But all he'd done was fall in with an even motlier crew of cutthroats and smugglers. More than once in the past six months he had awakened from a restless sleep, clawing at an invisible bond that sought to strangle the life from him. It was just a matter of time before he met the end he deserved and his body was tossed in some unmarked grave where the one person who might still care if he died would never find him.

He slowly sauntered toward Pamela. "You drive a hard bargain, Miss Darby. Are you sure you haven't a drop or two of Scot's blood runnin' through your veins?"

"Not that I'm aware of, Mr. Kincaid," she

replied, forced to tilt back her head to look him in the eye as he stopped a scant foot in front of her.

He had to admire her courage as well as her wits. Although she looked as if she would have liked nothing better than to bolt, she stood her ground as he cupped the softness of her cheek in his callused palm. "If I'm to inherit this kingdom you've promised me, lass, then perhaps you'd best start addressing me as 'm'lord.'"

Pamela sat with her back to the wall, watching Sophie sleep. A pale stream of moonlight trickled through the jagged gash in the stone, bathing her sister's angelic face in a wash of silver. Pamela smiled ruefully as a less than angelic snore escaped Sophie's puckered lips. She had been a sturdy seven-year-old when Sophie was born and she could still remember rocking the rosy-cheeked babe to sleep every night in her cradle while their mama took her final bows and gathered the roses thrown to her by her adoring admirers.

Pamela hugged the woolen blanket tighter around her shoulders and rested the back of her head against the wall, allowing her eyes to drift shut for a few precious seconds. Her own body was beginning to ache with exhaustion. She longed to stretch out next to Sophie on the makeshift pallet, but she had no intention of leaving her sister unguarded with that motley crew of bandits and smugglers still making merry in the vault below.

As she felt her head beginning to nod toward her chest, she jerked her eyes open and gave herself a brisk shake. She gazed around the dusty tower, wondering if it had once been a bedchamber shared by some lusty lord and his lady. Except for a crude table and chair, there was nothing left of its furnishings but piles of splintered sticks. A fretful squeaking emanated from the walls, warning her that she and her sister were not the tower's only occupants.

Perhaps it was only fitting that she be denied the sleep of the innocent. Now that she'd convinced Connor to help her swindle the duke out of his title and riches, she supposed she was no better than a common thief herself. She sighed, envying Sophie her untroubled conscience. She had always sworn she would walk through the fires of hell to protect her sister, but this was the first time she'd felt the flames tickling her toes.

Her heavy eyelids were beginning to drift shut again when she heard the ghost of a sound outside the wooden door. She jerked, suddenly wide awake. The blanket slipped from her shoulders as she rose to her feet, afraid she was about to be rewarded for her vigilance by an uninvited visitor.

She cast about for a weapon but all she could find was the leg from a splintered bedstead. She tested its weight in her hand, grimacing in dismay. Even a toy gun would have been a better comfort.

Stealing a glance at Sophie to make sure she was still sleeping, Pamela crept toward the door. She wouldn't have been surprised to find it locked — leaving them at the mercy of whoever held the key. But when she tugged the iron handle, the door inched open.

She pressed her eye to the narrow crack.

Connor Kincaid was sprawled in a wooden chair at the top of the stairs, his long legs stretched out in front of him to bar the passageway, and a pistol laid across his lap. His eyes were closed, but there was a lingering tension in his muscles that belied his casual sprawl, warning that he was not a man to be trifled with, even in sleep.

Pamela's first thought was that he didn't trust her. That he believed she might try to renege on their bargain and stage an escape.

But then she realized the mouth of the

pistol wasn't pointed toward the tower but toward the stairs. Connor wasn't holding them prisoner. He was guarding them.

Holding her breath, Pamela gently eased the door shut, marveling at her discovery. Connor had promised her he wouldn't let her sister come to any harm and in this — if in nothing else — he was evidently a man of his word.

She briefly considered returning to her own guard post but an enormous yawn seized her, making Sophie's nest of blankets look even more inviting. She hesitated for a moment, then padded over and curled up next to her sister. She gently tucked the blanket around Sophie's shoulders before falling into a deep and untroubled sleep.

CHAPTER 7

The future Duke of Warrick leaned back in his chair, eyeing the straight razor in Pamela's hand with palpable suspicion. "If you think I'm goin' to let you within an inch of my throat with that blade, lass, you'd best think again." He reached up to massage the faded scars that marred the corded muscles of his throat. "I'd as soon trust my neck to the hangman."

"If you don't allow me to clean you up for our journey, you may have to," Pamela replied. "It will be much easier to smuggle you out of Scotland if you look more like a duke's son than an unmannered ruffian."

He glared at her through the tangled strands of hair that fell over his brow, looking more like a man with murder on his mind.

Morning sunlight poured through a jagged gash in the stone in the tower chamber where she and Sophie had passed the night, gilding the dust motes that danced through the air. Unfortunately, the sun's golden rays also highlighted the deadly gleam of the blade in her hand. She supposed she might have inspired more confidence in Connor if that hand had been completely steady. But his black scowl could have unsettled even the most skillful of barbers.

"Why don't you just tell this new family of mine that I was raised by wolves?" Connor suggested, running one hand over the rugged curve of his jaw. Although less than a day had passed since Pamela had stroked that jaw herself, his crop of stubble was already blossoming into full-blown whiskers. "Then they'll expect me to be nice and hairy."

"Based on your fine temperament, I may tell them you were raised by badgers. Rabid badgers," she added sweetly as his scowl deepened.

She dipped a shaving brush into the cracked ceramic mug sitting on the crude wooden table and whipped the soap within into a milky froth. Perhaps his face would be less forbidding when covered with a mask of shaving soap.

Swallowing her trepidation, she approached him with the cup and brush in one hand and the razor in the other. Unfortunately, she was so focused on keeping her hands steady that she failed to mind her feet. The toe of her boot clipped the edge of a broken flagstone and she went stumbling toward him, helpless to slow her momentum.

One minute she was on her feet; the next she was in his lap. His hand shot out to close around hers, stilling the razor's blade a mere hairsbreadth from his Adam's apple.

Eyeing her warily, he gingerly extracted the razor from her quaking hand. "I do believe I'll shave myself, thank you very much. I'd hate to be decapitated before breakfast. It might spoil my appetite."

His lap was entirely too warm. Entirely too inviting. Pamela was beset by an absurd desire to press herself against his chest like a baby cat eager for the stroke of her master's hand. Judging by the possessive way his arm had curled around her hip, she was afraid he would be only too willing to oblige her. He had a way of looking at her with those piercing gray eyes of his that made her feel as if she was the lead actress on the stage of her life. After surrendering that role to both Sophie and her mother for as long as she could remember, it was both a seductive and dangerous sensation.

Scrambling awkwardly to her feet, she

peered into the cup. "I don't know why you're complaining. I didn't spill a single drop of the shaving soap."

He confiscated the cup from her hand before scooting his chair around to face the jagged spar of mirror propped against the wall. "I don't know why the Brits bother sendin' the redcoats to drive us off our lands." He rested the cup between his thighs and brushed shaving soap along the curve of his jaw. "If they armed you with a razor and your sister with a parasol, they could conquer us without firin' a single shot."

Pamela leaned against the edge of the table, observing his reflection in the mirror. "Why do you hate the English so much?"

"Does a Scotsman need a reason to hate the English?"

"No. But I believe you do."

He flicked her the briefest of glances, his eyes flashing silver in the sunlight. The razor looked far more menacing in his grip than it had in hers. Dismissing her question, he frowned at his reflection. "What if I don't look anythin' like this Warrick fellow?"

"That's the beauty of my plan. No one knows what he would look like. He was only a few weeks old when he disappeared. He was as bald as an onion and his eyes were still that muddy blue all babies are born with. Besides, it's all in the art of illusion. If growing up in the theater taught me anything, it was that people will see what they want to believe and believe what they want to see."

Connor drew the blade down his cheek, clearing away a patch of bristling whiskers to reveal a swath of smooth, sun-bronzed skin. "So what will my new name be?"

Pamela straightened. "You shall henceforth be known as Percy Ambrose Bartholomew Reginald Cecil Smythe, Marquess of Eddywhistle and future Duke of Warrick."

Pamela had expected him to be intimidated by such an impressive list of monikers and titles. She did not expect his striking face to curdle in an expression of horror. "*Percy?* The duke named the poor lad *Percy?* Why, you were right about the rotter! His wife should have shot him. If anyone calls me Percy, I'll shoot them myself!"

She sighed. "I don't think that would make for a very positive first impression. Christian names are very rarely used among the nobility. Your peers will probably call you Warrick and your inferiors will simply address you as 'my lord.' "

"And which will you be?" he asked.

"As always, your superior," she replied

103

without missing a beat.

He snorted. "Then perhaps you can tell me where I've been all these years."

"As I see it," Pamela said, pushing off from the table to pace behind him, "when the duchess was stricken with the fever and realized she was going to die before she could reach the shelter of her grandfather's cottage, she had no choice but to place you in a basket and leave you on the doorstep of a kindly old merchant and his barren wife."

Connor's voice rippled with mild sarcasm. "And I suppose I've been tendin' the store ever since then."

Pamela swung around to eye his brawny shoulders. She'd never encountered a man who looked less like a shopkeeper and more like one of the paid brawlers at Gentleman Jackson's boxing club.

"I think not," she said, conceding his point. "After the kindly couple died, you struck out on your own, determined to make your fortune in this world. When I found you, you were . . ." She tapped her pursed lips with one forefinger, searching her mind for a suitable occupation.

"Robbin' hapless travelers of their underwear?" he offered.

She glared down her nose at him. "Oh yes, why don't we just come right out and tell the duke you've been masquerading as Connor Kincaid — robber prince of the night, terror of the highways and scourge of the Highlands?"

"You left off despoiler of innocent females."

Pamela might have been able to tell if he was joking had he not chosen that moment to scrape away the whiskers beneath his nose, revealing a delectably kissable cleft.

For a breathless moment, she could only stare.

"If we make them believe I truly am the duke's heir, you do realize that the same villain who killed your mother may very well try to kill me."

Pamela clapped her hands together and beamed at him. "Yes, I know! Isn't it marvelous?"

His reflection cocked one eyebrow at her.

She hastened to explain. "What better way to expose the wretch than to catch him in the act?"

"The act of slippin' hemlock into my brandy or slittin' my throat while I'm sleepin'?"

She waved away the heavy note of mockery that laced his tone. "Don't be ridiculous. If this murderer doesn't want to get caught, he'll have to stage a convincing accident.

And since we'll be expecting him to do just that, we'll have ample time to see that he's brought to justice. If you see anything suspicious at all, just send word to me and I'll fetch the authorities."

"*Before* he kills me."

"That's what I'm hoping," she agreed cheerfully. "After all, he won't be expecting you to be as dangerous as he is. *More* dangerous," she quickly amended as Connor narrowed his eyes at her in the mirror. "And while we're waiting for him to show his hand, you can learn to pass yourself off as a gentleman in society. The duke will no doubt want to complete your education. Why, just think of it — you can even learn to read!"

Connor gave her another of those enigmatic glances in the glass. "Indeed."

"He'll probably hire a fencing instructor and a dancing master."

Connor shot to his feet. "I don't mind the swordplay, lass, but you didn't say anythin' about prancin' around a ballroom in ruffles and tights."

Reaching up to clap her hands on his shoulders, Pamela gently urged him back down in the chair. "Have no fear, sir. Tights went out of fashion several seasons ago."

Realizing that she had allowed her hands

to linger against the muscled breadth of his shoulders, Pamela snatched them back and tucked them behind her. "Even though you've been living among the Scots for most of your life, the duke will be just arrogant enough to believe you should still be showing signs of your noble English blood. You should probably go ahead and make an effort to stop dropping your g's."

"I don't know what in the bluidy hell ye're talkin' aboot, lass."

Pamela had already opened her mouth to correct him when another deft stroke of the razor revealed his brazen dimple. Tilting her nose in the air, she said primly, "Regardless of how coarse his tongue might be while in the company of other men, a gentleman would never swear in the presence of a lady."

"Is that so?" As he captured her gaze and held it, Connor's voice both softened and deepened, its provocative timbre raising gooseflesh on her arms. "Then I'll have to trust you to help me mind my tongue."

Warmth purled low in her belly as she remembered how that tongue had traced the yielding softness of her lips before sliding between them to have its way with her. She tore her gaze away from his before she could blurt out something incredibly foolish like, "It would be my pleasure."

She injected a deliberate note of briskness into her voice. "I suppose I should warn you that you'll still be a wanted man in London. It won't be the hangman you'll have to beware but a horde of ambitious young women eager to become your duchess. I'm sure their attentions will become even more relentless when they discover that you're young, virile and" — she shrugged as if his blatant physical charms were of absolutely no interest to her — "passably good-looking."

"How kind of you to notice," he said dryly. "So are these the willin' — I mean the *willing* women you promised me?" he asked, correcting himself before she could.

"I'm afraid not." Pamela shook her head sadly. "If you find yourself in a compromising position with an unmarried young lady, you may end up being forced to wed her against your will."

"So I'm only allowed to find myself in compromising positions with married young ladies?"

"Oh, no!" she exclaimed. "That won't do at all. A jealous husband might challenge you to a duel. You could cause a terrible scandal that could expose us both."

He sighed heavily. "So despite your promises I should resign myself to a life of celibacy more suited to a monk than a duke."

"Oh, there are always women of questionable moral character who will welcome a gentleman's attentions — lusty widows, courtesans" — she sniffed as if the smell of some overbearing perfume lingered in the air — "Frenchwomen."

"Ah yes, Frenchwomen." A nostalgic smile curved Connor's lips. "I robbed a coach once with a buxom young French maidservant on board. When I demanded her mistress's jewels, she threw herself in front of my pistol and begged me to take her instead." His smile deepened a devilish degree. "Begged quite insistently as I recall."

Pamela's own lips felt oddly stiff, as if they belonged to someone else. "I'm sure you were only too happy to accommodate her."

"I'm afraid I had to disappoint the lass." His smile vanished as the blade glided over his jaw, revealing its hard, unyielding planes. "Pleasure is fleeting. Gold is the only thing that lasts forever."

"What about love?" she asked softly, regretting the sentimental words the instant they passed her lips. "Isn't it supposed to be eternal?"

"Love's a luxury reserved for fools, poets and the rich. A poor man would rather have a bowl of warm stew in his belly and a pair of new soles for his boots."

"What of your parents? Did they not love each other?"

Steel flashed in the gaze he gave her, reminding her how it had felt to face down this man over the barrel of a gun. "They did. But it wasn't eternal. It only lasted until the redcoats murdered them."

Pamela was almost relieved when she heard the cheerful patter of her sister's boots on the stairs. "I've found the costume, Pamela!" Sophie sang out, her buttery curls bouncing as she came waltzing into the chamber. "I couldn't find the garters for the stockings so I'm loaning him a pair of mine."

It appeared that Brodie had already fallen beneath her sister's spell. The burly smuggler was trotting at Sophie's heels like a well-trained lapdog, his arms piled high with garments.

"Costume?" Connor repeated ominously, rising and turning to toss the razor and the cup on the table.

Nodding toward his all-black ensemble, Pamela said, "I had Sophie fetch you some more appropriate traveling garments from my trunk. And not a moment too soon, it appears," she added as he used the tail of his shirt to wipe the remainder of the shaving soap from his cheeks and chin. His unruly hair came tumbling around his face before she could gauge the full effect of his shave. "We had no idea what sort of financial straits we might find the duke's heir in, so I took the liberty of borrowing this costume from the theater where Sophie gave her last performance." Her *very* last performance, Pamela thought grimly.

Sophie whisked a shirt from the top of the pile of garments in Brodie's arms and held it up in front of her. "Petruchio wore this one in *The Taming of the Shrew*. Isn't it dashing?"

Eyeing the elaborate fall of lace-trimmed ruffles adorning the collar and cuffs, Brodie snickered. "Aye, lass. Our Connor'll be so comely in that, even I won't be able to resist the lad's charms."

"I'd suggest you try," Connor growled with a marked absence of any charm.

Hoping to avert disaster, Pamela bustled forward to relieve Brodie of the next garment on the pile. Unfortunately, it turned out to be a waistcoat fashioned from bright lavender silk.

"You needn't look so dismayed," she told Connor, struggling to hide her own consternation. "All the most fashionable gentlemen

111

are wearing them."

Connor scowled at the meadow of yellow flowers dotting the shiny fabric. "The gentlemen or the ladies?"

Brodie choked back a guffaw.

"Perhaps you'd prefer to wear your mask," Pamela said stiffly. "And in place of an elegant walking stick, you could carry your pistol so you could shoot anyone who dares to offend your stubborn pride. In lieu of a nicely tied cravat, we could simply drape a noose around your thick neck."

Muttering something mercifully unintelligible beneath his breath, Connor strode forward. Sophie skittered backward, clearly aware that he could snap her in two just as easily as he had her parasol.

But he simply snatched the shirt from her hands, the waistcoat from Pamela's and the rest of the garments from Brodie's arms before storming from the chamber.

When Connor reappeared in the doorway, Pamela didn't know whether to clap a hand over her mouth or her eyes.

The actor who had originally worn the costume was obviously a much smaller man than Connor. *Much* smaller. In *every* way. The lavender waistcoat gaped open over Connor's broad chest with no hope of button and hole ever meeting. His well-muscled shoulders had already split the delicate stitching of the shirt. As they watched, the seams of the buff breeches clinging to his powerfully built calves and thighs like a second skin threatened to give way as well.

"Cover your eyes, Sophie," Pamela ordered.

Her sister quickly obeyed but Pamela glanced over to catch her peeping through her fingers. Pamela wasn't sure she could blame her. Nor could she deny her own fascination with the battle being waged between the fragile fabric and the magnificent masculine specimen that was Connor Kincaid.

Another man might have looked ridiculous standing there in clothes tailored for a man half his size. Connor simply looked dangerous. Although it was Brodie who finally burst into hearty hoots of laughter, it was Pamela who bore the brunt of Connor's accusing gaze.

"I have a *much* better idea," he bit off, turning on his heel and marching back down the stairs.

Connor was gone even longer this time. So long that Pamela feared he had reconsidered their unholy little alliance and was even now racing away from the castle on his stallion, abandoning her and Sophie to the dubious mercies of Brodie and his companions.

While Sophie taught Brodie the words to a bawdy ditty she had learned while in the chorus of *Winifred Wooster, Fishwife of Ulster,* Pamela waited in front of the ugly gash that had once been a window. Last night she would have sworn the sea surrounding the castle was as dark and unfathomable as India ink. But the sunbeams slanting through the clouds revealed a shimmering swath of blue-green water that made her think of white sandy beaches and swaying palm trees she would never see. If not for the frigid snap of the wind against her cheeks, she would have sworn she was in Barbados, not Scotland.

A rainbow melted out of the misty horizon right before her eyes. Despite the sun streaming through the window, it was still raining somewhere beyond that magical arch of color. The bruised tint of the distant sky made the rainbow's ethereal hues appear even more vivid. As she watched, a second rainbow — just as impossible and equally glorious — appeared just to the left of the first.

For the first time she wondered if a man who had awakened to the breathtaking beauty of the Scottish landscape every morning of his life could ever be truly happy beneath the gray soot-laden clouds of the London sky.

When she heard a footfall at the top of the stairs, she turned, prepared to tell Connor that it had all been a terrible mistake. That she and Sophie would return to London to fight their own battles without his help.

She heard a gasp. If not for the bedazzled expression on Sophie's face, she would have sworn it was her own.

Connor stood in the doorway. The ill-fitting breeches had been replaced with the soft woolen folds of a green and black kilt. His knees were bare but tartan stockings hugged his muscular calves, disappearing into a pair of polished black shoes crowned with silver buckles. A ruffled jabot flowed down the front of his ivory shirt, accentuating the rugged masculinity of his jawline. A plaid that matched his kilt in both pattern and fabric was draped over one broad shoulder and secured with a copper brooch.

He'd smoothed his hair away from his face, securing it at the nape with a black velvet queue. The sunlight streaming into the chamber burnished the streaks of honey in the rich maple of his hair to pure gold.

Without the whiskers to mask it, the sun-kissed planes of his face were even more striking. He had only his stubborn scowl and slightly crooked nose to rescue him from being too pretty.

He did not look like a duke. He looked like a prince.

When in the company of Sophie and their mother, Pamela had often felt like a dowdy wren next to a pair of preening peacocks. Now she felt more like a humble dormouse in danger of being snatched up by the talons of a magnificent hawk and gobbled down in a single bite.

Brodie let out a low whistle. "For a second there I thought it was the ghost o' Bonnie Prince Charlie hisself!"

"Have you ever thought about treading the boards, sir?" Sophie asked Connor, unable to resist giving her silky eyelashes a fresh flutter. "Why, you'd make a marvelous MacBeth!"

They both fell back a step as Pamela glided toward Connor. When she reached his side, she took up a corner of the plaid, unable to resist touching him — even if it was only to finger a fold of the rich wool. "Where did you find such garments?"

"On the back of a haughty Englishman who liked to play at being a Scottish lord.

He kicked all the Scot tenant farmers off his lands and replaced them with sheep." Connor's devilish dimple reappeared. "One afternoon when he went strolling through the heather in his kilt and plaid to admire his fine flocks, he found me waiting for him instead."

Pamela felt her heart plummet toward her boots. "So you killed him," she said flatly, letting the corner of the plaid fall from her fingers as if it was still stained with his victim's blood.

"He was unarmed, so I demanded his purse and ordered him to strip. The last I saw of him, he was rolling down a hill as naked as on the day he was born, cursing me, the Scottish curs who had spawned me and my future offspring." Connor chuckled. "It probably took days for his valet to pluck all the thistles from his —"

Pamela cleared her throat, shooting a warning glance at her wide-eyed sister.

"— *toes*," Connor finished with deliberate care as Brodie rolled his eyes and Pamela nodded in approval.

The sunlight winked off of something shiny nestled in the folds of Connor's jabot. Intrigued, Pamela reached into the ruffles and drew forth a gold locket suspended on a delicate length of chain.

She held the lovely trinket up to the light. "Did this belong to your haughty Englishman as well?"

Connor removed the locket from her hand, his touch gentle but intractable. "No."

That one softly spoken word felt almost like a rebuke. He dropped the locket inside his shirt where it would be safe from prying eyes, including hers.

Pamela lowered her lashes, feeling unaccountably embarrassed. The locket must not be ill-gotten gain but some sentimental keepsake from a woman he had once loved and perhaps still did. Why else would he wear it next to his heart?

"So when do we leave for London?" Brodie asked.

"We?" Connor, Pamela and Sophie all said in unison.

"Aye," Brodie replied, blinking innocently at them. "Ye can't expect a fine gentleman like our Connor here to travel without his devoted valet, can ye?"

Pamela opened her mouth to protest, but Connor caught her by the arm and tugged her onto the landing, where they could converse in private.

"It wouldn't hurt for me to have an ally in the house," he said, keeping his voice low. "Someone I could trust."

"So why take *him?*" Pamela whispered between clenched teeth.

"Brodie has a good heart." Connor frowned at his friend, who was at that very moment showing Sophie how he could make his serpent tattoo dance by flexing his upper arm. "A wee brain, but a very good heart. I can trust him to have my back in a fight."

Eyeing Brodie's barrel chest and massive forearms, Pamela sighed. "If you insist, we can bring him along. But he'll never fit into the lavender waistcoat and I have no intention of letting him marry my sister."

"Don't worry about that," Connor assured her, his expression grave. "He'll have plenty of chances to kidnap a bride while he's in London."

Her mouth fell open. "But we can't allow him to . . ." She trailed off, beginning to recognize the twinkle of mischief in Connor's eyes. A reluctant grin curved her own lips. "Why, you shameless —"

A deafening explosion rocked the tower, sending her careening into his arms.

"What was that?" she gasped, clutching at the soft folds of his plaid.

Connor gazed down at her, his face so grim it sent a chill of foreboding down her spine. "If I'm not mistaken, I believe the redcoats have come to rescue you."

CHAPTER 8

"Get the women to the vault!" Connor snapped, shoving both Pamela and Sophie into Brodie's burly arms.

He turned and went flying down the spiral stairs, cursing himself as every kind of fool. He should have known better than to bring the women to this den of smugglers and thieves. The local authorities had been looking for an excuse to raid the ruins for months, and he'd finally given them a reason to bring the wrath of the redcoats and their cannons down on them.

A second blast rocked the tower, rattling the rusty iron bars in the windows. Connor missed a step and slammed into the wall. Biting off an oath, he dug his fingers into his throbbing shoulder. He had to stop them before one of those warning shots went astray, taking off the top of the tower before Brodie could get the women to safety.

He stumbled into the courtyard, not

surprised to find it deserted. At the first sign of trouble, the outlaws who shared this haunt would have scattered like rats, disappearing into the secret catacombs beneath the castle to wait for high tide and a chance to launch their boats. By nightfall the ruin would once again belong only to night swallows and ghosts.

If not for the two women trapped in the tower, Connor might have vanished with them. Simply melted into the mist and sailed away to a place where the law would never find him.

"Hold your fire!" someone shouted as he went striding beneath the ruins of the castle gatehouse and onto the broad grassy bluff that bordered the bridge.

Just on the other side of the bridge a battalion of redcoats was swarming over the meadow. A sooty plume of smoke drifted heavenward from the mouth of a massive cannon, profaning the misty blue of the morning sky. The soldier who had been preparing to relight the cannon's fuse looked to his commander for confirmation before dousing his torch in a bucket of water.

Even from this distance, Connor recognized the man's short-cropped steel gray hair and squat, bowlegged stance. He felt a sneer curl his lips. Colonel Alexander Munroe was the worst sort of traitor. One born a Scot but who had sold his soul to the English for the power and privileges of military rank. He was nothing but a puppet of the local gentility. He and his regiment spent their days driving poor tenant farmers off the lands their families had worked for generations and their nights being welcomed as conquering heroes into the homes of those they served.

Munroe barked out a command. The soldiers raised their muskets to their shoulders, training them on Connor.

Munroe walked to the very edge of the chasm before shouting, "Put your hands in the air, sir, before we blow you and this wretched eyesore to kingdom come!"

Rolling his eyes, Connor reluctantly complied, wondering what Pamela would think of the colonel's dialogue.

He waited patiently while Munroe gathered a healthy complement of his men around him and came marching across the bridge. Even though they kept their muskets at the ready, Connor saw several of the soldiers cast nervous glances at the churning sea below.

As soon as they stepped off the bridge, Connor called out, "And a good morn to you, Colonel. To what do we owe the honor of your visit?"

Munroe stopped a few feet in front of him, his men fanning out to flank him. "I'm looking for two women."

Connor smiled pleasantly. "Aren't we all? Although most of us have to be content with only one."

Several of the soldiers chuckled, but their mirth was quickly stifled by a black look from their commander.

"I can certainly see why you're still looking," Connor added, nodding toward the cannon on the opposite side of the bridge. "Your courtship technique leaves much to be desired."

One of the men cleared his throat and stared fixedly at the ground, having learned his lesson.

Munroe's bushy gray eyebrows drew together in a scowl. "I've no time for your pathetic attempts at levity, sir. Two women were abducted from their hired carriage last night on the Stirlingshire Road. Two *Englishwomen*," he added, making it clear that the disappearance of two Scottish women would have been beneath his concern. "According to a witness, they were taken by a man who perfectly matches your description." He reached into his scarlet frock coat and pulled out a tube of paper. He unfurled the scroll with a brisk snap of his wrist, revealing the broadsheet that had been nailed up in every market square from Inverness to the Orkneys. "By *this* very man, according to our witness's account."

"Hmmm . . . fine looking fellow, isn't he?" Connor leaned closer to study the crudely sketched likeness. "Though it's a wee bit hard to tell with that mask hiding so much of his face. He could almost be anyone." Connor nodded toward a strapping young soldier to Munroe's left who matched him in height, breadth of shoulder and strength of jaw. "Including him."

The soldier flushed and began to sputter. "Why, C-Colonel, I would never —"

"Silence!" Munroe barked. "I seriously doubt my lieutenant spent last night abducting and ravishing two innocent women."

As the soldier's flush deepened, Connor grinned. "*Two* innocent women? I can't say I'm not flattered, Colonel, but you may be giving me credit for more stamina than I possess." He started to lower his hands. Munroe's men tensed, their fingers twitching on the triggers of their muskets. Connor kept his hands at the level of his shoulders. "There's no need for such caution. As you and your men can see, I'm not only outnumbered but unarmed."

Munroe's skeptical *harrumph* told him what he thought about that. They both knew a man his size was never truly unarmed. "Seize him!" the colonel commanded, stepping back so the men under his command could do his dirty work for him.

As half a dozen soldiers lowered their muskets and swarmed around him, roughly jerking his arms behind his back, Connor felt a pang of regret to think of how crushed Pamela would be when she realized he would not be able to help her find her mother's murderer or win her reward from the duke. He wondered if she would shed a pretty tear when they led him to the gallows or if she'd join the rest of the English on the lawn with their picnic baskets and parasols to watch him hang.

One of the soldiers was closing an iron cuff around his wrist when suddenly the chains went clanking to the ground. Connor jerked up his head to find the men gaping in the direction of the gatehouse in open-mouthed fascination.

He took advantage of their distraction to swing in the same direction.

His own jaw dropped. Pamela and Sophie should have been safely secured in the vault by now, awaiting their rescue by these fine young English soldiers. Yet here they came, strolling across the grass in their perky little bonnets with their arms linked and their yellow and blue skirts rippling in the breeze, looking like twin buds of English woman-hood. All they lacked was a parasol to twirl.

As they meandered into musket range, Connor's hands closed into fists. "When I get my hands on Brodie . . ." he muttered beneath his breath.

Munroe looked equally flummoxed. He turned his glare on Connor. "Just what is the meaning of this, sir?"

"Damned if I know," Connor murmured, watching warily as Pamela detached herself from Sophie and wended her way through the soldiers to his side.

While the soldiers cast Sophie dazzled glances, which she received with downcast lashes and a demure smile, Pamela stood on tiptoe and pressed a chaste kiss to Con-nor's cheek, her lips soft and warm. "Hello, darling. You didn't tell me we had gentle-men callers." Tucking her small hand in the crook of his arm, she beamed at Munroe and his men. "So have you come to tour the ruins as well on this fine April morn?"

Connor gazed down at her, unable to believe he had once thought her face only pleasing. With her amber eyes sparkling and that wicked little smile playing around her lush lips, she was absolutely ravishing. And ravishable.

"They wouldn't have brought a cannon if they had come to tour the ruins . . . dear," he gently pointed out.

Pamela shaded her eyes against the sun to view the distant cannon. "Are they in the middle of some sort of military exercise? Might we be allowed to watch while we enjoy our picnic?" she asked hopefully.

Munroe's lips were pressed into a tense line. "We're not here on an exercise or to see the ruins, miss. We're here to rescue you."

Pamela arched one graceful wing of a brow, giving him an incredulous look. "From what? The only thing I care to be rescued from on this fine spring day is the incessant threat of rain."

"Bring the witness," Munroe snapped through clenched teeth, sending one of his men scurrying back over the bridge.

He reappeared a few minutes later, dragging the wiry old coachman behind him. Feeling Pamela's nearly imperceptible flinch, Connor covered the hand still nestled in the crook of his arm with his own and gave it a reassuring squeeze.

Munroe snatched the coachman out of the

soldier's grip and shoved him forward. "Are these the two women who hired your conveyance?"

The coachman slanted the women a nervous look, as if fearing one of them might whip a pistol out of her garter and shoot him between the eyes. "Aye, sir, they are."

The colonel nodded toward Connor. "And is this the man who accosted them last night?"

The coachman scratched his head, eyeing Connor's freshly shaven jaw, neatly groomed hair, and the plush wool of his kilt and plaid. "Now that I canna say for sure. It was full dark and the scoundrel was wearin' a mask."

A tinkling peal of laughter escaped Pamela. "Of course this wasn't the man who accosted us. As soon as my fiancé arrived, that rascal ran off like the spineless coward he was."

Munroe's start was visible. "Your fiancé?" He flicked Connor a disgusted look. "Do you mean to tell me that you're engaged to this rogue?"

Pamela's smile vanished, her eyes going as chilly as the North Sea on a frosty December morn. "I'll have you know that this *rogue* isn't only my fiancé. He also happens to be the Marquess of Eddywhistle and the future

Duke of Warrick. We had arranged to meet here to tour the castle ruins this morning. It was our extreme good fortune that he was on his way to his lodgings last night just as our carriage was being robbed on that deserted road." She swept her reproving gaze over Munroe and his soldiers. "A road you and your men should have been patrolling so that decent Englishwomen like me and my dear sister here could travel without fear of losing our purses." She lowered her eyes before adding softly, "Or something of even more value."

Several of the soldiers ducked their heads or averted their eyes, shamed by her delicate blush. Connor slipped an arm around her shoulders, gently urging her face into the shelter of his shirt. "There, there, dear," he murmured, giving Munroe a reproachful look. "I promised you we'd never speak of that grim night again."

The colonel was all but spitting with frustration. "I'm sorry, miss, but I find this entire tale to be utterly preposterous!"

Connor edged forward, lowering his voice to a dangerous pitch. "Surely you wouldn't be calling the lady a liar, would you? Because as a gentleman and her fiancé, I would have to demand satisfaction."

Munroe gritted his teeth for a long moment. When he spoke again, his voice was soft and persuasive and his words were directed toward Pamela alone. "I mean no disrespect, miss, but I have every reason to believe that this is the man we've been hunting for months." He waved the broadsheet at her. "A man wanted by the law and condemned by the Crown to hang by the neck until dead for the heinous crimes he's committed."

"Heinous?" Pamela repeated softly, the slight quaver in her voice warning Connor that she was no longer acting. "Just how heinous?" She laughed nervously. "Has he spat upon the Holy Bible? Drowned a litter of kittens in a bucket?"

"Oh, he's committed atrocities far worse than that," Munroe replied gravely. "Atrocities not fit for the ears of a lady."

"Indeed?"

As Pamela melted from his grasp so she could take the broadsheet from Munroe's hand, Connor battled an overpowering urge to seize her and hold her fast. To wrap his arms around her and whisk her away to a place where no man — including this lying redcoat bastard — could ever take her away from him.

As she studied the likeness sketched on the broadsheet, he could almost hear her weighing Munroe's words, hear the scales tipping in the colonel's favor. There was no reason for her to doubt Munroe's words, no reason for her to have faith in him.

Her hand trembled ever so slightly as she rolled up the broadsheet and slipped it into the pocket of her skirt. "If you don't mind, sir, I'll hang on to this so I can recognize the rogue should our paths ever cross. If this man is half the villain you say he is, then I pray you'll find him and take him into custody very soon." She slipped her arm back through Connor's, smiling up at him. "Are you ready, darling? I do so love dining al fresco in the morning."

Connor returned Pamela's smile with a grin of his own. He'd bested the redcoats numerous times in the past few years, but never felt such a fierce rush of satisfaction.

They were turning away from Munroe and his men when the colonel's hand shot out and ripped away Connor's jabot and collar, revealing the faded rope burns that marred the side of his broad throat.

Munroe's lip curled in a triumphant sneer. "And just how do you explain those marks, *my lord?*"

Connor lightly touched his fingers to the scars, his nostrils flaring in an aristocratic sniff. "My valet must have tied my cravat too tightly." Plucking the jabot from Munroe's hand and draping it around his own neck, he inclined his head in a polite bow. "If you'll excuse us, gentlemen, our picnic awaits."

Leaving Munroe frothing at the mouth with rage, they turned and strolled toward the castle as if they hadn't a care in the world. Sophie fell into step beside her sister, casting a wistful look over her shoulder at the gawking soldiers.

They were halfway to the gatehouse when Munroe shouted, "You won't be able to hide behind a woman's skirts forever! I don't care if you're calling yourself a marquess or a duke or the Prince Regent himself, if you ever set foot in the Highlands again, as God is my witness, *I'll see you hanged!*"

Connor inclined his head toward Pamela, speaking softly so his words wouldn't carry on the wind. "One word from you, lass, and he would have seen me hanged today."

"And just where would I have found another Scotsman with a thick neck and a thicker skull to impersonate the duke's son?" She cast him a sideways look from beneath her lashes. "Besides, you just don't seem the sort to drown a litter of kittens in a bucket."

"If you must know, I'm rather fond of kittens. But don't tell anyone. I'd hate to spoil my reputation." As they passed beneath the gatehouse, he scowled up at the tower. "So just how did you convince Brodie to let you pull this incredibly foolhardy stunt? After I strangle him with my bare hands, I'd like to know how sorry I should be."

Pamela gave Sophie a pointed look. She responded with a feline smile.

"Ah," Connor said. "So what did she do? Promise to marry him and give him a cottage full of wee bairns?"

Sophie shuddered. "I should say not. But I did offer to teach him all the words to 'Haughty Maude, the Banbury Bawd.' "

Pamela stole a worried glance over her shoulder, where Munroe and his men were staging their reluctant retreat. "Do you think he meant what he said? That he would see you hanged if you ever set foot in the Highlands again?"

"I think we'd best leave for London as soon as Brodie can find that spineless coachman of yours and drag him back here."

As Sophie went ahead of them into the tower, Connor tugged at Pamela's arm, urging her to a halt in the cool shadows of the doorway. He braced his forearm against the

stone arch above her head, shamelessly using the muscular wall of his body to im-
prison her there.

"Now that I've seen you act with such
skill, lass, how will I ever know when you're
telling the truth?"

Her lips may have trembled at their prox-
imity to his but that didn't stop them from
curving in a wistful little smile. "You won't."

She ducked beneath his arm and lifted the
hem of her skirts to proceed up the stairs,
leaving him alone to ponder her warning.

CHAPTER 9

"I'm sorry, miss, but the duke refuses to receive you."

Pamela leaned out of the hired carriage parked in the long curving drive of the palatial estate, eyeing the footman's bland face in disbelief. "How could His Grace refuse to receive us? Did you tell him I've brought word of his son?"

The footman let out an inelegant snort that was at direct odds with his starched scarlet livery and powdered wig. "You and every other charlatan between here and Paris. Why, in the past week alone, three Frenchmen and a Belgian dwarf have come knocking on the door, claiming to be His Grace's long lost heir. One impertinent fellow even slipped through the duke's bedchamber window while he was sleeping. He insisted the heart-shaped birthmark on his" — the footman's patrician nostrils flared in distaste — "*person* would prove him to be the true heir. It took three footmen to drag him from the duke's presence and toss him out on his" — he sniffed again — *"person."*

Pamela leaned back in the carriage seat, struggling to hide her dismay. It had never occurred to her that there would be other attempts to dupe the duke, other imposters.

Despite the footman's disapproving sneer, she refused to accept that they'd come all this way — enduring days of grueling travel — for nothing. She was no Belgian dwarf to be dismissed without an audience or tossed out on her . . . *person.*

She leaned forward again, giving the footman her warmest and most winsome smile. "I can assure you that we have no desire to waste the duke's valuable time — or yours. I truly believe he will be interested in what we have to share."

The footman's skeptical gaze swept her from bonnet to boots. Although she'd worn her finest frock — a sherry-colored walking dress that complemented the color of her eyes — she knew her lace-trimmed collar and cuffs and matching silk spencer were at least three seasons out of date. And while the addition of a plume of fresh feathers had restored a jaunty air to her battered bonnet, her trusty kid half boots still bore the scuffs and scars of trekking through the rugged climes of Scotland.

Her pride chafed beneath the footman's scornful gaze, much as it had when Connor had exposed the frayed seams of her drawers.

"Do forgive me, miss," he said, looking decidedly unrepentant, "but I sincerely doubt a woman of your . . . *standing* could have anything of interest to offer my master."

Pamela bit back a squeal as a pair of warm masculine hands closed around her waist from behind, lifting her clean off the carriage seat and depositing her feet on the ground with an ease that left her breathless. She opened her mouth to protest being treated in such an undignified manner, but snapped it shut when she saw the smirk vanish from the footman's smug face.

He went stumbling backward as Connor emerged from the carriage, unfolding his imposing form to tower over the both of them. The footman's wide-eyed gaze traveled up, up, up — past Connor's broad chest to the impressive width of his shoulders, finally coming to rest on his intractable face.

"Perhaps you didn't understand the lady," Connor said, his velvety burr even more beguiling when contrasted with the footman's clipped tones. "She wishes to see your master and she has no intention of standing out here in the drive all afternoon awaiting his pleasure. Nor do I."

The footman swallowed, his Adam's apple bobbing up and down in his pasty throat. "But — but — His Grace is not receiving callers. He ordered me to turn you away."

"And I'm ordering you to march right back in there and tell him we're not going anywhere until he agrees to hear the lady out." As Connor leaned over Pamela's shoulder, the footman grew even pastier. "And if someone has to come tell us the duke has been foolhardy enough to refuse her again, you might want to make sure it's not you. Because I can promise you 'twill take more than three footmen to toss me out on my . . . *person.*"

Lest there be any doubt about that, Brodie squeezed down out of the carriage behind them, the brass buttons of his own navy livery straining to contain his barrel chest. A powdered wig sat askew on his broad brow, one copper braid peeping out from beneath it.

As Brodie bared his gold tooth, growling deep in his throat, the footman scrambled backward, nearly tripping over his own buckled shoes in his haste to escape them.

He was halfway to the door when he stammered out, "Who — who shall I say is calling, sir?"

When Connor hesitated, it was Pamela who answered. "Someone His Grace would very much like to see."

Situated on the outskirts of London, Warrick Park had been the ancestral home of the dukes of Warrick for over three centuries. The main house was a graceful three-story structure in the Georgian style, its mellow red brick dressed out in elegant limestone. Tidy rows of white sash windows gave the mansion a far more welcoming mien than it deserved. Two Elizabethan wings from some earlier incarnation of the house fanned out from the structure on either side.

All of this understated grandeur was surrounded by acre upon acre of perfectly groomed parkland. It was clear from the cropped grass, clean-swept paths and neatly trimmed shrubbery that every effort was being made to subjugate the whims of nature to the mastery of man. Such a Herculean goal no doubt required a regiment of gardeners working around the clock. Pamela suspected that in the autumn they were probably ordered to catch the falling leaves before they hit the ground. She caught a glimpse of a Doric temple perched on the edge of a pristine blue lake through a sweeping stand of willows — another place where man had put his stamp upon nature.

As a pair of footmen escorted her and her party to the graceful portico sheltering the front entrance of the house, a balmy breeze warmed by the afternoon sun stirred the loose tendrils of hair at her nape. While she and Sophie had been traipsing around the Highlands, spring had arrived in England. Tender green buds misted the branches of the oaks lining the drive. A carpet of new grass bordered the drive — its baby blades the invigorating shade of fresh mint.

Pamela stole a look at Connor from beneath the brim of her bonnet. Did he appreciate the day's genteel grace or did he miss the tumultuous beauty of his own home — the brisk winds whipping down from the north, the ever-present threat of rain, the tantalizing promise of the rainbows to follow?

There were no forbidding thunderheads here, only delicate white wisps of cloud drifting across the placid blue pool of the sky. Connor should have looked out of place surrounded by the trappings of civilization, but his long stride was every bit as confident as it had been in the Highland forest.

The footmen flanked the entranceway, sweeping open the tall double oak doors to usher them into a three-story entrance hall floored in Italian marble. A pair of grand staircases curved up to the second floor balcony, their polished mahogany balusters gleaming in the sunlight streaming through the enormous arched window over the door.

Pamela drew in a shaky breath. She was the one who did not belong here. She belonged backstage at some musty theater, safe from the glaring footlights and gawking eyes. It was her mother who could have played such a role with relish, who would have tossed back her golden curls and strode into this magnificent mansion as if she owned it.

But her mother was gone, Pamela reminded herself grimly, the curtain brought down on her life by an unseen hand before the final act was done. She lifted her chin, giving one of the footmen a regal look before handing him her parasol and gloves.

The footman from the drive nervously eyed the woolen folds of the plaid draped over Connor's shoulder. "May I take your . . . um . . . blanket, sir?"

"I believe I'll keep it," Connor replied. "If

the house is as chilly as your master's hospitality, I might have need of it."

Both Sophie and Brodie were gaping at the entrance hall in openmouthed astonishment. Pamela could almost see Brodie tallying up the value of the brass sconces and silver candlesticks in his head.

"Your manservant and maid are welcome to wait in the servants' hall," the other footman offered with a derisive sniff. "I doubt you'll be very long."

Sophie shot her a sulky glance, looking less than subservient. It had been Pamela's idea to hide her sister's curves beneath a plain white apron and tuck her glossy curls under a lace-trimmed mobcap. Being a bad actress was synonymous with being a wretched liar, and masquerading as a servant gave Sophie an excuse not to open her pretty little mouth and give them all away. Pamela had never been so grateful that they looked nothing like sisters.

"I'd prefer to keep my maid with me," Pamela informed the footman.

"And my man with me," Connor said in a tone that brooked no argument.

Brodie bared his gold tooth in a ferocious grin. Both footmen shuddered.

They followed the servants down a long corridor paneled in rich cherry wainscoting.

Pamela was keenly aware of Connor's presence at her back. She'd always felt as sturdy as a moor pony next to the sylph-like Sophie, but Connor had a way of making her feel as delicate as a dove.

She had hoped they'd be received in some gloomy drawing room where the low light might work to their advantage. But the footmen escorted them to a sunny solarium with tall French windows lining two walls and a flourishing jungle of plants clustered in the corners. The wainscoting on the remaining two walls had been trimmed in gold leaf and painted a cheery cream.

"Miss Pamela Darby and . . . *party,*" one of the footmen announced, his contemptuous tone making his feelings about their motley little crew abundantly clear.

Before Pamela's eyes could fully readjust to the bright light, both he and his companion went scurrying off, plainly relieved to make their escape.

"Darby, eh? A rather common name for such a bold and reckless girl, is it not?"

Those acid tones ate right through Pamela's confidence, making her feel as if they'd already been found out. As if a battalion of constables was waiting to spring out at them from behind the jungle of plants and whisk them all off to Newgate in a barred wagon.

"Do come in, Miss Darby. Since I have no intention of allowing you to ruin my afternoon tea, you and your *party* might as well join me."

Blinking against the glare, Pamela moved toward the sound of that raspy voice, drawn like a fly into the glistening strands of a spider's web.

Their host sat against the far wall in a pool of sunshine. At first she thought he might actually be perched on a throne, but another blink revealed it to be some sort of wheeled chair fashioned of wood and iron. Despite the cozy warmth of the room, he wore a shawl draped over his shoulders and a burgundy lap rug tucked around his legs. His hair was long and lank — pale brown with a startling shock of silver at each temple. His hollow eyes and gaunt cheeks betrayed the ravages of both illness and time, but his appearance might not have been so shocking were it not for the portrait hanging just behind his head.

A portrait of a young man in the very prime of life. Dressed in riding clothes, he stood beneath the leafy canopy of an elm tree with one foot on a rock and a rifle cradled in the crook of his arm. An adoring pack of hunting spaniels danced around his legs. He was gazing at the artist with a regal arrogance that might have been intolerable had it not been tempered by the teasing quirk of his lips and the devilish sparkle in his hazel eyes.

Their host glanced over his shoulder, following the direction of Pamela's gaze. "Handsome devil, wasn't I? And don't think I didn't know it, either. Very few women could resist my charms."

Pamela would have loved to oppose his point, but when gazing at the man in that portrait it was easy to see how a woman could have fallen madly in love with him . . . and despised him with equal fervor for breaking her heart. Even though Connor wasn't truly his son, she feared it was a quality they had in common.

She dragged her gaze away from the portrait to find its subject surveying her from beneath the mocking wing of one silvery eyebrow as he lifted a delicate china cup to his lips. There was something about his bright-eyed candor that invited her own.

Taking a deep breath and a dangerous chance, she said, "It's an impressive piece but rather forlorn, don't you think? It would be far more striking if paired with a similar portrait of your duchess."

The duke choked on his tea.

Even in his diminished state, the duke's

presence was so commanding Pamela didn't notice the woman seated in the brocade wing chair to his right until she leaped up and began to pound on his bony back. Hers was the sort of beauty that had bloomed early and faded too fast, leaving the bright gold of her upswept hair tarnished and the skin of her throat as fragile as crepe.

She glared at Pamela, her dark blue eyes snapping with indignation. "I realize my brother's manners may have grown a bit rusty since his confinement, but that doesn't give you the right to come in here and upset him with such nonsense. We do not speak of *that* woman in *this* house."

The duke waved his sister away with an irritable flick of his hand, his eyes still watering as he coughed violently into a linen serviette. Pamela felt a pang of conscience when she saw the bright flecks of blood staining the pristine linen.

"Don't mind Astrid," he rasped out, dabbing at his bottom lip with the cloth. "My sister is just biding her time, waiting for me to die so she can claim my inheritance for that worthless whelp of hers."

As the duke's sister retreated to her chair, still eyeing Pamela with open enmity, Pamela felt her heart flutter with a dangerous excitement. It was all she could do not to shoot Connor a triumphant glance.

The duke glowered at her from beneath his silver brows. "If you must know, you cheeky chit, there are no portraits of my duchess. I had them all removed years ago. Now sit . . . *sit!*" He waved a hand at the settee and chairs grouped in front of his makeshift throne, dismissing her companions with a contemptuous look. "No point in wasting your breath on introductions. I find them tiresome and unnecessary since I already know everyone I care to know and many I wish I'd never met."

Pamela settled herself on the settee. Sophie was about to plop down beside her when Pamela cleared her throat pointedly. Puffing out a long-suffering sigh, Sophie moved to stand at the far end of the settee, her hands clasped in front of her like a dutiful servant.

Connor gingerly lowered himself to a delicate Hepplewhite chair, stretching his long legs out in front of him. Brodie stationed himself directly behind Connor's chair, standing at rigid attention like an enormous bewigged bulldog.

The duke nodded toward Sophie. "Why don't you make yourself useful, girl, and help my sister serve?"

When Sophie simply nodded and moved

to join Astrid at the tea cart, the duke asked Pamela, "What's wrong with the chit? Is she mute or just as slow witted as she looks?"

"Neither, your grace," Pamela replied, thankful she was a much better liar than Sophie. "She's simply shy."

The duke's sister poured while a sullen Sophie distributed the cups of tea, then brought around a tea tray laden with pastries. Although Connor declined both, Brodie reached over Connor's shoulder, plucked a cream-filled cake from the tray and popped it in his mouth whole, chewing with relish. Pamela winced as the silver spoon vanished from the clotted cream as well, disappearing up his sleeve without a trace.

While Sophie returned to her station beside the settee, the duke squinted at the drooping feathers on Pamela's bonnet. "Although your dowdy ensemble might suggest otherwise, I suppose you're fresh from Paris and itching to collect my little reward?"

Thankful to have something to occupy her trembling hands, Pamela took a genteel sip of her tea. "Not Paris, your grace, but Scotland."

"Scotland! Why would anyone waste their time in Scotland? Why, the Scots are nothing but a bunch of skirt-wearing barbarians too ignorant and insolent to recognize their betters." He cast Connor's kilt a sly glance. "No offense, lad."

"None taken," Connor murmured, his eyes narrowed to glittering slits.

Pamela downed the rest of her tea in a noisy gulp. She knew she'd best plead their case before Connor stormed out or stabbed their potential benefactor in the throat with a pastry fork. A pastry fork probably pilfered from the tea tray by Brodie.

Resting her empty cup on the delicate pier table at her elbow, she said, "I didn't waste my time in Paris, your grace, because I knew your son wasn't to be found there."

The duke bestowed a benevolent smile upon her. "And just how did you come to this rather unique conclusion, my dear? Based upon our limited interaction thus far, I can only assume it wasn't as a result of your keen wits."

Connor rose halfway out of his chair but Pamela steadied him with a pleading look. He sank back down in the chair, his smoldering glance warning her she would not be so successful a second time.

Pamela reached into her reticule, drew forth her mother's letter and held it out to the duke. "Perhaps your wife's words will speak with more eloquence than I can."

"Oh, for heaven's sakes, Archibald!" his sister exclaimed. "Why don't you let me ring for the footmen and have these scoundrels removed? I know you're bored half out of your mind and enjoy torturing them for your own amusement, but there's really no need to waste your breath or your time by reading some ridiculous forgery that —"

"Hush, Astrid!" the duke barked. "Still that flapping tongue of yours for five seconds and fetch me that letter."

His sister reluctantly obeyed, marching over to Pamela and sweeping the letter from her outstretched hand. It was all Pamela could do not to snatch it back. The duchess's letter might have cost her mother dearly but it was still all she and Sophie had left of her.

The duke scowled down at the letter, turning it over in his hands. The wax seal might have crumbled over time but it was still recognizable as his own.

Pamela held her breath as he unfolded the pages, knowing he would recognize his wife's flowing script as well, no matter how blurred or faded.

When he was done scanning its contents, he crumpled the letter up in his fist and shook it at Pamela, his expression fierce.

"Who was this Marianne person? Why would my wife exchange such shocking intimacies with her?"

"She was your wife's dear childhood friend." Pamela sat up straighter in her chair, unable to keep the prideful note from her voice. "And my mother."

The duke leaned his head against the back of the chair as if suddenly too weak to hold it upright. "Dear God, she's really dead, isn't she?"

At first Pamela thought he was referring to her mother, but in the space between one breath and the next, she realized he was speaking of the duchess . . . his wife.

She exchanged a dismayed glance with Connor. It had never occurred to her that in some small corner of what passed for his heart, the duke might have been seeking news of his runaway wife as well as his heir. The realization made her feel even more wretched with guilt.

"I'm afraid so, your grace," she said gently. "She never arrived at her grandfather's cottage. She didn't survive the journey to the Highlands."

"I suppose I've always known it." He sighed, his blue-veined lids fluttering shut over his weary eyes. "The headstrong minx probably died just to spite me." When he

152

opened his eyes again, they were as dull and flat as his voice. "Since it's the reward you're seeking to line your greedy little purse, I'm guessing you've brought me word of my son as well."

Pamela drew in a deep breath, praying God would forgive her for damning them all with her lie. "I've done better than that, your grace. I've brought you your son."

CHAPTER 10

The duke jerked upright in his chair, feverish spots of color darkening the hollows of his cheeks. His hazel eyes burned with an unholy fire, and for an elusive instant he bore more resemblance to the vital young man in the portrait behind him than the wizened, prematurely aged man he had become.

He opened his mouth but only a racking cough came forth. Lady Astrid leaped up from her chair and began to pound him on the back, shooting Pamela an accusing glare. "Look what you've done to him, you wicked girl! You ought to be ashamed of yourself! Why, such a strain could prove too great for his weakened heart!" As Astrid tenderly mopped his brow with her own handkerchief, then poured a fresh cup of tea and pressed it to his lips, Pamela frowned. Her concern for her brother's welfare seemed to be genuine. "Just say the word, Archie," she told him when his wheezing had subsided, "and I'll dismiss these charlatans and their preposterous claims and send for the physician."

Pamela could not stop herself from flinching in pity when the duke fitfully batted his sister's hand away. She retreated to stand at his right shoulder, wounded dignity evident in every line of her rigid posture.

The duke's piercing gaze was no longer fixed on Pamela but on Connor.

"You," he croaked out, pointing a palsied finger at Connor. "You don't look the sort who'd be content to hide behind a woman's skirts while she fights your battles for you."

Pamela began, "Your grace, I —"

"He's right," Connor said, rising from his chair. "I've done all the hiding I care to do."

The duke's voice was little more than a growl. "Then get over here, lad, and let me have a look at you."

Pamela held her breath, knowing Connor wouldn't take kindly to being ordered about. Especially in such an imperious manner.

But after a brief hesitation, he sauntered over to the duke's chair and simply stood there, gazing down at the man.

"Don't just stand there hovering over me like the angel Gabriel come to condemn my black-hearted soul," the duke rasped, crooking a finger at him. "Come down here where I can see your face."

His command left Connor with only one choice. Knowing that all of their fates hinged on this moment, Pamela dug her fingernails into her palm as he dropped to one knee in front of the duke's chair, bringing them face to face and eye to eye.

Pamela couldn't see Connor's face, but she had a clear view of the duke's. It had gone as still as a death mask as he searched Connor's face, his burning eyes its only trace of life.

It wasn't until he lifted a trembling hand to cup Connor's cheek that she realized with a jolt of wonder that the sparkle in those eyes was no longer malice, but tears. "I should have known the moment you walked in the room," he whispered, drinking in Connor's features with a feverish thirst. "You have the look of your mother about you. Her eyes . . ."

To Connor's credit, he did not shy away from the man's touch but simply placed his own hand over the duke's to steady it.

Pamela bowed her head, battered by a dizzying mixture of shame and triumph. The plan she'd set in motion when she and Sophie had fled London was finally coming to fruition. She truly hadn't wanted to trick a sick old man, but by doing so, she had given Connor a chance to unmask her mother's killer, and she had ensured her sister's future. Her role here was done. At least for now.

From this day forward, any communication between her and Connor would have to be conducted through whispered messages delivered by Brodie. There was no place in the life of a future duke — even a counterfeit one — for an actress's daughter born on the wrong side of the blankets. She trusted Connor would keep his end of their devil's bargain and help her expose her mother's killer, but once that task was done, their association would come to an end as well. He would be free to live out his life as the next Duke of Warrick and she would be free to retire to the seaside to bake shortbread and collect cats.

Suddenly desperate to escape this tender reunion that was no reunion at all, she surged to her feet. "Forgive me, your grace, but I realize you and your son are strangers to each other and must be eager to get reacquainted. I'm glad my search was fruitful and I was able to return him to you. I'll leave the address of my lodgings and you can have your solicitor contact me about delivery of the reward." She turned blindly toward the door, trusting Sophie would follow.

"Don't be so hasty, Miss Darby. Or so modest."

That commanding voice stopped her in her tracks. Because it did not belong to the duke, but to Connor. She slowly turned to find him standing at the duke's side. If Pamela didn't know better, she would have sworn he belonged there. The duke still clung to his hand, as if reluctant to surrender it for fear he would vanish back into the wild, never to be seen again.

There had been some indefinable shift of power in the room. One that left Pamela feeling as breathless and bewildered as the duke's sister looked.

Connor's cool gray eyes were more inscrutable than ever before, his heathered burr more musical to the ear. "Surely you don't plan to rush off before my" — he hesitated for less than a heartbeat "— my *father* and I can properly thank you for bringing us together."

She dredged up a nervous smile. "I'm sure the reward will express your gratitude far more effectively than your words ever could."

Connor smiled at her, the dimple in his

cheek even more devastating when complemented by the beguiling crinkles around his eyes. The smile was eerily similar to the man's in the portrait behind him. "Just listen to her, your grace. The lass would have you believe she's nothing but a greedy opportunist, when the exact opposite is true."

"It is?" Pamela whispered weakly.

"It is?" Sophie echoed, forgetting all about her own vow of silence.

"Aye, it is." Gently extracting his hand from the duke's grip, Connor sauntered toward Pamela, his grace as beautiful to behold as any predator's. And just as dangerous. "She's trying to hide her generous heart from us all so she won't spoil our reunion. She doesn't want you to know that I was truly lost until she found me." Pamela held her breath as Connor took her hand and brought it to his mouth, brushing his warm, moist lips over her knuckles with an intimacy that made her shiver. "I know what we agreed upon, lass, but I can no longer keep our little secret."

Pamela gasped, believing he was about to blurt out that he was an imposter and get them all tossed into jail, if not hanged.

She was too numb with dread to protest when he slipped an arm around her waist and steered her toward the duke, who had been watching their exchange with avid fascination. "I didn't come here today to claim my birthright, your grace," he said earnestly. "All I would seek on this day is your blessing." Too late, Pamela saw the spark of devilry in Connor's eyes. A spark she had seen once before when he had pressed the prop pistol to her heart and pulled the trigger. "Miss Darby's only use for the reward will be for her dowry, because much to my humble gratitude and amazement, she has agreed to be my wife."

CHAPTER 11

"That miserable scoundrel! That wretched blackguard! That — that —" Pamela struggled to recall some of the insults so generously offered to her by the smugglers in the outlaw's den. "That swiving, whoremongering son of a —" She slammed a hare's foot into a dish of rice powder, sending a choking cloud of the stuff into the air and setting Sophie off on a chain of delicate sneezes. "Why, I should have let Colonel Munroe hang him with his own jabot!"

Sophie shooed the cloud of powder away, then went back to trying to arrange the thick coils of Pamela's hair into some sort of manageable coif. "If I'm not mistaken, I believe it's customary to accept a marquess's marriage proposal with a tad more grace."

"That's the second time the conniving wretch has led me straight into a trap. And the last, I should add." Pamela leaned forward on the skirted stool, scowling at her reflection in the dressing-table mirror. She was starting to look nearly as feverish and mad as the duke. "I still can't figure out why he would do such a wicked thing."

"What?" Sophie sighed wistfully, tucking a curl behind Pamela's ear and securing it with a mother-of-pearl comb. "Declare his love for you in front of a roomful of people and announce that you've agreed to be his bride?"

"Precisely! I knew he was a born villain but I never expected him to sink to such monstrous depths. Did you see the way that nasty Lady Astrid was looking at me? You'd have thought I was something he'd dragged in on the heel of his boot! And I thought the duke was going to have an apoplexy and drop dead right then and there. They no doubt believe I've decided the reward's not good enough for me. That I've set my sights on the duchy itself!"

Sophie leaned over Pamela's shoulder, clutching the silver-backed hairbrush to her bosom. "Perhaps he spoke from the heart. Perhaps he's fallen *madly* in love with you and can't bear the thought of living another hour of his life without you by his side."

Somehow her sister's teasing words cut deeper than Connor's betrayal. Because for an elusive moment — when Connor had gazed deep into her eyes and tenderly brushed his lips over her hand — her own heart had dared to entertain such a ridiculous notion.

But then she'd seen that wicked sparkle in his eyes and remembered that she was not her mother. Or even Sophie, for that matter. She would never be the sort of woman who inspired such passion in a man. Connor's earnest words were meant to mock everyone in that room, including her.

She sat up straighter on the stool. "I can assure you that Connor Kincaid loves only himself and what he stands to gain from our unholy little alliance."

"Well, if you don't want to marry him, then I will. Or at least I would if he knew I was alive." Sophie sighed. "I've never met a man so immune to my charms. You'd almost swear his heart already belonged to someone else."

"Perhaps it does," Pamela replied softly, remembering the gold locket he had handled with such tender care and still wore next to his heart. "Ow!" she added as Sophie yanked another coil of her hair into submission. She rubbed her smarting head, glaring at her sister in the mirror. "I can't believe Mama allowed you to dress her hair for all those years. It's a miracle she didn't end up bald."

"*Maman* didn't wriggle nearly so much or have such impossible hair," Sophie retorted, stabbing a hair pin into Pamela's tender scalp. "And you shouldn't be complaining. After all, you get to go have a proper supper while I'm left to languish here all alone."

Although Sophie made it sound like the foulest of dungeons, their elegant suite with its cozy sitting room, dressing room and adjoining bedchamber was more spacious than any lodgings they'd ever shared with their mother. In truth it was Pamela who envied Sophie. She would have liked nothing more than to crawl into the charming hand-painted half-tester and pull the sumptuous bedclothes up over her head.

"If you don't stop whining," she said, "I'll demote you to scullery maid and you can go gnaw on a chicken bone in the kitchens."

When her sister failed to laugh at her jest, Pamela sighed and swung around on the stool to face her. "I'm truly sorry about all of this, darling. If I'd have known we were going to be staying for more than afternoon tea, I'd have told them you were my sister, not my servant. I know this role won't be an easy one for you to play, but at least I'll know you're safe and not at the mercy of some leering nobleman. I promise you that

I'll reveal your true identity just as soon as . . ." She hesitated, still determined to shield Sophie from the truth about their mother's grim fate. "As soon as it's prudent."

Although she appeared to be somewhat mollified by Pamela's sympathy, Sophie's nostrils still flared in a wounded sniff. "You could have at least had the decency to tell them I was a *French* maid."

Pamela swiveled back around on the stool, grinning at Sophie in the mirror. "You know, there are ladies who beat their maids regularly with a hairbrush to improve their dispositions."

Sophie tossed her head, her less than genteel snort telling Pamela what she thought of that idea. But she finished dressing Pamela's hair with a minimum of yanking and poking, finally stepping back from the stool with a flourish of the hairbrush and a triumphant, *"Voila!"*

Pamela touched a hand to her hair. She had to admit her sister had worked wonders with the scant resources at her disposal. Sophie had laced one of her own pink ribbons through the heavy coils before twisting them into a graceful Grecian knot at Pamela's nape. The look might have been too severe if not for the clusters of glossy ringlets she'd coaxed forward to frame Pamela's face.

Gripping the edge of the dressing table, Pamela drew in a shaky breath. Her face might be too pale and her eyes too bright, but at least her hair was perfect.

Now all she had to do was go downstairs and face her treacherous fiancé — and possibly the villain who was going to try to kill him.

Connor restlessly prowled the length of his extravagant suite, waiting to be summoned for supper. Although the towering mahogany four-poster that dominated the bedchamber was larger than some of the jail cells he'd frequented over the years, he still felt as if the walls were closing in around him. At least each time the law had tossed him in jail, he'd known there was some chance of escape. He slipped a hand beneath his collar, rubbing the scars left by the hangman's noose.

He'd spent too many years roaming the mountains and moors, wild and free. He could barely breathe in here.

It was the perfect den for a gentleman. The plaster walls had been painted a warm burgundy and were trimmed in forest green wainscoting. The furniture was all carved from rich warm cherry or gleaming mahogany the exact shade of Pamela's hair. A pair of comfortable chairs upholstered in buttery brown leather sat in front of the black marble hearth.

The air was redolent with the masculine scents of wood and leather, and there wasn't a speck of dust to be seen. It was almost as if the suite had been waiting for him.

Not for him, he corrected himself grimly. For the duke's son.

When the duke had touched his cheek and gazed at him as if he was the answer to the man's every prayer, he had expected to feel a rush of triumph, not an overwhelming wave of pity and guilt. In that moment he would have given anything to be back in the Highlands, thundering across the moor on his horse with the law fast on his heels.

His clansmen had once looked at him the same way — as if he had the power to make all of their dreams of reuniting Clan Kincaid come true. For almost a decade they had ridden by his side, thwarting the redcoats at every turn. They had been closer than brothers, the cords of loyalty that bound them thicker than blood. But eventually Connor had realized that the only place he was leading them was straight into a noose. So five years ago, on a misty Highland morning, he had mounted his horse and ridden away, leaving his men and his dreams far behind.

Wheeling around, he strode to the window overlooking the gardens, desperate for a gulp of fresh air to fill his starving lungs. He grasped the window sash in both hands and tugged it upward. It did not budge. Judging from the thick layer of white along its seam, the window had been recently painted.

Cursing the careless handiwork, Connor looked around for something to help him pry it open. He strode to the hearth and returned with an iron poker. He was on the verge of loosening the paint's grip on the sash when the poker slipped in his sweaty hands. Its tip went crashing through one of the lower panes, sending tinkling shards of glass raining down on the cobbled walk far below. A cool rush of night air came pouring into the room. Connor swore, staring in dismay at the destruction he had wrought.

"Ye're supposed to use the poker on the fire, lad, not the window."

Connor turned to find Brodie grinning at him from the doorway. With his knee breeches, white stockings and buckled shoes, he looked more like an overgrown schoolboy than a valet.

Connor pointed the poker at him. "Sneak

up on me like that again and I'll use it on your thick skull."

His high spirits undampened by the threat, Brodie strutted across the room to the bed, clanking with every step. He opened his coat and a veritable treasure trove of booty came spilling out onto the counterpane, including a pair of silver candlesticks, a delicate gold thimble, a small bird cage, a porcelain butter dish, and a filigree clock.

Connor blinked at the impressive haul. "I don't suppose the butler asked you to bring all that up here to polish it."

Brodie plucked a silver spoon from the pile and admired his reflection in the shining bowl. "I'm just plannin' for the future. If this duke o' yers decides to toss us out on our ears tomorrow, I've no intention o' leavin' empty-handed. Besides, he has so much o' this pretty stuff lyin' about, it'll be months before he misses so much as a thimble."

Connor returned the poker to the hearth before Brodie could steal it. "I hate to point this out, but if I'm to be master of this house someday, those are *my* things you're stealing."

"In that case I'll just consider it a wee advance on me salary."

"I'm not paying you a salary."

"Then I'd best go back for that silver-plated snuff box I saw in the library."

Brodie started for the door, but Connor stepped neatly into his path, forcing him to execute an abrupt about-face.

"Aren't you supposed to be polishing my boots or something?" he asked as Brodie made himself at home on the bed — reclining against the headboard and lighting a fat cigar he'd no doubt pilfered from the duke's private stock.

"Ye don't have any boots yet. The cobbler's comin' first thing in the mornin'."

Raking a hand through his hair, Connor wheeled around and resumed his pacing. "So I've been told. Along with the tailor, the linen draper, the haberdasher, the hatter, the stationer, the jeweler, the fencing master and some fellow whose sole purpose in life seems to be helping me pick out the right case for my toothpicks." He swung around to glower at Brodie. "I don't even have any bloody toothpicks!"

Brodie fished a silver toothpick from his heap of treasure and offered it to him. "I don't know why ye're so crotchety, lad. Ye've barely been here for an afternoon and ye've already found yerself a bride. How do ye think that makes me feel?"

Connor folded his arms over his chest. He

didn't want to confess the stab of panic he had felt in that moment when Pamela had turned to walk out of the solarium. Didn't want Brodie to guess that his ears had suddenly echoed with the damning clang of cell doors slamming shut. "You know very well that I've no intention of marrying Miss Darby. I just wasn't about to let her stroll out of here and leave us imprisoned in this gilded cage. For all I know she could be planning to make off with the reward, then send the authorities an anonymous note telling them I'm an imposter."

"So you don't trust the lass then?"

Connor felt his face harden. "Of course I don't trust her. She's English, isn't she?"

"Well, that's a relief, isn't it? I always thought I'd see ye hanged before I saw ye leg-shackled to some lass for the rest o' yer life." Brodie blew out a smoke ring, watching Connor from beneath his heavy eyelids as it floated toward the medallioned ceiling. " 'Twas a wee bit odd, wasn't it, when the duke said ye had eyes just like yer mother? Gave me a bit of a shiver, it did."

Connor shrugged off another uncomfortable pang of guilt. "Gray eyes are common enough. Both of my parents had them. Besides, Pamela was right about one thing. People tend to see exactly what they want to see instead of recognizing what's right in front of them."

Pamela lost her way three times on her way to the dining room. The maid who had knocked on her door to inform her that supper was being served had pointed her in the right direction, then vanished down a back staircase. Pamela quickly discovered that Warrick Park was a maze of long, soaring corridors and immense rooms that led one into another with no particular pattern or predictability.

Her stomach growled a protest as she took another wrong turn. She hadn't eaten since that morning and was beginning to fear that some haughty footman would find her bones months from now at the end of a dead-end corridor.

After an arduous trek through a portrait gallery lined with generations of dour Warricks who all seemed to be sneering down their aristocratic noses at her, she was finally rewarded for her persistence. As she approached a tall oak door, a bewigged footman dutifully threw it open, pausing only long enough to cast her ensemble a withering glance.

Slowing her steps, she smoothed her skirt, suddenly wishing she had remained lost until supper was over. Since she'd worn her best frock to their audience with the duke that afternoon, she'd had no choice but to don her second-best frock for supper.

The white poplin gown with its blonde lace flounce was more suited to morning wear. The gown's deep, square-cut neckline only served to make her feel more woefully exposed. Fearing the sharp-eyed duke and his sharp-tongued sister would recognize paste jewelry when they saw it, she'd had no choice but to leave her throat and the creamy swell of her bosom unadorned. At least no one could see the toe peeping out of her ragged right stocking or would know that she'd squeezed her long feet into Sophie's only decent pair of slippers.

Tilting her chin to a defiant angle, she swept past the footman and into the dining room. If she embarrassed Connor in front of his new *family,* he had only himself to blame. In truth, it would serve him right if she made him the laughingstock of all London!

She had time for only a fleeting impression of a long linen-draped table with the duke seated at its head and Lady Astrid at its foot before Connor rose to greet her, his imposing figure filling her vision. He was still wearing the stolen shirt, kilt and plaid he had donned that morning in the seedy inn where they'd passed the night. It galled her that he could travel most of the day, suffer any number of insults and indignities, and still look so deliciously fresh.

The burnished maple of his hair was neatly bound at the nape by a velvet queue and his jaw was perfectly smooth, which meant he'd already shaved a second time that day. Perhaps he'd ordered a footman to do it for him, she thought unkindly, already missing the surly ruffian with the wild hair and beard-stubbled jaw.

"Good evening, darling," he murmured, taking her hand. The tender smile that tilted his lips was belied by the wary glitter of his eyes. "I was hoping you wouldn't be too weary from our journey to join us."

"Don't be ridiculous, *pumpkin,*" she replied, her own adoring smile and the voluminous folds of the tablecloth hiding the fact that she was grinding the heel of her slipper into his instep. "You know that every moment we're apart is sheer torture for me."

Connor hid his grimace of pain with equal skill, leaning forward to brush her cheek with a chaste kiss. She turned her head at the last moment, hoping to force his mouth into her hair. But he anticipated the move, adjusting the angle of his descent so that the very corner of his mouth brushed hers with a possessive tenderness that made her toes curl.

The duke cleared his throat with a harsh bark. "I'd stand if I could, girl. But since I can't, you may as well sit."

He watched from his wheeled chair — his skin sallow but his eyes unnaturally bright in the glow of the candlelight — as Connor escorted her to a chair midway down the table, then returned to the place directly opposite hers. Given the size of the table it was fortunate the room had good acoustics, Pamela thought. If not, they would have all had to bellow at each other.

Lady Astrid dredged up a wan smile. "You should both be honored. It's been months since my brother has felt well enough to join us for supper."

Pamela stole a puzzled glance at the long rows of empty chairs that lined either side of the table. Since there was no one else there, she could only assume that Astrid's "us" was equivalent to the royal "we."

She felt a twinge of dismay. Although she wasn't exactly looking forward to coming face to face with her mother's murderer, she had hoped to be presented with a more promising list of suspects. Lady Astrid certainly didn't look the sort to dirty her lily-white hands by burning someone to death.

Before she had time to pursue that grim thought, a quartet of footmen appeared, each one bearing a steaming china bowl of haddock soup.

They had barely finished delivering them when Connor picked up his bowl and brought the rim to his lips. Oblivious to the horrified stares of the footmen and Lady Astrid, he took a deep sip of the broth, then sighed with satisfaction.

The duke pounded on the table like an overgrown baby, his lips curving in a doting smile. "Just look at that, Astrid! He has a healthy appetite. I've always admired that in a lad! Heaven knows I had a host of healthy *appetites* when I was his age."

Connor slowly lowered the bowl, suddenly realizing he was the object of every eye in the room.

"Oh, I'm sure he'll be in keen demand at every soiree and supper party," Lady Astrid replied, her thin lips pursed in a moue of distaste.

Unable to bear the woman's smug condemnation or the flush slowly creeping up Connor's throat, Pamela defiantly picked up her own bowl and took a loud slurp of the soup. Lowering the bowl, she beamed at the duke. "My compliments to the cook, your grace. 'Tis a delicious broth."

"Yes, it is, isn't it?" the duke agreed. He reached for his spoon, then waved it away with an impatient gesture and scooped up his bowl in both hands. They were trembling so violently that one of the footmen had to rush forward to help him steady the bowl before he spilled its contents in his lap. He did not stop drinking until he'd drained it dry.

Lady Astrid was gaping at them as if they'd all lost their wits. But when her brother lowered his empty bowl to glower at her, she put down her spoon with a defeated sigh and picked up her bowl. After a delicate sip or two, she set the bowl aside and dabbed at her lips with her napkin. "I don't wish to spoil my appetite. I do believe I've had quite enough for one evening."

Judging by her pained expression, she was talking about more than just the soup. They sat in awkward silence while the footmen whisked away their bowls and returned with the main course.

While one of the footmen filled their wineglasses, another servant circled the table with a silver tray, carefully placing a plump slab of braised trout on each plate. Pamela licked her lips, terrified the delectable aroma was going to make her stomach growl.

Judging by the voracious glint in Connor's eye, he was probably even more famished than she was. His brow furrowed as he surveyed the bewildering array of forks, knives and spoons grouped around his plate. He finally selected the most threatening-looking knife in the bunch and prepared to stab the piece of fish with it.

Pamela delicately cleared her throat. As he glanced up at her, she chose the small fork nearest her plate and used it to tuck a bite of the succulent fish between her lips. Connor hesitated for a moment, then laid aside the knife and followed suit.

"My son has already told me about the kindly couple who took him in after" — the duke hesitated, his face clouding — "after he lost his mother. But he thought you might want to explain how you happened upon him."

Pamela wondered what Connor would do if she blurted out, "Oh, he was robbing my carriage at gunpoint."

Instead, she smiled brightly and said, "Well, as he might have already told you, I'd followed up every lead and exhausted nearly every avenue in my search for him. It never occurred to me that I would find him studying for the clergy."

"The clergy?" both the duke and his sister exclaimed in amazement.

"The clergy?" Connor echoed, choking on a piece of fish.

"That's right." Pamela clasped her hands together beneath her chin as if in devout prayer. "I finally found him at the abbey in St. Andrew's, studying the commandments of God and living like a monk."

The dangerous set of Connor's jaw warned her he was currently contemplating breaking several of those commandments, starting with *Thou shalt not kill.*

"A monk, eh? Well, he certainly didn't inherit those tendencies from his father." The duke took a thoughtful sip of his wine. "I never thought we might have an archbishop in the family."

"Then your hopes won't be dashed, your grace," Connor assured him, "because I've decided to set aside my studies so I can devote my full attention to learning the duties expected of your heir. And to pleasing my darling bride, of course."

He lifted his wineglass to Pamela, the smoldering look he gave her over its beveled rim leaving little doubt as to just how *full* and *pleasing* his attention could be.

She inclined her head, hoping the flicker-

179

ing candlelight would hide the heat rising in her cheeks.

"Just how soon do the two of you hope to wed?" the duke asked.

"June," Connor said at the exact same moment Pamela blurted out, "Late December. Of next year."

Connor chuckled. "You'll find my bride-to-be has a rather droll sense of humor. Since our courtship was so hasty, the lass believes we should take some time to get to know each other before we wed."

"It sounds like a very practical notion to me," Lady Astrid remarked with her first hint of approval.

"Ah, but since when have practicality and passion ever gone hand in hand?" Connor gave Pamela another one of those scorching looks. "She knows very well that I've no intention of waiting that long before making her mine."

No longer able to hide her blush, Pamela crossed her feet at the ankles, wishing her legs were longer so she could kick him in the shin.

"Can we expect your family at the wedding, Miss Darby?" Lady Astrid inquired.

"I'm afraid not, my lady. I'm an orphan," she confessed, watching Astrid's face for any visible flicker of guilt.

"How tragic," the woman replied, washing down a dainty bite of the fish with a sip of wine.

Pamela sighed and finished off her own wine. At this rate it would be December of next year before she exposed her mother's killer.

But at the sound of a loud commotion outside the dining room door, Lady Astrid's indifference vanished. She rose halfway out of her chair, her spine ramrod stiff but her lips trembling.

"Sit down, Astrid," her brother snapped. "The servants will handle it. That's why we pay them so handsomely."

Quelled by his icy stare, Astrid sank back down in her chair, gripping the edge of the table with white-knuckled hands.

As the harsh cacophony of masculine voices swelled, Pamela shot Connor an alarmed glance. His hand was already inching beneath the table, probably to reach for a pistol he was no longer wearing. Or worse yet, she thought with a flare of panic, to reach for a pistol he was still wearing.

"Take your paws off me, Phillip!" someone shouted, the voice faintly slurred. "You've no right to keep me away from them!"

At that moment the dining room door came flying open and a man came staggering into the room. He yanked his arm free from the footman who had been struggling to restrain him.

The stranger glanced around the table, his contemptuous gaze finally coming to rest on Connor. "So, what they're saying in town is true, is it? After all these years, my uncle's long lost heir has finally returned to the adoring bosom of his family to claim his inheritance." He swept out one arm and sketched Connor an unsteady bow, his voice dripping with scorn. "I came as soon as I heard the news. I couldn't be more delighted to make your acquaintance, *Cousin Percy.*"

CHAPTER 12

Pamela winced in alarm as Connor rose to his full height to face the stranger. She had not forgotten his threat to shoot anyone who dared to call him Percy.

"Forgive me, your grace," the footman said, his gloved hands trembling as he faced the duke and tugged his rumpled coat straight. The poor servant's face was scarlet and his wig askew. "I did everything I could to discourage him."

The duke dismissed the man with a curt flick of his hand. "It's all right, Phillip. I know just how impossible my nephew can be."

No wonder Lady Astrid looked so pale and miserable. This drunken interloper was no stranger, but her son — the "whelp" the duke had spoken of during their interview. The whelp who would have inherited the duke's title and fortune if not for her mother's letter and the unexpected return of his *cousin.*

Both his eyes and hair were as dark as midnight. His unruly curls tumbled over his brow in fashionable disarray. Although Pamela judged him only a year or two older than Sophie, his air of dissipation and the cynical twist of his lips made him appear far older. He was dressed in clothes that would have been the envy of any young buck strolling down Bond Street on a Saturday night, but his cutaway tail coat was missing a button and his cravat hung loose around his throat. The aroma of brandy wafted off of him like French cologne.

Now here was someone who looked capable of murder, Pamela thought, her lips tightening.

He was tall, broad-shouldered, and whipcord-lean, but still had to cock back his head to look Connor in the eye. Which he did, with equal measures of boldness and insolence. "So I hear you've been living in Scotland all these years. And to think, my uncle has always said the Scots never produced anything of value but decent whisky and target practice for our English soldiers."

Pamela sucked in an audible breath, knowing perfectly well that Connor didn't need a pistol to defend himself. He could simply clout the young man into next week with one blow from his massive fist.

"And I was told the English never produced anything of value at all." Connor looked the man up and down. "Apparently, it's true."

The man's dark eyes narrowed in an expression eerily similar to Connor's. "Why, you —"

"May I introduce you to your charming cousin Crispin, son," the duke said dryly, polishing off his wine. "It's fortunate you returned before he could gamble, drink and whore away my entire fortune."

"Archibald!"

His sister's scandalized tones appeared to have little effect on the duke. He simply held out his wineglass so a footman could refill it. "No need for histrionics, Astrid. It's not as if the lad was going to live long enough to inherit anyway. Given his delightful disposition and his penchant for cheating at cards and dallying with married women, someone is bound to kill him before I croak my last. He may be one of the finest swordsmen in all of London, but that's not going to stop some jealous husband from shooting him in the back."

Lady Astrid shrank back into her seat, two

spots of color burning high on her cheek-bones.

Crispin gave his uncle a sullen look before shifting his attention to Pamela.

He prowled around the table, his gait none too steady, and dropped to one knee beside her chair. He brought her hand to his lips, a sunny grin infusing the lean planes of his face with charm. "And just who is this captivating creature?"

"That *captivating creature* is my fiancée," Connor said, "and I'll thank you to keep your hands off of her."

The lass belongs to me.

As Connor's words from the castle ruins echoed through her memory, Pamela felt that same delicious shiver dance across her flesh. Once again, he'd uttered the lie with such conviction she was almost tempted to believe him.

Stealing a glance at Connor from beneath the sinful length of his dark lashes, Crispin lowered his voice to a clearly audible stage whisper. "Be forewarned, my lady. He'll probably want to get an heir on you as quickly as possible so I'll still have no chance of inheriting should he meet with an unfortunate accident."

Neatly extracting her hand from his grip, Pamela offered him a chilly smile. "I've always heard that it's habitual drunkards who should take the most care. They're the ones most likely to tumble down a flight of stairs and break their necks . . . or leave their cigars lit and burn to death in their beds."

She caught a flicker of something in his eyes. Something wounded and wary. And more than a little dangerous.

"I shall take care to heed your warning, Miss . . . ?"

"Darby. Miss Pamela Darby."

"Darby? I know that name. Where have I heard it before?" He frowned thoughtfully, then snapped his fingers. "I know! There was an actress at the Crown Theatre for years by the name of Marianne Darby."

"Marianne Darby was my mother," Pamela informed him stiffly.

"Indeed?" A guileless smile broke over his face. If he was toying with her, he was quite an amazing actor himself. "She was a brilliant talent — absolutely luminous on the stage. Her Desdemona was a revelation! It probably won't surprise you to learn that I've always had a fondness for actresses and opera dancers. Enchanting creatures, every last one of them."

Pamela wasn't aware that Connor had come striding around the table, until he caught Crispin by the elbow and hefted him to his feet. She supposed Crispin should be grateful he hadn't hauled him up by the back of his collar.

"It's not too late for you to catch a play tonight," Connor said. "I believe your performance here is done."

Wisely recognizing that Connor was no footman to be shaken off or dismissed with the arrogant flick of a hand, Crispin sighed. "My cousin is right. The night is young and so am I." Ignoring Connor's glower, he once again bowed over Pamela's hand, touching his lips ever so gently to her knuckles. "Until we meet again, *chérie.*"

Then he was gone, leaving her to wonder if she had just come face to face with her mother's murderer.

Pamela flung herself to her back with a gusty sigh, glaring up at the canopy above her head. Considering that she'd spent the last month fitfully napping on carriage seats or sharing prickly heather-stuffed ticks with Sophie in seedy Scottish inns, the sumptuous half-tester with its feather mattress and crisp linen sheets should have lulled her to sleep within minutes. But she was so restless the bed might as well have been studded with nails.

Her belly was full. She had servants eager to do her bidding. Sophie was snoring gently in the adjoining dressing room, safe for the moment from any lascivious noblemen who might try to prey upon her. Pamela should have been sleeping with the satisfied contentment of a newborn babe.

But every time she closed her eyes, she saw a kaleidoscope of faces whirling through the darkness: the duke's expression of helpless wonder when he had gazed upon Connor's face for the first time; Lady Astrid's white-faced mortification when her son had come staggering into the dining room; Crispin's lean, saturnine features twisted in a sneer as he gazed up at Connor.

And the smoldering look Connor had given her when he had pledged to devote his full attention to pleasing his bride.

Biting back a moan, she kicked away the heavy counterpane. Given her wanton response to Connor's kiss, she feared his full attention was not something she could withstand. At least not without surrendering the last of her tarnished principles and proving she truly was her mother's daughter.

She squeezed her eyes shut to block out the moonlight streaming through the sash window, longing for the solace of sleep.

Even as a delicious languor began to creep

through her limbs, she could still see Connor's face — his smoky gray eyes, the crooked bridge of his nose, that incorrigible dimple set deep in his rugged jaw. When her eyes fluttered open, it took her a dazed moment to realize he was actually there, looming over her in the moonlight — no phantom, but flesh and blood.

CHAPTER 13

Pamela opened her mouth but Connor's hand was there, warm and firm against the parted softness of her lips, stifling any sound she might have made.

He leaned close to her ear, the silky rasp of his voice raising gooseflesh on her arms. "Don't scream, lass, or you'll bring the whole house down on our heads."

Given that a notorious highwayman was sitting on the edge of her bed with his hand over her mouth, it occurred to her that screaming just might be the wisest course of action.

But when he slowly withdrew his hand, she only whispered furiously, "What do you think you're doing?"

His dimple made a devilish appearance. "Sneaking into my betrothed's bedchamber to steal a good-night kiss?"

He was dressed as he had been at their first meeting — all in black, one with the shadows. His hair was loose, its unruly tendrils framing his face. He still smelled like fresh pine and wood smoke. She could not help but wonder if he still tasted like whisky and danger.

She propped herself up on her elbows, shaking her hair out of her eyes. "How did you get in here?"

"Through the window."

She followed the direction of his gaze, her mouth falling open in surprise. The window that had been safely secured only minutes ago was now standing ajar, inviting in a cool night breeze and any scoundrel or rogue who happened to be passing by.

She snapped her mouth shut and returned her wary gaze to his face. She couldn't afford to forget that he was a thief any more than she could afford to forget that he was a man accustomed to taking what he wanted, consequences be damned.

"Did you ever think of using more conventional means — like the *door?*"

He scowled. "Where's the challenge in that? Besides, it would hardly do for some footman or maid to catch me sneaking into my fiancée's room in the dead of night. We have to think about your reputation."

"Oh, I'm sure you already have everyone thinking about my reputation. My reputation as a man-hunting, gold-digging little strumpet who's set her greedy cap on snaring a duke." Remembering that Sophie was slumbering in the next room, she lowered her voice to a hissed whisper. "What on earth possessed you to tell them you were betrothed to the penniless daughter of an actress?"

"Ah, but you forget, lass — you're not penniless anymore. That reward would make quite a handsome dowry."

"As if I would squander it just for the privilege of marrying you!"

He gently cupped her cheek in his hand, tracing the plump curve of her bottom lip with the callused pad of his thumb. "I could have told them we were already wed. Then you'd be sharing my bed on this night."

"Oh, I might be sharing your bedchamber, sir, but never your bed."

As Connor gazed down into Pamela's upturned face, her defiant words were belied by the shimmer of uncertainty in her eyes, the inviting way her lips parted ever so slightly beneath the coaxing pressure of his thumb. In that moment he could barely remember his paltry excuse for coming here, could almost believe he really was an overeager groom desperate to sample his bride's charms. There wasn't a man alive who would condemn him for that — not when Pamela lay rumpled and warm beneath his hand, her eyes snapping with amber sparks and her unbound hair cascading like mahogany silk down her back.

He wanted nothing more than to bear her back against the softness of the mattress with the hard length of his body. To bury his face in the sweet-smelling silk of her hair and fill his hands with the ripe sweetness of her breasts. To ease up her nightdress, coax her creamy thighs apart and take her like a thief in the night. To slip away while she was still aching for his touch, leaving her to wake in the morning and wonder if it had all been some extraordinary dream.

But Connor had learned long ago that whatever he stole now, he would have to pay for later. And as he gazed down into Pamela's wary eyes, he was afraid the price for one night in her arms might be more than his heart was willing to pay.

He reluctantly lowered his hand, telling himself he must have imagined the flicker of disappointment in her eyes. "You're the one who warned me I'd still be a wanted man in London. What better way to ward off all those eager young women than to let them believe I'm already taken? Then we can focus all our efforts on finding your mother's killer."

"And once we do? What then?"

He shrugged. "You can break my heart. Beg off our engagement and leave me a wasted shell of a man ruined for any other woman."

She lowered her lashes, uttering a soft laugh. "As if anyone would ever believe a woman like me would refuse a man like you."

He tilted her chin up with one finger. "Well, in that case . . ."

Then he did what he'd been aching to do from the moment he'd slipped into her chamber. From the moment her sister had interrupted them on that cold, rocky road in Scotland. He twined his hand through the silky coils of her hair and touched his lips to hers.

Pamela shuddered as a tide of yearning, unexpected and powerful, swept through her. This time there was no Sophie to save her from her own folly with a well-timed blow from a parasol. There were only the two of them and the coaxing sweetness of his mouth against hers.

She couldn't have said how she ended up flat on her back beneath him. One minute she was still propped up on her elbows, the next her arms were twined around his neck, her fingers tangled in the coarse silk of his hair. He was a shadow covering her, blocking out the moonlight as he pressed her deep into the softness of the mattress with the long, hard length of his body.

His mouth slanted over hers again and again, deepening his kiss with each pass until she welcomed the smoldering velvet of his tongue into her mouth. He tasted even better than she remembered — smoky and sweet and intoxicating. She moaned against his lips, no longer able to resist tracing the edge of his chipped tooth with her tongue.

That single shy motion dragged a ragged groan from his throat. "Och, lass, what are you tryin' to do? Drive me wild?"

When his mouth descended on hers again, she knew she had succeeded without even trying. His kisses were no longer tender and coaxing but fierce and hungry, demanding a response she was only too eager to give. He possessed her mouth like a born thief, stealing her breath, her heart, her will to resist him.

She didn't even protest when he eased her nightdress off her shoulder so he could press his lips to the delicate wing of her collarbone, taste the pulse throbbing beneath the gossamer skin of her throat. His teeth tugged at her earlobe, sending a dark shiver of delight pulsing between her thighs.

His mouth caught her moan, feeding it back to her with a ferocious tenderness that left her limp with yearning. Made it even easier for his knee to nudge those thighs apart so he could settle his weight between them. He rocked against her, his kiss mimicking the motion with each rhythmic thrust of his tongue, until those shivers of delight began to multiply into something even more extraordinary and far more dangerous. She heard herself sob his name in a voice that didn't even sound like her own.

Despite everything that had passed between them, it was still a shock when his hand dipped into the bodice of her nightdress and closed over her breast, bringing them flesh to flesh for the first time. He filled his palm with the fullness of her breast and gently squeezed, then brushed the callused pad of his thumb over the rigid bud of her nipple, sending a fresh throb of desire deep into her womb.

Shame began to war with Pamela's pleasure as she realized the worn folds of her nightdress and the thin buckskin of his trousers were all that separated her from ruin. Had her mother once surrendered to such a magnificent man, never knowing that he wouldn't just be the first, but the first of many?

Pamela's dismay began to swell into panic. Her hand closed around Connor's wrist, but she might as well have been tugging at a tree stump. "Please, Connor, no! Please don't!"

Connor was so drunk with desire that it took him a dazed moment to realize Pamela's hand was seeking to drag his fingers away from the softness of her breast instead of urging them closer. That she was no longer begging him to continue, but to stop.

He slowly lifted his head to gaze down at her, both of them going so still that the only sound in the room was the harsh rasp of their breathing.

With his hand still cupped around the glorious fullness of her breast and his groin aching in the cradle of her thighs, he wasn't in any mood to play fair. "You promised me all the willing women I cared to woo."

She drew in a shuddering breath. "Is that what you're doing? Are you wooing me, Mr. Kincaid?"

Her words cut him to the quick. Only seconds ago she had moaned his Christian name as if he had the power to satisfy her every desire. "If you must know, *Miss Darby,* I'm not in the habit of wooing women."

A heartbreaking little laugh escaped her. "Of course you're not. They probably woo you."

"That's not what I meant. I'm in the habit of paying for them."

Pamela's eyes widened, her beautiful, well-kissed mouth forming a soundless "Oh."

Although he made an earnest effort, he was still too aroused to keep the rough edge from his voice. "What do you want from me, lass? Flowers? Tender words? Promises I won't be able to keep?"

He would give her all that and more if she would just let him slip her nightdress over her head so she could be naked beneath him. So he could be inside of her. Hell, in that moment he'd have promised her the dukedom itself had it been his to give.

When she finally spoke, her words were little more than a whisper. "I want you to go."

Even as she uttered the words, Pamela wished she could take them back, wished she didn't have to see the icy mask settle over his face, leaving it as beautiful and merciless as it had been the first time she'd glimpsed it in the moonlight.

He was up and off of her in a heartbeat, leaving her shivering in the cool night air. She sat up in the bed and raked her tumbled hair out of her eyes, wishing desperately for the courage to call him back.

He turned at the window, a shadow framed by moonlight. "If I were the real marquess, could I command you to let me stay?"

Pamela hugged one knee to her chest, finding it a poor substitute for the warmth of his body. "If you were the real marquess, you wouldn't want to stay. You'd have no need of a woman like me."

Although she would have thought it impossible, his voice deepened even further. "Oh, I have need of you."

Then he was gone, leaving her to collapse on the mattress, her lips still yearning for his kiss, her body still aching for his touch.

CHAPTER 14

When Connor awoke the next morning, it hardly improved the ragged edges of his temper to hear a cheerful song come floating out of the adjoining dressing room:

> Once there was a bonny lass
> With hair as red as cherries.
> Her eyes were blue as a summer loch,
> Her lips as ripe as berries.
>
> I begged her to be me bride
> While down on bended knee.
> She hiked up her skirts and dropped her drawers
> And made a mon o' me!

Connor sat up with a groan, casting his blankets aside. Golden sunlight poured through the row of sash windows on the far wall, searing his bleary eyes. A morning breeze perfumed with the intoxicating scent of apple blossoms drifted through the broken window pane.

He'd tossed and turned for half the night after his visit to Pamela's bedchamber, his body aching with its undiminished need for her. He didn't know what made him the bigger fool — sneaking into her bedchamber like the common thief he was or letting her convince him to steal away empty-handed.

When he had finally dozed off, his fitful sleep had been haunted by images of Pamela reaching for him, her eyes misty with longing, her lips moist and tender from his kisses. Those enticing dreams were just as quickly replaced by shadowy nightmares where her desperate hands sought to shove him away. Where he ignored her frightened eyes and hoarse pleas and roughly took his pleasure in every manner imaginable without giving a single thought to hers.

When dawn had finally arrived, he had fallen into a sleep as dark and dreamless as death. Which made it doubly hard to awaken to such a merry sound.

He rolled out of the bed, stretching and yawning like a great cat. He slipped on his trousers and padded into the dressing room to find Brodie splashing about in a long copper tub. Tendrils of steam wafted from the water as Brodie reached around to scrub his back with a long-handled brush, still humming beneath his breath.

Connor cleared his throat.

Brodie swung around to beam at him, lacking the good grace to look guilty. "And a good morn to ye, lad! I hope ye don't mind, but as yer valet, I took the liberty o' ringin' for yer bath."

"*My* bath?" Connor repeated pointedly.

Brodie dropped the brush in the water and rubbed a ball of soap beneath his hairy underarm, lathering enthusiastically. "Aye, and you'll be welcome to it, as soon as I'm done."

As Brodie ducked his entire head beneath the water to rinse the soap from his braids, Connor eyed the layer of scum on its surface and briefly considered holding him under until the bubbles stopped surfacing. But he couldn't figure out where he would hide the body.

He was gazing thoughtfully at the window seat, trying to judge its width and length, when Brodie reappeared, shaking water from his eyes like a wet spaniel.

Connor sniffed, noticing the succulent aroma of bacon hanging in the air for the first time. His stomach rumbled. Last night at supper he had discovered it was nearly impossible for a man to fill his belly when forced to use a tiny fork for every bite.

It didn't take him long to spot the tray resting on Brodie's cot — the tray stacked with empty china plates. Gazing at the scattered crumbs, he sighed. "I see you also took the liberty of ringing for my breakfast."

"Aye, and I must say it was quite tasty! Though the rasher of bacon was a wee bit overdone. I thought I might have a chat with the cook today." Brodie waggled his copper eyebrows at him. "I hear she's not married and might be in the market for a husband."

"I hear she weighs fifteen stone and can twist a chicken's head off with her bare hands."

Brodie's grin turned into a leer. "I always did love a lass with a strong grip."

Connor clenched and unclenched his fists, fighting the urge to demonstrate the impressive strength of his own grip by fastening his hands around his friend's throat and squeezing the life out of him.

Before Connor had time to avert his eyes, Brodie rose from the bath. The sight of his hairy, dripping body displayed in all of its naked glory effectively spoiled Connor's appetite. The serpent tattooed on Brodie's massive deltoid seemed to be winking at him.

"Would ye mind handin' me that towel, laddie?"

"Oh, not at all," Connor replied, snatching up the linen bath sheet draped over a nearby stool and tossing it directly over Brodie's head. "Is there anything else I can do you for you while I'm here? Polish your boots? Starch your shirt? Braid your back hair?"

Brodie tugged the towel off his head and rubbed it over the curling hair that furred his massive chest. "Well, now that ye mention it, I could use some help trimmin' me toenails before they send up yer tailor. The puir fellow's already been waitin' for an hour, but this one toenail has been rubbin' against the top o' me boot for —"

Connor would never learn how long the pesky toenail had been plaguing Brodie because at that precise moment he grabbed Brodie's arm and hauled him right out of the tub. He dragged him across the bedchamber with Brodie sputtering, swearing and dripping all the way. Connor threw open the door, shoved him into the corridor, then slammed the door in his ruddy face.

As Connor leaned against the door, blockading it with his body, he heard a maidservant's shrill scream and a loud crash, followed by Brodie's jovial, "Why, hullo there, lass! Would ye like to see my snake dance?"

Connor shook his head, hoping for the poor maidservant's sake that Brodie was talking about the serpent tattooed on his upper arm.

"Now don't go runnin' away like that, lass! I do believe I'm goin' to need a bigger towel!"

Connor quickly discovered that one of the benefits of being a marquess was that you were allowed — and perhaps even encouraged — to keep people waiting. He rang for a fresh bath and breakfast before informing a footman to send up the tailor.

He also discovered that having his bath and breakfast pilfered by the most shamelessly incompetent valet in all of England was the least of the indignities he would be forced to endure that day. The tailor spent hours poking and prodding him and showing him bolt after bolt of fabric, all of which looked identical to him. While the man chattered on and on about the benefits of nankeen over merino — names like Byron and Beau Brummel tripping from his nimble tongue — his assistant climbed all over Connor with a measuring tape, cooing in admiration over the breadth of his shoulders and the circumference of his forearms.

When the assistant dropped to one knee at Connor's feet and pressed the tape to his inner thigh, rolling his eyes in near ecstasy, Connor decided he'd had quite enough of being jabbed with pins and groped by strangers for one day.

Gripping both the tailor and his assistant by their high starched collars, he ushered them toward the door.

"But, my lord," the tailor protested in dismay, his skinny arms filled with bolts of cloth, "how are we to carry on? We haven't even decided between the superfine and the kerseymere yet!"

"Surprise me," Connor snapped. "Or better yet — I'll take them all. Just send the bill to the du— to my father."

Pleasure suffused the tailor's long face. "Oh, yes, my lord! It would be my great honor to —"

Connor slammed the door in both their faces, cutting off their fawning bows in mid-motion.

He was still slumped against the door, savoring a precious moment of peace, when a footman's brisk voice informed him that the hatter had arrived.

It turned out the tailor was only the first in a long parade of London merchants eager to use their wares to transform him into an elegant gentleman worthy of his title. Connor was forced to look at so many different incarnations of the beaver hat he decided it would almost be easier to wear an actual beaver on his head. The hatter was followed by a haberdasher with a dizzying array of handkerchiefs, stockings and ivory-handled walking sticks, a stationer with reams of expensive parchment and vellum, and a jeweler with a gleaming display of crested rings and silver snuff boxes.

By the time another footman arrived to inform Connor that his fencing master was waiting for him in the ballroom, he was more than ready to run someone through with a sword, preferably himself.

Eagerly excusing himself from the crestfallen young man appointed to help him pick out the perfect toothpick case, he hurried down the stairs, thinking a little swordplay might be the very thing to soothe his temper.

"Bloody hell, man, you don't honestly expect me to fight with that thing, do you?"

As that familiar roar reached Pamela's ears, she froze in the middle of the deserted corridor, cocking her head to listen.

"I might be able to darn my stockings with

it, but it's not good for much else. Unless, of course, you'd like me to shove it up your arrogant —"

As that threat met with a virulent outpouring in fluent French, Pamela lifted the hem of her gown and took off at a dead run, following the clash of those raised voices. She didn't have to lift her hem much since it was already four inches too short. Having exhausted her own supply of suitable frocks, she'd been reduced to commandeering Sophie's favorite morning gown — an act that had left her sister weeping piteously into her pillow and muttering unkind remarks about strained seams and overstuffed sausages.

Remarks which seemed only fitting with the bodice stays of the gown digging deep into Pamela's ribcage, making each step a misery. By the time she flung open the tall double doors at the end of the corridor, she was gasping for breath and dangerously close to swooning — a condition that was only aggravated by the sight that greeted her.

Connor stood at the center of the cavernous ballroom, facing a slender, effete Frenchman who had a long, thin sword in his hand and a murderous gleam in his eye. The man was still spewing out a torrent of

French, most of it, mercifully, incomprehensible to Pamela's untrained ears.

Connor might have been unarmed, but he still towered over the sputtering Frenchman by half a foot. He was dressed as simply as a highwayman posing as a gentleman could be — in black trousers and a white lawn shirt with full sleeves and flared cuffs. He wore no waistcoat and his cravat was knotted in a simple loop at his throat. A black satin queue secured his gleaming hair at the nape.

It should have been illegal for a man to look so good without even trying, Pamela thought, biting her lip in consternation. Or at least immoral.

The enraged fencing master spotted her first. He spread his arms in a dramatic appeal, the waxed ends of his thin black mustache quivering with indignation. "Do you hear the words of this barbarian, mam'selle? He dares to insult the size of my sword!"

As he brandished the long, thin blade of the delicate epee at her, Pamela had to choke back a snort of laughter. It wasn't that difficult to imagine Connor darning his stockings with it.

"*That* is not a sword." Glowering at them both, Connor marched over to the wall and swept down one of the massive broadswords displayed next to an empty suit of armor. He strode back to the fencing master, wielding the enormous blade with one hand. "*This* is a sword!"

"Ha!" the Frenchman barked, dismissing the weapon with a flick of his hand. "Only if one has no skill! No grace! No honor! That blade is fit only for digging your grave after a French foil pierces your cowardly heart."

"Oh, really?" Connor took a step forward, the menacing gesture wiping the sneer right off the Frenchman's face. "Then perhaps you'd like to match your blade against mine and we'll just see whose grave we'll be digging come sunset."

As the fencing master lowered his sword and went skittering backward in alarm, Pamela boldly stepped between the two men.

She flattened her palm against Connor's chest, giving him a beseeching look. "Now, darling, you know I faint at the mere mention of blood, much less its sight. There's really no need for such posturing. I'm sure that everyone, including Monsieur . . ." She gave the fencing master a questioning look.

"Chevalier," the Frenchman offered with

a toss of his head and a sulky flare of his nostrils.

"I'm sure that everyone, including Monsieur Chevalier, would agree that your blade is superior." She drew even closer to Connor, lowering her voice to a conspiratorial whisper. "As well as *much* larger."

Connor gazed down at her, his scowl slowly melting to an expression that was even more dangerous. At least to her.

He covered her small hand with his, binding them together so she could feel every powerful beat of his heart beneath the thin lawn of his shirt. "If you're so convinced my blade is *superior,* lass, then why don't you give me the chance to prove it?"

In that moment the fencing master was forgotten. The two of them might have been all alone in the ballroom, engaged in their own private dance. A dance he had started last night, but she had not had the courage to finish.

She drew in a shaky breath rich with his scent, which now included the enticing aroma of bayberry soap. "As Monsieur Chevalier has just reminded us, one careless blow can destroy even the most steadfast of hearts."

"But just how cowardly is the heart that won't even risk that blow?"

Before Pamela could respond to the blatant challenge in Connor's eyes, the temperamental fencing master blew out a disgusted "Pfft!" and sheathed his sword in the scabbard at his belt. "It's obvious my talents are being wasted here. Please give the duke my regrets." He tossed Connor one last sneer. "And my condolences."

Snatching up the rest of his equipment, he went storming toward the French windows along the west wall of the ballroom that had been propped open to welcome in the afternoon sunshine and balmy spring breezes. Only then did Pamela realize they'd never been truly alone. They'd had an audience all along.

Crispin was lounging against the wall between two windows, lazily swishing the graceful epee in his hand back and forth. As the fencing master marched past him and disappeared into the garden, he ducked his head and offered Connor a sly grin. "Hello, cuz. You seem to have lost your fencing partner. Mind if I step in?"

CHAPTER 15

Dread quickened in Pamela's heart as Crispin came sauntering across the parquet floor. The blade of his epee, graceful and deadly, glinted in the sunlight streaming through the French windows.

She turned back to Connor, her whisper low and urgent. "You mustn't do this."

"And why not?" Connor responded, an all too familiar gleam in his narrowed eyes as he watched Crispin approach. "I thought we'd already determined my blade was up to any challenge."

"You know very well why not. If he's the one who murdered my mother, then you couldn't give him a better opportunity to finish you off. You heard the duke last night at supper. He called him one of the finest swordsmen in London."

"I'm not from London," Connor reminded her.

She dug her fingers into the front of his

shirt. A few more steps and Crispin would be within earshot of her frantic whisper. "You didn't see the look in his eye last night when I was taunting him. You mustn't do this! Please, Connor, I'm begging you!"

Connor gazed down into Pamela's imploring eyes, wishing he could have heard those very words tumbling from her luscious lips when he was holding her in his arms last night. Then he could have given her everything she wanted . . . and more.

Ignoring a pang of regret, he gently disengaged her fingers from the front of his shirt and set her away from him. "Don't fret, lass," he said, raising his voice so that it could be clearly heard. "I promise to go easy on the lad for your sake."

Crispin barked out a laugh. "Don't make any promises you can't keep. Because I've no intention of going easy on you, not even for the lady's sake." He turned his brash smile on Pamela. "If you don't wish to watch us make fools of ourselves to impress you, I'd advise you to go. There must be a piece that requires practicing on the piano or a sampler that needs stitching."

"Oh, I wouldn't miss this for the world," Pamela replied, her tone so frigid Connor wouldn't have been surprised to see icicles sprout from the chandeliers. "I can assure you that I'll be here to witness *every* parry and thrust."

Crispin shot Connor a bemused glance. "That doesn't surprise me. It's been my experience that the female is frequently the more bloodthirsty of the sexes. Not that any blood will be shed today, of course," he hastened to add.

He strode over to the tall cherrywood cabinet on the other side of the suit of armor to retrieve a *fleuret,* the knob used by fencers to blunt the deadly points of their swords. When he turned around, the delicate *fleuret* was already fastened to the tip of his blade. "You'll find I'm not as squeamish as Monsieur Chevalier. You're welcome to use the weapon of your choice." He gave the massive broadsword in Connor's hand a derisive look. "Even if it does put you at a disadvantage."

Connor said, "I would think the disadvantage would be yours since there's no way for me to blunt the edge of my sword."

Crispin gave him another of those shameless grins. "Ah, but you'll have to get close enough to me to use it first." A thoughtful look crossed his face. "There must be something we can do to make this contest even more enticing — a prize, perhaps?"

"What sort of prize did you have in mind?"

Crispin slanted Pamela a provocative look. "Since I sincerely doubt you'd be fool enough to wager the dukedom, how about a kiss from your lady?"

Pamela gasped, outraged at his audacity. She crossed her arms and tapped her foot, waiting for Connor to inform the scoundrel that her kisses were not cheap favors to be rewarded to the winner of some ridiculous contest.

"A kiss it is," Connor agreed.

Pamela's mouth fell open, then snapped shut. As the two men lifted their weapons and began to warily circle each other, she backed away from them until she felt her shoulder blades hit the wall. Crispin's attempt to dismiss her had only fueled her suspicions. Although she would have liked nothing better than to flee the ballroom with her hands over her eyes, she had no intention of leaving Connor at his mercy.

When it came to size and strength Connor had every advantage, but Crispin was quick and light on his feet, anticipating each of Connor's moves with the elegance and poise of a dancer.

It didn't take Pamela long to realize that Connor was also surprisingly light on his feet. He moved with the feline grace of a predator — all muscle, stealth and power. When Crispin feinted, he dodged, using the broad blade of his sword to parry each of Crispin's thrusts.

Crispin danced around him, taking great care to stay out of his impressive reach between attacks. Both of them knew that one sound blow from Connor's sword could cut the delicate blade of the epee right in two.

"You're a far more worthy opponent than I'd supposed, Cousin Percy."

"I really wish you wouldn't call me that," Connor replied, using the flat side of his blade to strike a savage blow that left the finely honed steel of the epee singing in Crispin's hand.

"What would you prefer I call you?" Crispin bared his clenched teeth in a smile. "Bart? Reggie? Cecil?"

"I was called Connor in Scotland. But since I'm going to be a duke and you never will be, you might try simply addressing me as 'my lord.' "

Pamela gasped as that single, well-executed blow drew first blood. Crispin's smile vanished. His dark eyes flashed in his pale face as he lunged forward, doubling the ferociousness of his attack.

"And what should I call you?" Connor asked. *"Cuz?"*

Backing toward the French doors, he neatly blocked each of Crispin's blows, his own lazy smile deepening.

As Crispin's upper lip curled in a snarl, Pamela realized Connor was deliberately baiting him, seeking to taunt him into making a mistake, perhaps even into revealing his part in her mother's death. She squeezed her eyes shut, praying that mistake wouldn't be fatal for either one of the men.

Her eyes flew open at the shrill clash of steel on steel. Gripping the basket-hilt of his sword in a white-knuckled hand, Crispin had launched into a vicious sally, leaving Connor with no choice but to continue his retreat. Pamela flinched as Crispin lunged, his blade narrowly missing Connor's ear.

Crispin's forward momentum caused him to stumble. He quickly recovered his balance, but the ragged rasp of his breathing had deepened. Sweat darkened the back of his waistcoat.

The men circled each other again, reversing positions. Pamela realized that Connor hadn't been retreating at all, but simply biding his time while Crispin wore himself out. Now he pressed his advantage, swinging the blade of the mighty broadsword in one relentless arc after another, driving Crispin right out the open French windows and into the garden.

Pamela snatched up her skirts and followed, her heart pounding in her throat.

As the two men abandoned the flagstone path for a grassy clearing flanked by a sweeping pair of willows, Pamela spotted the duke and Lady Astrid taking tea on an elevated terrace just off the drawing room.

Lady Astrid froze in the motion of pouring her brother another cup of tea. Was that fear or excitement glittering in her eyes? Pamela wondered, her sense of foreboding deepening.

There was no mistaking the sparkle of glee in the duke's eyes. He put aside his tea and clapped his wiry hands, leaning forward in his wheeled chair. "Why, look at this, Astrid! You didn't tell me you'd arranged for an afternoon entertainment! How grand!"

Although the footmen stationed on either side of the terrace did not dare to relax their rigid stances, their eyes eagerly followed the contest taking place in the clearing below. The grunts of exertion and the ear-jangling clang of steel against steel drowned out the peaceful burbling of a marble fountain.

Pamela drew as close as she dared and

pressed her back to an apple tree in full bloom, her nerves shredded by the unbearable suspense.

Now that he had an audience, Crispin seemed to have regained both his confidence and his footing. He went on the attack, his blade a steely blur in his capable hand. But Connor continued to block him at every turn, finally landing a blow of his own that came close to wrenching the epee from Crispin's hands.

Something came skittering down the path toward Pamela. She bent to pick it up only to discover it was the *fleuret* from the tip of Crispin's sword. The *fleuret* he had slid onto his blade while his back was still to them.

Her breath froze in her throat. Without the *fleuret,* the deadly point of the epee was exposed. If some terrible *accident* should befall Connor now, no court in the land would be able to convict Crispin. There would be no way to prove he had sought to do his opponent deliberate harm by improperly applying the *fleuret.*

He wouldn't even have to run Connor through the heart. Piercing one of his lungs would kill him just as quickly.

As her imagination conjured up a stark image of Connor sprawled in the grass, gasping for breath as his life's blood soaked through the pristine white of his shirt, she felt as if an invisible blade had pierced her own heart.

She lunged forward, shouting Connor's name.

He glanced in her direction, a puzzled scowl clouding his brow, and she realized that distracting him had been a terrible miscalculation. Time seemed to slow until Pamela could see every delicate white petal of the apple blossoms drifting down from the boughs above, the hint of cruel satisfaction in Lady Astrid's expression, the fierce concentration on Crispin's lean face as he drew back his blade for the fatal thrust.

Without giving herself time to think, she threw herself between the two men. Crispin balked at the last second, pulling back on his thrust. The razor-sharp point of the epee whipped across Pamela's forearm, slicing open both fabric and flesh.

Then Connor's strong arms were there, breaking her fall as she stumbled to her knees.

"You wee fool!" Connor sank to the ground with her, his voice hoarse. "What are you tryin' to do? Get yourself killed?" His hands were no longer as steady as they'd been on the hilt of his sword, but shaking with reaction as he tugged up her sleeve to reveal the bloody welt on her arm.

She offered him a brave little smile. "My sleeve bore the brunt of it. It's nothing — just a scratch. Although Sophie's going to have my head for ruining her gown," she added beneath her breath.

Crispin was gazing down at them, a bewildered expression on his face. He shook his head. "I'm so sorry . . . I never intended . . ."

"Oh, really?" Pamela replied coolly, squinting up at him. "Just what did you intend?"

She held out her hand, slowly opening her clenched fingers to reveal the *fleuret.* The *fleuret* that was essentially useless unless applied with the greatest of care.

Both Crispin and Connor's gazes flew to the tip of the epee in Crispin's hand. Its lethal point seemed to sparkle in the sunlight.

Pamela felt every muscle in Connor's body go rigid. Despite that tension, his hands were astonishingly gentle as he removed her from his lap and settled her on a nearby carpet of apple blossoms.

He reached for his sword and rose to face Crispin, his expression resolute.

Crispin began to back away from him, shaking his head helplessly. "I swear it was nothing but an accident. I never meant to hurt her. Surely you can see that."

Connor paced him step for step, his momentum never slowing.

Lady Astrid came to her feet, the color draining from her face. "Archibald! Do something! You must stop them!"

But the duke simply retrieved his cup and took a delicate sip of tea, his dark eyes bright with fascination as he watched the proceedings. The two footmen rushed to peer over the edge of the terrace, no longer able to maintain their own pretense of indifference.

As Connor drew back his sword, Crispin lifted his own weapon to block the coming blow, but did nothing else to defend himself.

Connor's two-handed blow severed the thin blade in two. The basket-hilt of the epee went tumbling from Crispin's hand, leaving him unarmed and at Connor's mercy.

Connor just kept coming. Even as Crispin scrambled backward, nearly losing his footing in the slick grass, Connor drew back the massive broadsword a second time.

"Oh, Lord," Pamela whispered. "He's going to cleave his head clean off."

Although her every instinct urged her to hide her face, she could not take her eyes off of Connor. His eyes burned in a face as beautiful and terrible as the visage of an avenging angel cast down from heaven to deliver God's wrath.

Crispin's eyes widened as Connor swung. At the last possible second, Connor turned the blade to its flat side, striking Crispin a jarring blow to the side of the head.

Crispin went down like a stone, howling an oath. Lady Astrid sank back down in her chair, pressing a napkin to her bloodless lips.

It took Crispin several minutes to shake off the initial effects of the blow and sit up. He glared at Connor, clutching his left ear.

Connor offered him a hand but he smacked it away. "Monsieur Chevalier was right," he snarled. "You'll never be anything more than a barbarian."

"And you'll never be anything more than the nephew of a duke and a drunken ne'er-do-well who cheats at dueling as well as cards."

"Bravo, lads!" The duke's dry applause echoed through the garden. "Such dramatic flair, such delicious melodrama! I haven't been so entertained since Mrs. Siddons played Portia in *The Merchant of Venice.*" He made a shooing motion with his hands. "If I were you, I'd take your bows and exit stage left now. You should always leave your adoring audience clamoring for more."

Shooting his uncle a look of pure loathing, Crispin climbed to his feet and went staggering back down the path.

Propping his sword against a tree, Connor returned to Pamela's side. He knelt beside her, checking the shallow scratch on her arm for any sign of fresh bleeding. "Why would you do anything so foolhardy, lass? Weren't you the one who told me that one careless blow can destroy even the most steadfast of hearts?"

"Yes, but how cowardly is the heart that won't even risk that blow?" she quoted back to him. Shooting a wary glance at the terrace, she lowered her voice to a whisper. "Besides, where was I going to find another imposter if Crispin ran you through? You know actors aren't to be trusted."

Connor wrested the *fleuret* from her hand, studying it through narrowed eyes. "Apparently neither is the duke's nephew."

"For a minute there, I thought you were going to cut off his head," she confessed.

"For a minute there, so did I. But I knew I wouldn't be able to collect my prize if they carted me off to Newgate and hanged me."

"Your prize?"

"Aye . . . have you forgotten, lass? You owe the winner of the contest a kiss."

He leaned closer, his smoky gaze dropping to her lips. For a dazed moment, Pamela thought he was going to collect his prize right there in the garden in front of the duke, Lady Astrid, the gawking footmen and God.

But he simply plucked an apple blossom from her hair with his deft fingers before gently tugging her to her feet.

Crispin ducked into a back stairwell, determined to reach the haven of his bedchamber without any more of the servants witnessing his disgrace. He knew the two smirking footmen from the garden would waste no time telling everyone in the servants' quarters what they'd witnessed. By nightfall, it would be all over London that the Duke of Warrick's nephew had been bested in a fencing match by a Scots barbarian wielding an antique broadsword. His uncle wouldn't be the only one laughing at him then.

He dragged himself up the stairs, wiggling his aching jaw between two fingers to make sure it wasn't broken. His ears were still ringing and a vicious devil of a headache was just beginning to throb at the base of his skull.

He'd faced many a man over both swords

and dueling pistols in the past few years, but he'd never stared death directly in the eyes before. Somehow his cousin's mercy had been even more galling than his wrath. If he had been cut down where he stood, at least his uncle wouldn't have been able to deny him a place in the family tomb. His former lovers would have wept prettily into their handkerchiefs and his friends would have gathered at their favorite gambling hell to toast his fine head for liquor, his skill at the faro table and his droll wit.

Perhaps once he was gone, his mother would have understood how badly he had wanted to protect her after his father's death and his uncle would have realized how very hard he had tried to be a son to him. And how deeply it cut to watch while he embraced a stranger. Crispin snorted, his amusement at his own folly as bitter as the metallic tang of the blood in his mouth.

He rounded the corner of the second-story landing only to crash right into someone hurrying down the stairs. They bumped heads, then both sat down abruptly, a shower of rumpled linens tumbling around them.

Crispin clutched his brow, the sudden change in position setting off a hellish chorus of bells between his ears. "Bloody hell!" he swore as a ruffled mobcap bobbed in his bleary vision.

"Why don't you look where you're going, you clumsy oaf?" a musical female voice snapped. "Are you blind?"

Still gripping his head, Crispin scowled. He'd never before been spoken to in such an insolent manner by a servant.

But when his vision cleared and he saw her cornflower blue eyes and lush Cupid's bow of a mouth, he felt as if he had been struck not only blind, but deaf and mute as well.

Her impertinent little nose and the golden curls peeping out from beneath her mobcap also gave him a peculiar start of recognition. "Do I know you?"

"I should think not. I'm Pamela's s-s-servant. I'm her maid. Her maidservant. Yes, that's what I am. Her maidservant."

"Pamela?" It took a dazed minute for his mental faculties to reassert themselves. "Ah, yes — my cousin's fiancée — the ever so charming Miss Darby. Yet you address her by her Christian name. Tell me — does your mistress encourage such familiarity?"

"Does yours?"

At her cheeky retort, Crispin quickly discovered that it hurt to smile. But he still couldn't stop himself. "My mistress encourages all manner of familiarity. That's why she's my mistress."

The girl's mouth curved into a reluctant little half smile. "You're bleeding," she announced.

"I am?" He reached toward his face but her hand was already there, dabbing at his cheekbone with the corner of a sheet. Her touch was far gentler than her voice.

He welcomed her assistance, grateful for the opportunity to study the creamy curve of her cheek and the beguiling sweep of her honey-colored lashes at such an intimate range. He frowned, his bewilderment deepening. "Are you certain we haven't met before? It's not like me to forget a face as lovely as yours."

"I'm sure you've forgotten more lovely faces than you've remembered." She slanted him a provocative look from beneath those lashes, her parted lips only a tantalizing breath away from his.

He leaned forward, suffering a pang of regret when she quickly retreated. She began to gather up the scattered linens, her motions once again brisk with purpose. He scrambled to his feet to assist her, piling the sheets so high in her slender arms she could barely see over the top of them.

"Thank you for being such a gentleman,"

she said primly.

He chuckled. "I've been accused of many things in my day, but rarely that."

He stood back, allowing her to brush past him on the narrow stairwell. He watched her go, bemused by the proud tilt of her head and the saucy sway of her round little rump. He hadn't been so tempted to dally with a maidservant since his fifteenth summer when he'd lost his innocence to a buxom young chambermaid who had crept into his bedchamber each night after the candles had been extinguished.

"Wait!" he called after her as she reached the foot of the stairs. "Do you have a name?"

"Yes," she replied without slowing her steps. "I most certainly do."

Then she was gone, leaving him to sag against the wall and wonder why the ringing in his ears suddenly sounded like cathedral bells.

That night Pamela once again found herself tossing and turning as if the mattress of her cozy half-tester had been stuffed with stones instead of feathers. She was still haunted by the genuine horror she had glimpsed in Crispin's eyes while she sat bleeding at his feet. Perhaps he was simply dismayed that his plan to kill Connor had gone awry. But what if losing the *fleuret* from the tip of his epee really *had* been an accident? What if they were no closer to finding her mother's killer than they had been yesterday?

She rolled to her back, gazing up at the half-tester's canopy. The sooner they exposed her mother's killer, the sooner she and Connor could put an end to their travesty of a betrothal. She would be free to break off their engagement and disappear with her sister and the reward and he would be free to court a more suitable bride — some earl's pampered daughter or the haughty niece of a marquess, perhaps.

She flopped to her side, wincing at the sting of the scratch on her forearm. The sash window was safely secured, misty beams of moonlight the only intruder on this restless night.

The room suddenly felt unbearably stuffy. Pamela kicked away the blankets. After lying there for a few more interminable minutes, she rolled out of the bed, marched over to the window and threw up the sash. A cool night breeze poured into the room, caressing her fevered brow. She leaned out the window and searched the shadows below but detected no hint of movement.

Sighing, she returned to the bed. Folding her hands beneath her cheek, she lay gazing at the open window. Perhaps in the most secret corner of her heart, she had hoped Connor might come to collect his prize. If she drifted off to sleep now, would she awaken to find his shadow looming over her in the moonlight? And if she did, would she have the strength to send him away or would she open her arms to welcome him into her bed?

Groaning, Pamela scrambled back to her feet. She snatched up her faded dressing gown from the back of a nearby chair and shrugged it on over her nightdress. If they were going to trap her mother's killer, then she and Connor had much to discuss, did they not? And it was nearly impossible to do so beneath the watchful eyes of the duke, his suspicious sister and their nosy army of servants.

She eased open the door and peered both ways down the deserted corridor. Perhaps it was time to show Connor Kincaid he wasn't the only one who could sneak into someone's bedchamber in the dead of night.

As Pamela slipped into Connor's bedchamber, she had to resist the urge to let out a low admiring whistle. The bedchamber was so vast it made her own generous suite look like servants' quarters. She drew in a deep breath, savoring the masculine scents of leather and fine wood.

As she drifted across the gleaming cherry floor, she realized the mischievous moon had followed her from her room. It was peeping through one of the tall sash windows on the far wall, bathing the bed in a wash of silver.

The towering four-poster with its turned bedposts and ornately carved headboard crowned the center of the room. It wasn't the spectacularly overwrought bed that engaged her fascination, but the man who lay on his back with his long limbs sprawled among its rumpled bedclothes.

Pamela crept closer, swallowing a knot of trepidation.

Too late it occurred to her that Connor hardly seemed the sort to don a long nightshirt and tasseled nightcap. Instead, he reclined on his back with a mere ribbon of bedsheet draped carelessly over his hips.

Her mouth went dry. If she had any moral fortitude whatsoever, she would beat a hasty retreat straight back to her own bedchamber, her own lonely bed. But curiosity was already overcoming her caution, tempting her to draw within touching distance of Connor's sleeping form.

With his hair spilling across the pillow and

moonlight bathing the rugged planes of his face, he no longer looked like a gentleman but like some mythical creature of the forest — more satyr than man. It wasn't difficult to imagine him chasing down some squealing maiden who would beg him for mercy while secretly welcoming the forbidden pleasure only his touch could bring her.

She inched nearer to the bed, her treacherous fingertips itching to explore the silky whorls of hair dusting his chest. Moonlight caressed those broad planes, reminding her that he didn't sleep completely nude after all. He was still wearing the gold locket she had glimpsed in the ruins of Castle Mac-Farlane. And he was still wearing it over his heart.

He stirred in his sleep, drawing her gaze to the sculpted muscles of his abdomen, his powerful thighs. When he shifted again, sending that fragile ribbon of sheet into a dangerous slide, she jerked her mortified gaze back to his face.

His thick, spiky lashes rested flush against his high cheekbones. He must have been dreaming, because a roguish hint of a smile deepened the dimple in his right cheek.

Pamela shook her head, a wry smile curving her own lips. She still couldn't resist that dimple. It had proven itself her downfall, from the first time she'd seen it sketched on that handbill.

Reaching out her trembling fingers, she tenderly stroked his cheek.

She heard a click. One minute she was standing beside Connor; the next she was beneath him, both of her wrists manacled over her head by one of his powerful hands and the mouth of his cocked pistol pressed to the underside of her jaw.

CHAPTER 16

Pamela's voice came out of the darkness, strained and breathless. "If you pull that trigger, I'm guessing a bouquet of flowers won't burst out of the muzzle."

For a bewildered moment, Connor thought he was still dreaming. How else to explain the intoxicating scent of lilacs, and Pamela warm and soft beneath him in his bed? But if he was still dreaming, then why wasn't she as naked as he was? Why was there a worn layer of cotton separating the beguiling softness of her plump breasts from his bare chest? Why was his rigid arousal nudging her thigh instead of being buried deep inside of her? And why was the mouth of his pistol rammed against the tender underside of her jaw?

He felt her graceful throat convulse in a swallow. "If this is how you greet every woman who comes to your bed, Mr. Kincaid, I can see why you might have to pay for your pleasures."

He carefully uncocked the weapon that was under his control, but could do nothing about the one pressed to her thigh. Nor did he relinquish his grip on her slender wrists. "You'd sleep with a loaded pistol under your pillow too, lass, if someone in this house was trying to kill you."

"I can assure you that I didn't sneak in here to smother you with a pillow. Although I must confess the prospect has its merits."

He gazed down at her, fighting the temptation to silence her saucy little mouth with a kiss. But with her beneath him and completely at the mercy of his superior strength, he couldn't trust himself to be satisfied with a mere kiss — no matter how delectable.

Silently cursing himself for a fool, Connor freed her wrists and rolled off of her, dragging the sheet over his lap as he did so. Unfortunately, that only succeeded in making a rather pronounced tent. Hell, at this point even the counterpane wouldn't have helped.

He slipped the pistol back under his pillow, then scooted backward to lean against one of the bedposts at the foot of the bed. He figured the more distance he put between them, the sooner his boiling blood would cool.

Pamela sat up and rubbed her wrists, giving him a reproachful look. "I must say your hospitality leaves a little to be desired."

"How did you get in?" he demanded. "Did you climb through the window?"

"No. I walked through the door."

He scowled. "Damn that worthless valet of mine. Brodie was supposed to have locked the door when he came in. He must still be out making calf's eyes at the cook."

Pamela's eyes widened. "The squat woman with no neck and the ham hocks for hands?"

"That would be her. She chased him out of the kitchen with a meat cleaver this afternoon when he offered to show her his tattoo, but he insisted she was just toying with his affections and will make him a bonny wife someday."

Pamela shook her head ruefully. "Perhaps we should be more worried about the cook mistaking you for Brodie and cleaving you to death in your sleep than Lady Astrid poisoning your tea or Crispin pushing you down a flight of stairs."

As Connor remembered the raw panic he had felt when the point of Crispin's epee went whipping toward Pamela, he felt his face harden. "Oh, I think I can take care of young master Crispin. All you have to do is let me hold him down and pummel him until he confesses."

"I'm afraid you might enjoy that a little too much. Even if he turns out to be innocent."

Connor snorted. "Men like him are never innocent."

"Are you saying that because he's English or because he reminds you of yourself at that age?"

"At his age, I was still riding with my clansmen, trying to fulfill my father's dream of reuniting Clan Kincaid."

"Why did you give up on that dream?" she asked softly.

"Because I finally realized we weren't the heroes we'd always fancied ourselves to be. That we'd become the very thing we despised — common villains preying on the weak."

Pamela arched one eyebrow. "So you decided to pursue the more virtuous vocation of highwayman?"

"A highwayman doesn't have to lie to himself to make himself believe that all of his efforts are for some noble cause when the only worthwhile cause is filling his own purse. He doesn't have to play the hero and spend half his life pretending he can save his men and his clan when he can't even save himself."

Pamela should have been alarmed by the ruthless glint in Connor's eye, but she found herself creeping closer to him instead of fleeing. She already knew there was nowhere she could hide to escape his piercing gaze.

"Why did you come here tonight, Pamela?" he demanded in a low growl. "What do you want?"

No one had ever asked her that question before. Not her mother. Not Sophie. She'd been too busy tending to their wants and needs to consider her own, which was why she still had no answer for him. At least not one she could trust to words. All she could do was return his gaze and pray her heart was not in her eyes.

He reached out and idly stroked his thumb over her lips. "I was hoping you'd come to deliver my prize."

His touch coaxed a smile from her lips. "If Crispin had won the fencing match, were you going to let him kiss me?"

"If I had believed Crispin had a chance in hell of winning, I wouldn't have agreed to the wager. Because if he had kissed you," Connor told her solemnly, "I would have had no choice but to cut off his head."

There it was again. That thrilling note of possessiveness that made her feel as if she belonged to him. As if she would always belong to him.

She blew out a long-suffering sigh. "Well, you did win, so I suppose I have no choice but to honor the wager." She leaned toward him and pressed her eyes shut, already anticipating the tantalizing brush of his mouth against hers.

"Oh, no you don't, lass." Her eyes flew open to find him leaning against the bedpost with his hands folded behind his head and a lazy smile curving his lips. "The kiss is *my* prize. *You* have to give it to *me*."

"Oh!" Pamela had no idea why she suddenly felt so ridiculously shy. He had already kissed her numerous times and she had kissed him back with an alarming lack of restraint. But somehow that wasn't the same as initiating the kiss.

Judging from his smirk, he was probably expecting her to give him a virginal peck on the cheek. Pursing her lips into a tight little rosebud, she touched them to the very corner of his mouth. But then that rosebud flowered, her mouth going soft and inviting against his smooth, firm lips.

Connor sucked in a hissed breath but held himself utterly still, allowing Pamela to sample him to her heart's content. One kiss soon melted into another. And another.

Until his ragged groan emboldened her to trace the seam of his lips with the tip of her pert little tongue, to lick into his mouth with a tender hunger he ached to satisfy.

He threaded his hands through her hair, tugging her mouth away from his. Her lips were still parted, her eyes misty with longing.

"Were you planning on kissing Crispin with such unbridled enthusiasm?" he demanded, his breath coming hard and fast.

"You're the one who agreed to the wager. If he had won, I was going to make *you* kiss him."

He shook his head. "I always knew the English weren't to be trusted."

"Then don't trust me," she whispered, lifting a hand to his cheek. "Just kiss me."

Pamela didn't have to ask him twice. Connor slanted his mouth over hers with a ferocity born of desperation, mating her with the warm, rough sweetness of his tongue. For a breathless eternity, she could only cling to him, could only take what he would give her and wish for more.

It seemed he was only too eager to oblige her unspoken wishes. While continuing to lay claim to her mouth with long, lavish kisses, he cupped her bottom in his big warm hands and lifted her into his lap. Her dressing gown fell open and her nightdress rode up as her knees slid down on either side of his powerful thighs, leaving her straddling the firm ridge of flesh beneath the sheet. As he arched upward, pressing himself to the tender mound between her thighs, her head fell back and a moan of raw pleasure tore from her throat.

That moan turned into a whimper as he shifted her again, urging her around until she sat between his sprawled legs with her back to his chest. He reached around her, his sun-bronzed hands gently smoothing the skirt of her nightdress up to her waist, exposing her threadbare drawers to the silvery kiss of the moonlight and his touch.

Their encounter in the Highlands had given him an unfair advantage. He knew he only had to tug at her drawers and the frayed seams would give way. As he did just that, Pamela gasped a protest.

"I'll buy you more," he vowed, his voice a husky whisper in her ear. "Or better yet, you can just stop wearing them altogether. Then I could touch you whenever I wanted. Wherever we happened to be. You can't tell me it wouldn't make those long, horrid meals with the duke and his asp of a sister more bearable."

A wicked little shiver raked Pamela as she

imagined Connor slipping his hand beneath the tablecloth and beneath her skirts to stroke her there, without their fellow diners ever suspecting a thing.

His hands were chapped and callused from hours of riding, which only made their tenderness more impossible to resist. His large fingers parted her curls, then her delicate folds, touching her in that wild and secret place with an exquisite care that made her want to weep.

As he stroked and petted her, she shuddered with longing, a sob of pure pleasure wrenched from her trembling lips.

"Shhhh, lass," he murmured in her ear, desire thickening the musical cadences of his burr. "I just want to touch you. I'll not hurt you. I swear it."

How could she tell him he was already hurting her? That he was carving off a piece of her fragile heart with each nimble stroke of his fingertips, each deft flick of his thumb over the throbbing little bud nestled in the crux of her silky curls? As he wrapped one arm around her waist, imprisoning her in a vise of delight, she could feel his unabated desire for her, riding high and hard against the cleft of her rump.

She stole a furtive glance downward, captivated against her will by the forbidden wonders his fingers were working in the moonlight. There was something both shocking and erotic about being in his arms while bared all the way to the waist. As she watched his longest finger glide toward the very heart of her while his thumb continued its maddening rhythm, her treacherous body betrayed her deepest secret — that she wanted him as badly as he wanted her.

Connor groaned, nearly undone by the thick tears of nectar Pamela's body was weeping for him. He wanted nothing more than to accept her unspoken invitation. To whisk away the sheet that separated their naked flesh and urge her forward and to her knees, where she could better accept what he was aching to give her. He wanted to rub himself in the delectable cream welling up between her legs, then bury himself so deep inside of her she would no longer be able to tell where her body ended and his began.

But this wasn't some stranger he had paid to couple with him. This was Pamela. Brave, bonny Pamela who was bold and foolish enough to defy an armed highwayman with a toy gun, throw herself in front of Crispin's sword, and take the biggest risk of all by coming to his bed in the middle of the night, her feet bare and her hair unbound.

As he dipped his finger into her, marveling at how tight and hot she was, she arched into his hand. He wished it was his mouth — wished he could sample her musky sweetness, nip that swollen little bud with his teeth and use his tongue as a whip to drive her over the edge of ecstasy. But for now he had to satisfy himself with capturing her chin in a fierce grip and tilting her face to the side so their mouths could meld in a hot, hungry kiss.

As Connor's finger glided in and out of her, pushing deeper with each foray, Pamela writhed against him. He was persistent yet patient, and she was terrified he was just going to leave her teetering on the cusp of bliss until she expired from anticipation.

"There's no rush, sweetheart," he whispered against the corner of her mouth. "I've got all night to make you come."

But he wouldn't need all night. All it took was a second finger added to the first and a flick of his thumb and rapture went spilling through her in shuddering waves. She opened her mouth to cry out his name, but his hand was there, muffling her broken wail before she could wake the entire household.

As Connor felt the fevered silk of Pamela's body grip his fingers, he arched against her bottom, clenching his teeth against a spasm of raw lust. He was on the verge of losing control and spilling his seed without even being inside of her, something he hadn't done since he was a lad of sixteen.

It hardly helped his predicament when she wiggled around in his lap and threw her arms around his neck. As she rubbed her smooth cheek against his beard-stubbled one, he wouldn't have been surprised to hear the angels singing. What he heard instead was:

> Once there was a bonny cook
> With legs as stout as trees.
> One squeeze from those dimpled thighs
> Could bring me to me knees

"Oh, hell," Connor swore as the muffled voice came drifting through the door. He buried his face in Pamela's throat, his own voice so hoarse with lust he barely recognized it as his own. "If Brodie walks through that door right now, I swear to God I'm going to shoot him."

Pamela pushed against his shoulders, her hands gentle but firm. "I should go."

"Oh, no, you shouldn't. If you stay, I promise I won't shoot him." His mouth glided down her throat, savoring the salty sweetness of her sweat-dampened flesh. "I'll just hit him over the head with something very heavy. Maybe an iron poker or the clock from the mantel. We can hide his body in the window seat. It'll be days before they find him. The cook will thank us."

She cupped his cheeks in her hands, forcing his head up so he could meet her glowing gaze. "I don't want him to find me in your chamber."

"You could hide under here." Giving her a hopeful grin, Connor reached to lift the sheet covering his lap.

She grabbed his wrist, the shy downward flick of her gaze and her admiring swallow softening the sting of his disappointment. "I really don't think there would be room."

Connor sighed. Brodie was whistling now, the cheery sound swelling with each step. Biting off an oath, Connor tucked the sheet around his waist, swept Pamela up in his arms and went striding toward one of the windows.

Pamela clutched at his neck, her eyes widening in alarm. "What are you going to do? Toss me out the window?"

"Do you trust me?" he asked, balancing her weight with one arm as he shoved up the window sash with his other hand.

"No!"

His response to her vehement declaration

was to kiss her — long and deep and hard — until she was just as dazed and limp as she had been in those moments after his deft fingers had coaxed her over the brink. Before she could clear her mind enough to protest, he had wrapped his powerful hands around her wrists and was lowering her out the window.

For a dizzying moment, there was nothing beneath her pinwheeling feet. Then she felt her toes connect with something solid and realized he had lowered her onto a broad shelf of a ledge that jutted out over the window below his chamber. From there she could easily swing into a nearby sycamore tree — to a spot where the branches formed a broad cradle.

"You can climb down to the garden from there," he called softly down to her. "The branches are close together — like a ladder."

Clinging to his wrists for dear life, Pamela gave the distant ground a dubious look. "What if I'd rather spend the night up here?"

"Then you might have some explaining to do to the gardeners in the morning." He leered down at her. "Especially since you're not wearing any drawers."

She clamped her knees together, having

forgotten that small but important fact. Glowering up at him, she eased her wrists from his grasp, swung from ledge to tree and began to clamber toward the ground, feeling her way along each branch with painstaking care.

When Brodie eased open the door and slipped into the chamber, Connor was still standing at the window.

"Are you still up, lad? I thought you'd be long asleep by now."

"I was," Connor said, a smile curving his lips as he watched Pamela go scampering across the dew-drenched grass like some fey creature from his boyhood fantasies. "But a dream woke me up."

Ignoring the gawking footmen stationed at each end of the cherry sideboard, Connor added three coddled eggs, four rashers of crisp, juicy bacon and an entire school of kippers to the already heaping portions on his plate. He hesitated, eyeing each of the silver serving dishes in turn, then topped off his plate with a pair of steaming rolls and a slab of plum cake big enough to choke a horse.

Breakfast was the only meal where he was allowed to load his own plate and he had every intention of making the most of it.

There were also more foods he could eat with his fingers instead of having to mince off tiny portions with one of those ridiculous forks. He was beginning to understand why Esau had traded his birthright to Jacob for a mess of pottage. He'd been so famished since their arrival at Warrick Park that he would have gladly traded the duke's wealth and title for a hearty bowl of Scotch broth or a steaming portion of *tatties and neeps*.

After exchanging an amused glance with his fellow servant, one of the footmen dared to address him directly. "We were just wondering, my lord, what one eats for breakfast in Scotland."

"Babies," Connor replied without cracking a smile. "Plump, juicy English babies. Oh, and haggis, of course."

Leaving them with horrorstruck expressions, he carried his plate to the oval table beneath the windows where the duke and Lady Astrid were breaking their own fast.

As he sank into his chair, he stole a surreptitious glance at the mantel clock, then the door, knowing very well that he'd been doing so every three minutes since he'd entered the sunny morning room where breakfast was served.

He should have known his vigilance wouldn't escape the duke's sharp eyes.

"Eager to lay eyes on your charming fiancée this morning, are we? Don't be so impatient, son. Once the two of you are wed, you can keep her abed in the morning for as long as you like."

Lady Astrid glanced up from buttering a roll. "Really, Archibald. There's no need for vulgarity, is there?"

"On the contrary, Astrid. If a man is to keep his young bride satisfied, there's every need for it." He waved a fork in Connor's direction. "I recommend vigorous vulgarity, son, at least once a day and twice on Sundays."

Connor dabbed at his lips with his napkin to hide his smile. There were times when he found the old man almost tolerable. "I'll take great care to heed your advice, your grace."

If Pamela really was to be his bride, such counsel would be a pleasure to follow. Except he would prefer it to be at least twice a day and thrice on Sundays. Judging by her eager response to his touch, he didn't believe Pamela would object.

"Ah, yes, my brother is a fount of wisdom on all matters matrimonial." Astrid turned her acidic gaze on Connor. "It's a pity you can't ask your mother about that, isn't it?"

The duke snorted. "And just what would

you know about pleasing a mate? Your poor Sheldon burned himself to death in his bed just to escape your nagging."

Connor felt the tiny hairs at the back of his nape prickle to attention. He took a leisurely sip of his chocolate, keeping his face carefully bland to hide his keen interest in their exchange.

"My *poor* Sheldon was a miserable sot! If he had heeded my nagging, he wouldn't have been swilling brandy as if it were water or smoking those foul cigars of his in bed. Papa knew he was a hopeless bounder when he forced me to marry him. He just didn't give a —" Astrid froze, choking back whatever unladylike pronouncement she was about to make.

She inclined her head, the skin around her mouth going pinched and white. Connor felt a flicker of reluctant pity. Her hair might be going silver and her chin soft, but a hint of tarnished beauty still hovered about her like the ghost of the girl she had once been.

The duke dismissed her outburst with a contemptuous "harrumph" and turned his attention back to Connor. "I've arranged for you and Miss Darby to attend a soiree tomorrow evening at Lord Newton's town house. The tailor assured me that he and his assistants would be working around the clock and could deliver the first installment of your wardrobe in the morning. I'm afraid I won't be able to accompany you. I want to save all my strength for the ball I'll be hosting next week to celebrate your official reintroduction into society."

Connor frowned. "A ball? I don't suppose that would involve dancing, would it?"

Amusement sparkled in the duke's eyes. "It is customary to take a turn or two around the floor with the lady of your choice in your arms."

The lady of his choice. Connor stole another look at the clock to discover it was nearly ten o'clock. His frown deepened.

Perhaps Pamela was simply languishing in bed, exhausted from her midnight visit to his bedchamber. And his bed. His gaze flicked from the clock to the door. During their journey from Scotland, he had discovered that she was an early and cheerful riser, eager to face each new day and the adventures it would bring.

What if she wasn't languishing in bed but cowering in her bedchamber, too mortified to face him? He couldn't bear the thought that he might have shamed her with his touch. That she might have already come to regret the pleasure he had given her.

He shot to his feet, giving his overflowing plate one last yearning look.

"Where are you going?" Lady Astrid snapped as he strode toward the door. "Surely you're not going to drag poor Miss Darby out of her bedchamber. That would hardly be appropriate."

He made an abrupt about-face and marched back to the table. He retrieved a warm roll, then proceeded on his way, leaving the duke chuckling and Lady Astrid opening and closing her mouth like a beached herring.

By the time Connor reached the door of Pamela's bedchamber, the roll was long gone but his misgivings were not. He pressed his ear to the door, half afraid he would be greeted by the sound of Pamela's heart-wrenching sobs.

But all that greeted him was silence. He lifted his fist to knock, then lowered it. This was one time when he had no intention of giving Pamela the opportunity to refuse him.

Setting his jaw to a determined angle, he boldly threw open the door.

Pamela had been gazing down at the heaps of taffeta and muslin scattered across the unmade bed, but when the door flew open, she whirled around to face him.

Connor's heart sank. It was worse than he'd feared. Her beautiful eyes were swollen nearly shut, her nose was bright pink and her cheeks were still streaked with fresh tears. Her hair was in a dreadful tangle — half up and half down with combs and hairpins sticking out at all angles. And worst of all, she was gazing at him as if *he* were the one who had murdered her poor mother.

Although his feet felt as if they were weighted with lead, he couldn't stop himself from moving toward her. "There's no need for this, lass, and I won't have it," he said quietly. "You can't spend the rest of your life weeping in your bedchamber just because you spent a few stolen moments in mine."

Connor heard a startled gasp. Too late, he saw Sophie standing next to the dressing table, her mouth hanging open and her astonished gaze fixed on Pamela as if she'd never seen her sister before.

He stopped a few feet from Pamela, aching to close the distance between them if only so he could touch her one last time. "You've nothing to be ashamed of, lass. I'm the one who took advantage of you and your innocence. As you well know, I'm not an honorable man. But I can promise you that despite what happened between us last night, you're still a virgin. You'll bring no shame to your husband's bed." Although he made an honest effort, he could not quite keep the bitter note from his voice. "He'll never even have to know you let a dirty, thievin' Highlander put his hands on you."

Connor wasn't aware that Pamela had been gripping a hairbrush until it went sailing past his head, striking the door behind him with a dull thud.

"I'm not crying because I'm ashamed, you thick-witted Scotsman!" She glared at him, her voice rising to a wail. "I'm crying because I don't have anything to wear!"

CHAPTER 17

"What's wrong with what you're wearing right now?" Connor asked cautiously, prepared to duck should Pamela hurl another unexpected object at him — a lace garter or perhaps the dressing-table stool.

He'd seen her stand down an entire regiment of English soldiers armed with nothing but a smile. He never thought he'd see her trembling on the brink of hysteria over a rumpled heap of taffeta.

She eyed him disbelievingly. "Are you blind as well as daft? I only had two suitable frocks of my own and I wore both of those the first day we were here. I've already been reduced to borrowing Sophie's gowns."

Sophie snorted and rolled her eyes. "Borrowing? Destroying is more like it. She returned my favorite gown with the sleeve all slashed to ribbons! And that's not even counting the damage she did to my prettiest pair of slippers with her enormous feet."

Ignoring her sister's pout, Pamela waved a hand toward the pile of garments on the bed. "I've tried on every one of her gowns and each one is less flattering than the last."

"I've always been more inclined to notice the female in the frock than the frock itself," Connor admitted. "If you must know, most men would rather do away with the frock altogether."

"Well, I may have to do just that." Clutching her skirt in both fists, Pamela lifted the scalloped hem of the pastel pink confection she was modeling at the moment, giving him an enticing glimpse of trim ankles and a pair of bare feet that looked incredibly dainty to him, especially compared to his own. "Because this one is at least five inches too short."

"Indeed," he murmured, afraid to say more.

"And just look at this bodice. It's a disaster!" She dropped the skirt and cupped her hands beneath her breasts, hiking them upward. "If I so much as take one deep breath, my bosoms are going to pop right out for all the world to see!"

Since she had invited him to look, Connor gazed his fill at the luscious globes threatening to spill over the top of the low-cut bodice. He could still remember how warm and soft they'd felt in his hands. "And that would be a bad thing?" he asked, forced to bite the inside of his cheek to keep from smiling.

"It most certainly would! Especially since Sophie just told me she overheard the servants in the kitchen saying we've been invited to our first soiree tomorrow evening. I can't even find a gown to wear to breakfast. How am I supposed to dress for a soiree!"

"I'm not even sure what a soiree is," Connor confessed.

"It's a deliciously sophisticated French word for party," Sophie offered with a superior little smirk.

"We're not in France," Connor retorted. "Why don't they just call it a party?"

Pamela collapsed to a sitting position on the foot of the bed, her proud shoulders slumped in defeat. "It's going to create enough of a scandal when everyone discovers the future Duke of Warrick has pledged his troth to an actress's daughter who was born on the wrong side of the blanket. Once I make an appearance in my ill-fitting, unfashionable gowns, no one will believe you could have fallen in love with me. Not when they can plainly see how common I truly am." She bowed her head, her voice fading until it was barely audible. "I shall be ridiculous in their eyes and I will make you ridiculous, too."

Connor's amusement faded as Pamela's words slowly sank in. She wasn't ashamed of him. She was afraid she would shame him. Connor Kincaid. A dirty, thieving Highlander with rope scars on his throat and a price on his head.

He ached to touch her, but he was afraid of further bruising her already battered pride.

Knitting his hands at the small of his back to keep them off of her, he turned to address Sophie. "Look after your sister. Get her a cool rag for her eyes and ring for breakfast." He turned toward the door, then turned back. "Order her a hot bath as well . . . with some of those flowers or leaves they sprinkle in to make the water smell nice."

Sophie gaped at him, plainly insulted at being treated like the servant she was pretending to be. "Aye, my lord," she said, bobbing him a mocking curtsy. "Will his lordship be requiring anything else?"

He stole a look at Pamela, who was eyeing him with equal bewilderment. "No. You can trust me to take care of the rest."

Connor strode through the long corridors of Warrick Park as if he were already its master. As he rounded a corner without breaking his stride, a pair of young maidservants dusting the wainscoting exchanged a nervous glance and went scurrying out of his way.

He arrived back at the morning room to find it already deserted. A lone footman was removing dishes from the sideboard. When Connor cleared his throat, the man jumped as if he'd been shot. The silver platter in his hand slipped through his fingers and went crashing to the floor, scattering the remnants of the coddled eggs across the priceless Aubusson carpet.

Connor had no time to waste on apologies or pleasantries. "Where can I find the duke?"

"Your father, my lord?" The servant stole a furtive glance at the mantel clock. "At this time of the morning, you can usually find him in the portrait gallery."

Connor was already striding back down the corridor when he realized he had no idea where the portrait gallery was.

He stopped at the foot of the grand

staircase in the entrance hall, raking a hand through his hair in frustration. He could pinpoint his exact location in the Highland wilderness using nothing more than the angle of the sun and the thickness of the moss growing on the side of a tree, but he couldn't seem to navigate this damn maze of a house.

He was about to return to the morning room to demand directions when a rhythmic squeak came floating down the stairs. Connor had heard that sound before, each time some flustered footman rolled the duke's wheeled chair into a room with his master berating him the entire time for going too fast or not fast enough.

Connor took the stairs two at a time, turning left at the second-story landing. His brisk strides soon carried him to a long, spacious gallery with a balcony overlooking the darkened ballroom on one side and a wall lined with formal portraits of all shapes and sizes on the other. The flickering wall lamps failed to completely dispel the gloom.

The duke's wheeled chair had been silenced and a footman was just disappearing through a far door, having been dismissed by his master. The duke sat all alone, huddled in his chair with a shawl wrapped around his shoulders and a lap rug draped over his wasted legs.

He was gazing up at the wall, his attention so transfixed, he might have been the only living creature in the house.

Connor had to steel his heart against another one of those disturbing pangs of pity. This man was his enemy, he reminded himself. If the duke was alone, it was because he had driven away everyone who had ever loved him.

Connor's strides slowed. For the first time since arriving at Warrick Hall, he truly felt like the intruder he was. As he traversed that seemingly endless gallery, his steps as stealthy as a thief's, the Warrick ancestors in their ornate garments and gilded frames seemed to be sneering down their noses at him, mocking him for daring to pretend to be one of them.

His curiosity sharpened as he approached the duke's chair. He could not imagine any likeness that could have so captured the man's jaded attentions. His curiosity shifted to bewilderment as he realized the duke wasn't gazing up at a portrait, but at a large blank space on the wall between two portraits. Judging by the faded condition of the gold-flecked wallpaper that surrounded the perfect square, the space had not always been empty.

Connor would have sworn the man wasn't even aware of his presence, which was why he started when the duke said softly, "Everyone believes I had her portraits removed because I despised her for leaving me. But the truth was that I simply could not bear to look upon them. Couldn't bear to be reminded every miserable day of my life that I'd been fool enough to lose her." He shook his head. "I said such terrible things to her. Made such dreadful threats. I was trying to frighten her into not leaving me, but all I succeeded in doing was driving her away. What I should have done — what I was too young and proud and foolish to do — was fall on my knees and beg her to forgive me."

He sighed, his hollow-eyed gaze still devouring that empty wall. "I come here every day and gaze up at the place where her portrait used to hang and I can still see her. Those long, shiny curls she would let me brush before bedtime. Her laughing eyes. That maddening dimple that would only appear when she was teasing me."

Connor gazed up at the wall with equal fascination, almost able to see the woman the duke was describing.

The duke wheeled his chair around to face him. "I suppose you find me ridiculous. She would laugh in my face if she could see me now. She never did have any patience for my pride. Or my weaknesses."

"After she deserted you, why didn't you divorce her or have her declared dead so you could remarry and produce another heir?" Connor asked, genuinely curious.

"Because I knew there would be no point in it. She would always be the wife of my heart. Do you know that I never slept with another woman after she left me? All these years I've been faithful to a ghost." A bleak chuckle escaped him. "That would please her too, you know. She'd tell me I got just what I deserved for breaking our marriage vows — and her heart." He tipped his head back to meet Connor's gaze, his expression defiant. "How you must hate me!"

"I don't hate you," Connor told him, relieved to be able to pull a thread of truth out of his own web of lies.

The canny glitter had returned to the duke's eyes. "Ah, but you pity me, which is even more galling to a sick old man who was once as brash and robust as you. I suppose I should be grateful to you and your Miss Darby. Until you returned and told me what had become of your mother, I was still able to pretend she might come walking back through my door someday — as young and beautiful as on the day she left me. But now that I know she's well and truly gone, I have one more reason to welcome death. Although given the blackened condition of my soul," he added dryly, "there's little chance we'll ever be reunited, even on the other side of that great void."

"If you had the chance," Connor asked softly, "whose forgiveness would you seek? God's? Or hers?"

"Since I'm not likely to receive mercy from either one of them, perhaps I should content myself with asking for yours."

Connor went down on one knee in front of the chair, putting them at eye level just as he had on the first day he'd arrived at Warrick Park. He placed one hand on the man's bony knee, willing to beg if he had to. "It's not your remorse or your regrets I need today, your grace, but something else entirely."

The duke laid his hand atop Connor's, giving it a surprisingly hearty squeeze. "Anything, son. Anything at all."

When a timid rap sounded on her bedchamber door that afternoon, Pamela swung it open to find two young maidservants tittering and bobbing like a pair of fledgling pigeons.

"G'day, miss," chirped the plump, rosy-cheeked one with the carrot-colored curls peeping out from beneath her mobcap. "We've come to fetch you. Lord Eddywhistle requests your presence in the ballroom."

"Lord Eddywhistle?" Pamela repeated, momentarily baffled. Despite enjoying a hearty breakfast and a long hot bath, her head was still a little foggy from her embarrassing bout of tears. "Oh! You mean the marquess!"

"Aye, miss, the marquess." The tall, willowy maid tossed her pale yellow braid over her shoulder. "And it weren't so much a request, really, as a demand."

"Or a command," her plump companion offered helpfully. "I believe his exact words was" — she lowered her voice in a passable imitation of Connor's burr — " 'If the lass balks, remind her I'm goin' to be the duke someday and my word will be law.' "

Pamela cast a disbelieving glance over her shoulder at her sister. Sophie had been stretched out on her stomach on the bed, devouring the latest issue of *La Belle Assemblée,* which she'd nicked from Lady Astrid's bedchamber, but she was now watching the proceedings at the door with avid interest.

"He actually said his word would be law,

did he? That's odd," Pamela muttered. "I didn't think he was particularly fond of the law." She surveyed the maids' eager young faces. "You can tell Lord Eddywhistle I'll be down as soon as I can find something suitable to wear. Which could be next week," she added beneath her breath.

The maids exchanged a dismayed glance. "Oh, no, miss," the slender one said. "That won't be necessary. He said all you needed to wear was your dressing gown."

"Excuse me? He wants me to wear my dressing gown downstairs in the middle of the day?"

"Aye, miss." The plump little maid's brow puckered in a determined frown. "His instructions was very clear on that matter. Very clear indeed."

Pamela shook her head, wondering what could have possessed Connor to make such a peculiar request. After a moment's thought, she squared her shoulders and jerked a fresh knot in the sash of her faded dressing gown. She ran her fingers through the loose curls piled atop her head to find them still a little damp from her bath.

"I suppose we should go then. We certainly wouldn't want to keep our future lord and master waiting, would we?"

As she sailed from the chamber, accompanied by her beaming escort, Sophie scrambled down from the bed to follow.

Pamela went marching into the ballroom with Sophie trotting at her heels. Her temper had been rising with each step and she was determined to give Connor Kincaid a piece of her mind for daring to summon her in such a high-handed manner.

But when she crossed the threshold and saw what awaited her, the pieces of her mind scattered, leaving her without a coherent thought in her head.

The ballroom had been transformed. If not for the sparkling cut-glass chandeliers and the row of open French windows on the far wall, she never would have recognized it as the same room that had housed yesterday's duel.

Almost every inch of space was occupied by bolts of fabric in a dizzying array of textures and colors. Dressmaker's dummies were scattered throughout the room, their voluptuous forms draped in luxurious lengths of silk and satin. Even the ancient suit of armor standing guard against the far wall had been recruited to model a mink tippet and a saucy little willow bonnet crowned by a towering plume of ostrich feathers.

"Oh, my!" Sophie exclaimed, slipping right past Pamela. She eyed the watercolor fashion plates that had been propped up on gilded easels throughout the room, swaying on her feet as if she might swoon. "I'm willing to wager they smuggled these right out of Paris! Aren't they the most exquisite things you've ever seen?"

A sea of expectant faces greeted Pamela, but she only had eyes for one of them. She stood frozen in place as Connor came wending his way through their ranks to greet her.

"What have you done?" she demanded, sounding nearly as breathless and prone to swoon as Sophie.

He shrugged his broad shoulders, as if assembling a virtual army of dressmakers and linen drapers was something a highwayman did every day. "I summoned them to start work on your trousseau."

"Do you even know what that word means?"

"It's a French word for —"

"Hush, Sophie," Pamela and Connor snapped in unison.

Sophie's wounded pout quickly shifted into a gasp of delight as a display of elegant silk slippers in a variety of sizes and a rainbow of colors caught her eye. Their gemstone buckles sparkled in the sunlight.

"The hardest part was getting them all to agree to close up shop for two days and work around the clock," Connor admitted, "but I'm quickly learning just how persuasive a title and the promise of a generous reward can be."

Pamela already knew exactly how persuasive he could be, even without a title or the promise of a reward. Judging from the bliss she had experienced at his skillful fingertips only last night, he could probably persuade a woman to do just about anything he wanted her to do, no matter how deliciously wicked or wanton.

"I can't do this," she said, taking a hasty step backward.

"And why not?" He narrowed his eyes and squared his freshly shaven jaw in an expression she was coming to know only too well. "You don't dare refuse me. You said it yourself, lass. I can't have my bride embarrassing herself — or me — in front of all of London."

His bride.

For a dizzying moment, it was only too easy to imagine herself on his arm, wearing one of the elegant gowns sketched in the fashion plates as she gazed up at him adoringly. Only too easy to forget that they were only playing roles and that her part in their little farce would be over long before the curtain rose for the second act.

She eyed a bolt of shimmering sea-green crepe with open longing, reminding herself that even the most miniscule of roles required a costume.

"Very well, my lord," she said softly. "I shall strive not to disgrace your good name."

Grinning his approval, Connor crooked a finger at his waiting minions.

Connor felt a brief pang of sympathy as they rushed forward, descending upon Pamela in a flurry of pins and feathers and measuring tapes and Brussels lace, all chattering at once in English and French with a smattering of Italian tossed in. She shot him a panicked look before she was swallowed up completely.

Knowing his work here was done, he started for the door only to find Sophie standing all alone, her pretty face blanched nearly green with envy.

Following her wistful gaze to the dazzling array of slippers, Connor leaned down and whispered, "Why don't you pick out a bonny pair or two for yourself and pretend they're for your mistress? Since she ruined your finest pair with her *enormous feet,* I'm sure she wouldn't mind."

Sophie's face lit up and for a minute Connor was afraid she was going to forget all about her role of maidservant and throw her grateful arms around his neck. But she stopped herself just in time. Lowering her eyes, she bobbed a deferent curtsy. "Aye, my lord. Whatever you wish, my lord."

Connor watched her scamper over to the display of slippers, wishing her sister could be so easily seduced by a taffeta bow or a shiny buckle.

CHAPTER 18

Pamela felt as if she were floating down the grand staircase. Her white satin slippers gently hugged her feet without pinching. With each step the hem of her evening gown rippled over the lustrous pearl buckles that adorned them. The gown was fashioned from sea-green crepe with a pleated skirt that seemed to waltz with each graceful sway of her hips and a rounded bodice trimmed in blonde lace that displayed the creamy swell of her bosoms to their best advantage without threatening to evict them every time she drew in a deep breath.

She was doubly grateful for that when she spotted Connor waiting for her at the foot of the stairs. She sucked in an uneven breath, her heart betraying her with a stumbling lurch.

Apparently, while her new French modiste was cobbling together a handful of dresses she could wear until the rest of her trousseau was completed, Connor's tailor had paid him a visit.

His transformation from highwayman to gentleman was now complete. He wore the elegant doeskin breeches, striped gold waistcoat and black cutaway tail coat as if he'd been born to them. Since the clinging breeches were cut to just below the knees, a pair of plain silk stockings hugged his powerful calves. He wore polished black shoes and a snowy white cravat tied in a simple bow that complemented the sun-bronzed strength of his jaw.

Oddly enough, he didn't look any less dangerous than he had the first time they'd met. Instead of polishing away his rugged edges, the trappings of civilization only sharpened them.

Pamela breathed a sigh of relief to see he hadn't succumbed to the fickle whims of fashion by cutting his hair. He was still wearing it tied back at the nape. Her fingers twitched with a wicked urge to tug away that velvet ribbon and run her fingers through it.

As she neared the bottom of the stairs, trailing her gloved fingers lightly along the mahogany baluster, he sketched her a graceful bow. "Miss Darby."

"My lord," she replied primly, bobbing

him an equally graceful curtsy as she stepped off the last stair.

He straightened, his eyes gleaming with appreciation. As he leaned down to whisper in her ear, his warm breath ruffled the upswept coils of her hair, sending a delicious little shiver down her spine. "I trust you were finally able to replace all of those raggedy drawers of yours."

"Oh, my new drawers won't be ready until next week. So I decided not to wear any," she informed him, smiling sweetly.

His mouth fell open but before he could respond, a shrill creaking warned them that a footman was pushing the duke's wheeled chair across the marble floor toward them.

"I just came to see you off," the duke said. "Astrid is almost ready. She'll be along in a few minutes."

As Pamela exchanged a guarded glance with Connor, the duke rubbed his hands together, his eyes sparkling with an emotion that could have been either malice or glee. "I might be too weak to venture out myself, but you didn't think I was going to send the two of you off without a chaperone, did you? I'm not so close to the grave that I can't remember what it was like to be young and desperately in love."

Pamela plucked a speck of invisible lint

off the ivory silk of her elbow-length gloves, suddenly even more eager to avoid both men's eyes.

"So is it true what they're saying about her? That her mother was an opera dancer?"

"I heard she was an *actress*."

"Well, I heard her mother was a common little . . ." An inaudible whisper was followed by a flurry of malicious female titters. "That came straight from Lord Biffledown's wife. Apparently her husband had some *dealings* with the woman."

"What can one expect?" interjected a new voice that was so tart one could almost smell vinegar in the air. "After all, he's been living among those savage Scots for all these years. He probably believes a lady is any female who wears shoes and bathes once a month — whether she needs to or not."

One of the voices dropped to a sly murmur. "I've heard the Scots are cursed with insatiable carnal appetites. Perhaps he was afraid a true lady wouldn't be able to satisfy him."

"If what his tailor is bandying about town regarding his *measurements* is true, I wouldn't mind trying."

That droll pronouncement was greeted by a scandalized ripple of laughter and a flutter of fans.

Connor inclined his head toward Pamela and whispered, "I do believe that's our cue."

They stood in the foyer of Lord Newton's stately Wimpole Street town house, waiting for the red-faced footman to announce them. Pamela was staring straight ahead, her cheeks burning with humiliation and her spine stiff with pride. It hadn't surprised her in the least when Lady Astrid had abandoned them at the front door, drawing a hare's foot from her reticule and claiming she needed to powder the shine from her nose.

Connor offered her his arm. She tucked her gloved hand in the crook of it.

As the liveried footman stepped into the arched doorway that led into the drawing room, an expectant hush fell over the guests. "The Marquess of Eddywhistle and Miss Pamela Darby," he announced, his voice cracking like a lad's in the first throes of manhood.

Pamela felt a petty twinge of satisfaction as the circle of women who had been gathered by the doorway went scurrying off in different directions like a pack of wide-eyed rats that had just spotted a hawk circling overhead.

The spacious drawing room was occupied

by a veritable crush of guests. The pungent scents of the wax wall lights mingled with the heady aroma of the freshly cut flowers decorating the tables and a variety of perfumes to form a cloying potpourri in the overheated, overcrowded room. Pamela was grateful the stays of her new gown allowed her room to breathe. Had she been wearing one of Sophie's gowns, she would have probably fainted dead away.

As they drifted further into the room, accepting flutes of smuggled French champagne from a footman's tray, the idle chatter resumed but the curious stares only intensified. The very women who had been denouncing Connor as a savage Scot only minutes before were now eyeing him with open appreciation. Had she not been on his arm, Pamela suspected he could have found any number of willing women to woo before the night was over.

She lifted her chin, returning their avid gazes with a cool stare of her own. That was when a familiar face near the hearth caught her eye.

"Oh, no," she breathed, draining her champagne in a single gulp.

"What is it?"

"It's Viscount Pemberly. The man I told you about. The one who was trying to force

Sophie into becoming his mistress." Tightening her grip on Connor's arm, she sought to steer him in a different direction.

"Don't be so hasty, lass," he said, his jovial tone belied by the wicked gleam in his eye. "I've been wanting to make the fellow's acquaintance ever since you told me about him."

"You offered to kill him for me," she reminded him.

His grin only deepened. "Precisely."

Setting his own half-empty champagne glass on a footman's tray, Connor made a beeline for the hearth, leaving her with no choice but to accompany him or be dragged across the floor behind him. Given that the viscount's wife was hanging off his arm, Pemberly didn't look any happier to see her than she was to see him.

"Why, Miss Darby," he said, flashing his white teeth in a grimace of a smile. "How lovely to see you again. I just heard the news about your rather stunning reversal of fortune."

"And just how is it that you and the marquess's fiancée came to be acquainted?" his wife inquired with frosty politeness.

The viscount's handsome face flushed. "Now, dear, you know I've always been a devoted patron of the arts — especially the theater. I was a great admirer of Miss Darby's talented mother."

"And of her charming young sister, from what I've heard," Connor said, earning the nobleman an even icier look from his wife.

Pemberly suddenly seemed to be having great difficulty swallowing. He clawed at his cravat, seeking to loosen it. "And just how is dear little Sophie?"

Pamela glanced behind them, thankful Lady Astrid hadn't yet made her entrance. She couldn't very well tell the viscount she'd left her sister sulking in the window seat because Pamela got to go off to a party in her pretty new things while Sophie was expected to stay behind and turn down the bed.

Before she could respond, Connor edged closer to the viscount, the move emphasizing the disparity in their heights. "Dear little Sophie is under my protection now. If any man tries to make improper advances toward the lass, his own fortunes are going to suffer a stunning — and perhaps fatal — reversal."

The viscount winced as his wife dug her fingernails into his arm. "Come, Sherman," she said, her voice cracking like a whip. "I want you to take me home immediately. We have *much* to discuss."

Connor watched them go, a lazy smile flirting with his lips. " 'Twill be a slow death. And far more painful than any I could have devised."

Pamela laughed and shook her head, almost pitying the poor viscount. "Remind me to never make an enemy of you."

Connor brushed her cheek with the backs of his knuckles, his gaze searching her face. "Would you consider making a lover of me?"

At first Pamela thought he was teasing her, but all traces of humor had disappeared from his eyes. All she could see reflected in their smoky depths was her misty-eyed reflection. As Connor leaned toward her, her eyes fluttered shut and her mouth went dry with longing, already anticipating the taste of his lips, the velvety caress of his tongue against hers.

"Tsk, tsk," someone said, practically in Pamela's ear. "This is exactly why Uncle sent Mummy to chaperone the two of you. He'll be quite disappointed to learn she's faked a megrim and is languishing in Lady Newton's dressing room with a cool cloth on her brow."

They jerked apart to find Crispin leaning lazily against the mantel. His eyes were sparkling with a malicious glee that reminded Pamela of the duke.

She glared at him. "Did your uncle send you to chaperone us as well, or are we here to play nursemaid to you?"

"Neither. Actually, I was hoping my dear cousin here could settle an argument for me."

"What sort of argument?" Connor asked warily.

"One that could easily lead to bloodshed if not settled quickly and definitively."

Seizing Pamela by the hand, Crispin dragged her toward a group of guests gathered around the towering bookshelves at the far end of the drawing room, leaving Connor with no choice but to follow.

"Byron versus Burns," Crispin said to the rapt group of young people clustered around him. "Who was blessed with the most eloquent tongue? The most persuasive pen? A living libertine or a dead Scot? That is the question I must put before you on this night."

"I'll vote for any poet who can romance my Emily into letting me steal a peek at her ankles," a freckled young man called out, earning hoots of laughter from his male friends and a cuff on the arm from the blushing Emily.

While the laughter was dying down, Crispin slid a thin leather-bound volume from the shelf. "I shall begin tonight's experiment by reading to you from Lord Byron's *When We Two Parted*." He thumbed through the pages until he found what he was looking for, cleared his throat and began to read:

In secret we met
In silence I grieve
That thy heart could forget
Thy spirit deceive . . .

From her place next to Connor on the settee, Pamela had to admit that Crispin would have cut a striking figure on the stage. He seemed to grow taller and more confident when not forced to share the limelight. Several of the other guests had abandoned their conversations and were drifting toward their little group, drawn by the rich timbre of his voice.

If I should meet thee
After long years,
How should I greet thee?
With silence and tears.

An enthusiastic smattering of applause greeted the end of Crispin's reading. He took a bow, then tucked the book back on the shelf.

"As most of you already know, my long lost cousin here has spent most of his years living with that hale and hearty race known as the Scots." As Crispin's calculating gaze settled on Connor, Pamela felt a twinge of foreboding. "Since there is no greater pleasure than hearing a poem rendered in its native tongue, who better than my dear cousin to bring to life the words of Robert Burns — the most famous Scotsman of them all!"

As Crispin plucked a cloth-bound volume from the shelf and tossed it at Connor, Pamela felt her blood run cold. She had sought to spare him the embarrassment of her outmoded dresses, never dreaming he might endure a far worse humiliation at his cousin's treacherous hands. She'd had every intention of teaching him how to read before anyone discovered his lack of education, but they'd certainly had no opportunity for study since arriving at Warrick Park.

She snatched the book out of the air before Connor could catch it. Glaring daggers at Crispin, she said, "I'm sure the marquess has better things to do with his time than play at these ridiculous games."

Connor gently removed the book from her hand. "It's all right, darling. A Scotsman welcomes any chance to enlighten an En-

287

glishman when it comes to the romance of poetry."

His words were greeted with bemused glances and nervous chuckles. A hush fell as he rose to take Crispin's place at the bookshelf, his imposing presence commanding the attention of everyone in the drawing room.

"May I choose my selection?"

Crispin extended a gracious hand. "Be my guest."

Pamela held her breath as Connor flipped through the book several times before finally securing a page with his finger. Without introduction, he read:

From thee, Eliza, I must go,
And from my native shore;
The cruel fates between us throw
A boundless ocean's roar . . .

The words were as simple and heartfelt as when the poet had first penned them, but Connor's evocative burr transformed even the simplest syllable into music. He glanced at her, no longer making any attempt to hide the passion simmering in his eyes. Unlike Crispin, he was performing for an audience of only one. Pamela felt helpless tears start in her eyes as he continued:

288

But boundless oceans, roaring wide,
Between my love and me,
They never, never can divide
My heart and soul from thee.

As the echo of those last words faded, the entire drawing room erupted in thunderous applause. Judging by the number of handkerchiefs that suddenly appeared, Pamela wasn't the only one who had been moved to tears. The freckled young man was even rewarded with a tender kiss on the cheek from his Emily.

Both Crispin and Byron were forgotten as a chorus of eager voices rose to beg Connor for another Burns poem.

"That's enough for tonight, lads and ladies," he told them, "but I promise to return after my wedding to bring you a rousing rendition of 'O Aye My Wife She Dang Me.' "

The laughing men gathered around Connor to slap him on the back and offer him their congratulations. Pamela watched a stone-faced Crispin disappear into the crowd and decided to do the same. As Emily's beau charmed the girl into sliding behind the pianoforte to coax a winsome Bach concerto from its keys, Pamela rose and slipped through the crush of guests, seeking an escape from the merry chatter and prying eyes.

She didn't get very far before she heard Connor's clipped footsteps behind her. He caught her by the hand and tugged her around to face him.

She jerked her hand from his, lowering her voice to a raw whisper as she saw several heads turn their way. "Why didn't you tell me you could read?"

He shrugged. "You never asked. My father was a gentleman. He was the one who taught me."

Pamela felt her lips go numb with shock. "Your father was a gentleman? I had assumed your parents were . . ."

"Peasants?" he offered helpfully when she trailed off.

She could feel a guilty flush creeping up her throat. "Farmers. Shepherds. Crofters perhaps?"

Connor's voice was no longer expressive, but flat and devoid of emotion. "My father was Scots but he was born and raised in England. It was *his* father who sold out our clan at Culloden."

"For thirty pieces of English silver," she said softly, remembering those damning words from the courtyard of Castle Mac-Farlane.

"And an earldom," he confessed.

Pamela's ears were beginning to ring. "I suppose you neglected to mention the earldom as well."

Connor's face darkened. "That title was bought with the blood of my clansmen. My father rejected everything it stood for when he returned to the Highlands to try to reunite Clan Kincaid beneath the banner of their rightful chieftain. He gave up both wealth and privilege to live in a humble cottage and marry a penniless lass who adored him with her every breath." He glanced back at the laughing crowd still lingering around the bookshelf. "Even if I couldn't read, I could have recited that piece from memory. Robbie Burns was my father's favorite poet. I can't tell you how many times I heard him recite those very words to my mother while we sat around the hearth at night."

Pamela shook her head helplessly, feeling like even more of a fool. "And how was I to know that?"

"You couldn't know, because you assumed my parents were ignorant, uneducated ruffians. That's what the English always assume about the Scots."

She lifted her chin, stung by the unfairness of his accusation. "It wasn't as if you did anything to disabuse me of that notion. When we first met, you were pointing a loaded pistol at my heart. Did your father teach you to do that as well?"

"No. The redcoats who hanged him did."

They stood there, the gulf between them swelling until it was deeper and wider than any boundless ocean Burns could have described. Pamela sensed that words, no matter how eloquent or persuasive, were no longer enough to bridge it.

She took a step toward him. "What do you want, Connor?" she asked softly. "Do you want to punish me? Do you want to make me pay for their sins?"

Before he could give her an answer, the footman stepped back into the doorway. From the corner of her eye, Pamela saw a couple join him.

The footman cleared his throat forcefully to make sure he had everyone's attention before intoning, "Sir Simon and Catriona Wescott."

The golden-haired man standing beneath the archway was leaner than Connor but nearly matched him in both height and breadth of shoulder. He'd been blessed with the sort of effortless grace and dazzling masculine beauty that commanded every female eye in the room.

Despite the fluttering fans and lashes and the chorus of wistful sighs that greeted his arrival, it was painfully evident that he only had eyes for the woman on his arm.

Unfortunately, when Pamela glanced at Connor, she discovered to her shock that he too only had eyes for Simon Wescott's wife.

CHAPTER 19

Pamela's heart sank like a stone in her breast. Connor was gazing at the woman in the doorway as if he'd seen a ghost. A beautiful, fresh-faced ghost with upswept strawberry blond curls and cinnamon-tinted freckles scattered across her nose and cheeks. As her husband leaned down to murmur something in her ear, she squeezed his arm and laughed aloud, the adoration in her gaze making her gray eyes sparkle.

Connor lifted a hand to his chest, but there was no way for Pamela to know if he was touching the locket he always wore under his shirt or the heart that was probably thundering beneath it.

As the knight and his lady started across the room, exchanging smiles and greetings with everyone they passed, Pamela realized she and Connor were directly in their path. Connor did not budge and Pamela felt as if her own feet were rooted to the floor.

She held her breath as the woman drew nearer, waiting for her to see Connor, waiting for the start of recognition in her eyes that would shatter the secret hopes Pamela had been hoarding in her own heart.

The couple glanced at them as they strolled past, the man murmuring a greeting while the woman nodded and smiled at each of them in turn. Pamela managed to dredge up a polite smile in return, but Connor's expression never changed. He simply watched her pass, his face so still it might have been hewn from stone.

It wasn't until the pair had reached the hearth that the woman cast Connor a quizzical glance over her shoulder.

"Let's get the bloody hell out of here," he said, grabbing Pamela's hand and starting for the door.

Given his preoccupation with the lovely stranger, she supposed she should be thankful he even remembered she was there.

"What about Lady Astrid?" she asked, forced to take two steps for every one of his long strides.

"She'll find a way home," he said, waiting impatiently as the footman went to retrieve Pamela's cashmere shawl and swansdown muff. "Perhaps Lady Newton has a broom she could borrow."

■ ■ ■ ■

Connor didn't say a word while they were waiting for their driver to bring the carriage around. His stony silence continued on the long ride back to Warrick Park. Pamela huddled in her corner of the carriage, growing more miserable with each passing league. By the time the carriage rolled up the long curving drive and halted in front of the house, she was beginning to wonder if he was ever going to speak again.

He threw open the door and leaped down from the carriage the minute it stopped, ignoring the flustered groomsman who was waiting to assist them. Pamela half expected him to just leave her there — forgotten and alone — but he reached back in and closed his powerful hands around her waist, sweeping her out of the carriage and to her feet just as he had on the afternoon they'd arrived at Warrick Park for the first time.

He stood staring up at the lighted windows of the house as the coach rattled away toward the stables. "I can't bear to be locked up in a cage tonight."

Turning on his heel, he started down the hill toward the stand of swaying willows, tugging off his cravat as he walked. Pamela hesitated for a second, then followed. She could feel the evening dew soaking through the flimsy soles of her slippers with each step. Although Connor's stride was as steady and sure as it had been in the mountains, she began to pick up momentum as they neared the bottom of the hill, tripping over the hem of her gown and rending the delicate gauze.

Connor strode right past the graceful columns of the Doric temple beyond the willows, rejecting any claim of civilization on the land or the night. He didn't stop until he reached the edge of the lake. Resting his hands on his hips, he stood on the bank, gazing out over the moonlit water.

Pamela trailed him all the way to the water's edge, wrapping her arms around herself to hug back a shiver. She had left her cashmere shawl in the carriage, along with her lovely new swansdown muff.

When she could no longer bear Connor's silence, she said softly, "She's the one, isn't she? The one who gave you the locket you wear over your heart."

Connor glanced at her, bewilderment flashing like quicksilver in his eyes. "The locket was my mother's. It was the last thing she ever gave to me."

Pamela drew closer to him, still not daring to hope. "I don't understand. I saw the way you looked at her. As if you were aching to touch her just to make sure she was real."

He went back to gazing over the water, his eyes as distant as the silvery orb of the moon hanging in the eastern sky. "Oh, I know she's real. She's my sister."

"Your sister?" Pamela sank down to a sitting position in the wet grass, her relief so keen she no longer cared if he found her ridiculous. "That woman was your sister?"

"Aye." He shook his head, a bitter smile touching his lips. "Did you see her? She looked right at me and didn't even know me. I suppose I can't blame her though. She hasn't laid eyes on me since the night the redcoats came."

Pamela hugged one knee to her chest. Now that Connor's silence was broken, she was afraid to speak; afraid to so much as breathe for fear he would retreat back into his impenetrable shell. She sensed that he wasn't just breaking the silence of moments, but of years.

His burr seemed to deepen as if he was traveling further backward in time with each word. "When we heard the redcoats comin', I begged my father to let me stay. I was a gangly lad of fifteen who fancied himself a man. I demanded a gun so we could fight them side by side, but my father kept insistin' I had to take Catriona and hide, that I was her only hope. He wanted my mother to go too, but she refused to leave his side."

"They were nearly upon us then." Connor cocked his head as if he could still hear the swelling thunder of hoofbeats, could feel the ground beginning to quake beneath their feet. "For the first time ever, I defied my da. I shouted that I was nearly full grown and he had no right to tell me what to do. Then my father — my gentle, softspoken father who had never lifted a hand to me in anger — struck me so hard he broke my tooth."

Connor ran a finger over the chipped edge of the tooth that made his smile so dear to her.

"He grabbed me by the shoulders and shook me. He told me that if I didn't hide Catriona, the soldiers would do terrible things to her . . . unspeakable things. They wouldn't care that she was just a wee lass of ten.

"I couldn't speak by then. I could only nod. When I did, my father snatched me against him, nearly squeezin' the breath out of me. Then he shoved me away, shoutin', 'Go! Go lad! *Now!* ' "

Connor unfastened the top studs of his shirt, drawing forth the delicate chain with the gold locket dangling from the end of it. "That was when my mother pressed this into my hand, told me to guard it with my life so I'd always have a piece of her with me. So I'd never forget who I was." His fist tightened around the locket. "Then I grabbed Catriona and I went. There was a hollow tree at the edge of the woods where we used to play. I dragged her inside and held her against me. I made her bury her face in my shirt and I covered her ears so she wouldn't hear what was goin' to happen."

Pamela ached to cover her own ears, so she wouldn't have to hear it either.

"The redcoats came then. The lamps were still lit and I could see everythin' through the window of our cottage." All of the passion left his voice, leaving it as hard and brittle as flint. The very absence of emotion gave Pamela a harrowing glimpse into his anguish, his helpless rage. "They grabbed my father, took turns striking him until he hung limp between two of them, bloody and battered but still conscious. Then they went after my mother, laughin' and makin' jokes about what a fine time they were goin' to have with her."

Connor swung around to face her, the raw hatred in his eyes chilling her to the bone. "If I could have got to them in that moment, I swear to God I'd have killed them all with my bare hands."

"You couldn't leave Catriona." Pamela's voice was equally fierce. "You made a vow to your father. In your heart of hearts, you knew he was right. If you had let the red-coats get their hands on her . . ." She didn't finish. She didn't have to.

"When they came for my mother, she pulled a pistol out of her skirt and pointed it at them." One corner of Connor's mouth slanted upward in the ghost of a smile. "She looked so beautiful standin' there — tall and proud, facin' them down as if she was a queen and they were nothin' but a bunch of slaverin' goblins. For a breath or two, I even dared to hope." His smile faded. "But she only had one shot and there were nearly a dozen of them, circlin' her like a pack of wolves."

Pamela came to her feet, transfixed against her will. She wanted to throw her arms around his neck and press her mouth to his to silence him, to drag him down into the wet grass and do whatever it took to stop him from telling her what happened next.

"When she lifted the gun to her temple, I

heard my father shout, *'No!'* But she just smiled at him, the same way she always smiled at me when she was rufflin' my hair before bedtime or scoldin' me for wearin' my muddy boots in the house. You see, she *knew* they were goin' to kill them both and she wasn't about to make my father watch those animals take turns rapin' her before they did."

Connor's eyes were as dry and barren as a desert, but Pamela could feel hot tears trickling down her own cheeks.

"When she pulled that trigger, I felt Catriona's wee body jerk in my arms as if she'd been the one shot. I realized then that I'd been screamin' the whole time, but without makin' a single sound. As my mother fell, my father broke free of the redcoats and tried to get to her, but they knocked him over the head with the butt of a pistol. Then they dragged him outside and hanged him. I buried my face in Catriona's hair and kept it there until all was quiet."

As quiet as a beautiful spring eve with crickets chirping and a gentle breeze blowing across the surface of a lake. On that night so long ago there would have been nothing but the muffled sound of a little girl's sniffling, the eerie creaking of a rope and the wind sighing through the branches of the pines in a timeless lament.

"When we came creepin' out, the cottage was a smolderin' ruin. My father's body was still swingin' from the tree. I pulled Catriona into my arms one last time, tryin' to shield her from that sight." He bowed his head. "Then I buried my parents and put my sister on the mail coach to London with a note askin' my uncle to look after her."

"You were all alone," Pamela whispered, swallowing past the knot of anguish in her throat. "How did you bear it?"

She lifted a hand but he caught her wrist in a harsh grip before her fingertips could brush his cheek. "I don't want your pity, lass. And I sure as hell don't need your charity."

A helpless laugh escaped her. "Is that what you think I'm offering you, Connor? Pity? Charity? Because I can promise you that I didn't feel particularly charitable tonight when I saw the way you were looking at Simon Wescott's wife."

He blinked down at her, clearly taken aback by her words. "How did you feel?"

She returned his frown with one of her own. "I felt very cross indeed."

"Cross?" His grip on her wrist softened, but the ripple of amusement in his voice only made her feel more contrary. "Because you thought she'd given me that locket? Because you believed she was a woman from my past who still had some sort of claim on my heart?"

She tugged her wrist from his grasp. "Among other things."

Her frosty tone only deepened his dimple. "And now that you know she's my sister," he asked gently, "just how do you feel?"

Instead of telling Connor how she felt, Pamela decided to show him. Rising up on her tiptoes, she drove her hands into his hair and tugged his mouth down to hers.

CHAPTER 20

Connor groaned, accepting her unspoken invitation to ravish her mouth by thrusting deep with a velvety stroke of his tongue. Welcoming the hot, hungry press of his mouth against hers, Pamela threaded her fingers through his hair, raking the silky strands free from their velvet restraint as she had longed to do all night.

He might play the role of gentleman with convincing flair, but she knew in her heart he would always be that same wild boy who had taken to the mountains after his parents were murdered, with a gun in his hand and a dangerous gleam in his eye. She could taste that wildness in his kiss, smell it in the crisp, musky tang of pine and wood smoke that no amount of bayberry soap could ever completely wash away.

She realized in that moment that she didn't want to tame him. She wanted to drive him even wilder.

Judging by the growl that rumbled up from deep in his throat when she pressed the softness of her breasts to his muscled chest, he was more than eager to let her do just that. She ran the tip of her tongue over his teeth, savoring that chipped edge even more now that she knew what it had cost him. As her tongue grew bolder, tenderly mating with his, he slid his hands down her back to cup the lush curves of her bottom in his palms.

"You're wet," he murmured against the corner of her mouth.

"I can't help it," she replied, no longer willing to be shamed by her desire for him. "It happens every time you kiss me."

He lifted his head to give her a bemused look. "No, I mean your skirt. It's wet." He held her away from him, dismay replacing his bemusement as his gaze traveled down to the bedraggled hem of her gown. It was as if he was truly seeing her for the first time since they'd left the soiree. "What happened to your bonny gown, lass? And your new shoes?"

Pamela glanced down to discover that her white slippers were no longer white, but caked with mud. One pearl buckle was hanging by a thread and the delicate satin was already pulling apart from the soles. "I don't really know. I suppose when I was following you down the hill, I must have —"

"And where's your shawl?" Connor demanded, briskly rubbing the gooseflesh from her naked arms. "What are you trying to do, you wee fool? Catch your death of a chill?"

Before Pamela could remind him that he was the one who had dragged her out of the carriage without giving her time to retrieve her shawl or muff, he swept her up in his arms as if she weighed no more than a child and started for the Doric temple.

She twined her arms around his neck and rested her head on his shoulder, the heat radiating from his big, powerful body making her feel as if she would never be cold again. His arms were the same arms that had cradled his little sister's trembling body, his hands the same hands that had covered her ears to try to shield them from the brutal thud of fists and the sharp crack of the pistol that had ended their mother's life. He had done everything within his power to spare her the horror of that night, leaving him to carry its terrible burden all alone.

Pamela pressed her lips to the fading rope scars that marred the corded column of his throat. This was one night when he would not be alone.

He carried her up the broad flat steps of the temple. Moonlight filtered through the swaying branches of the surrounding willows, dappling the circular interior with shadows.

He sank down on one of the broad benches that ringed the overblown gazebo, cradling her on his lap. Thankful that he had already rid himself of his cravat, she lavished the strong line of his jaw with feathery kisses.

Uttering a soft groan, he reached down to tug off her sodden slippers and tossed them aside. "I'll buy you more," he vowed, the possessive glint in his eye making her shiver with anticipation. "A hundred pairs, each more expensive and bonnier than the last."

"What kind of thief are you? Why buy them when you could just steal them for me?"

Driven half mad by the wicked sparkle in Pamela's eyes, Connor tipped up her chin to reclaim the warm, wet silk of her mouth for his own. In that moment he would have stolen the crown jewels for nothing more than a honeyed sip from her lips.

But after several minutes of drinking deeply of that pleasure, he knew it would never be enough to satisfy him. He wanted more. He wanted it all.

She gasped into his mouth as he laid her back on the bench, following her down without once breaking their kiss. He had dared to hope she would open her arms for him, but when her legs fell apart as well, inviting his hard, hungry heat to nestle in the cradle of her thighs, he nearly exploded with want.

He braced his weight on his hands to gaze down at her, fighting to gain control of both his breathing and his lust. He had thought she was beautiful when she had come floating down the staircase earlier in the evening, but she was even more stunning now with the shimmering coils of her hair tumbling out of its pins, her luminous eyes reflecting the moonlight, her plump lips glistening with the dew of their kiss.

He rose up on his knees to shrug off his coat and waistcoat only to find her sturdy little hands already there, impatiently tugging away the garments. She tore at his shirt with equal enthusiasm, scattering the pearl studs across the floor of the temple.

"My tailor will never forgive you for that," he warned her as his shirt fell open.

"What about you?" she whispered, gazing at the well-muscled contours of his chest in rapt fascination. He sucked in a sharp breath as her fingertips raked lightly through his chest hair, then ventured lower to caress the taut planes of his abdomen. "Will *you* forgive me?"

He caught her hand, pressing it boldly to the rigid shaft straining against the front of his breeches. "I already have."

As Pamela shyly traced the width and breadth of him through the clinging doeskin, it was her turn to suck in a shocked breath. When it finally escaped on the wings of a sigh, Connor's mouth was there to catch it. He covered her again, laving her lips with deep, drugging kisses even as his hand glided beneath her skirt and up her thigh. She moaned as the very tips of his fingers brushed the damp silk between her legs.

"You told me you weren't wearing any drawers, you wicked, wee liar," he whispered, the words an endearment on his lips.

"Weren't you the one who warned me there was no honor among thieves?"

He punished her for her lie by touching her through the silk, using the sleek fabric to create an exquisite friction between his thumb and forefinger and the throbbing little bud beneath. Soon she was sobbing with pleasure, begging for his mercy. In answer to her breathless pleas, he slid his longest, thickest finger through the narrow slit in the silk and into her, ravishing her tenderly but thoroughly. She thought she would perish from disappointment when he stopped touching her altogether, leaving an aching void where his finger had been.

Ignoring her whimper of protest, he cupped his hands beneath her bottom and rose to his feet. She was so limp with desire she could only wrap her arms and legs around him and hold on. She would have been lying if she had claimed she didn't feel a primal thrill at how effortlessly he lifted her, how easily he could make her his own. To be such a man's woman — even for one night — was more than she had ever dared to dream.

She let out a helpless squeal of surprise as he set her down on the slab of cool, smooth marble that rested on a stone pedestal in the very center of the temple.

"It seems the duke has provided a table for dining al fresco." Connor's wolfish smile sent a dark shiver dancing down her spine. "Thoughtful of him, wasn't it?"

She didn't realize just how thoughtful until Connor tugged her gown over her head and gently eased her to her back. His hands made short work of the fragile silk of her drawers, leaving her exposed to the cool night air and his heavy-lidded gaze.

As Connor gazed down at his moonlit goddess, the night breeze drifting through the graceful columns failed to cool the fever coursing through his blood. Both the fever and the blood were pooling in his groin, leaving it hot, heavy, and near to busting the seams of his breeches.

He couldn't believe that his dream of having Pamela naked beneath him was finally a reality. Well, except for the blush silk of her stockings and the lace garters hugging her creamy legs just above the knee. A smile slanted his lips. He was a generous man. He could afford to leave her those.

"My modiste will never forgive you," she murmured, eyeing the tattered scrap of silk in his hand that had once been her new drawers.

He tossed the fabric away. "What about you, lass? Will *you* forgive me?"

Before she could answer, he parted her thighs, lowered his head and put his mouth on her.

In that moment, Pamela would have forgiven him anything.

For Connor the slab of marble became a pagan altar where he could worship Pamela to both his heart's and his body's content. She tasted of ambrosia and nectar and all the forbidden delights once denied to mortal man. He savored every creamy, luscious sip, knowing he could never truly drink his fill of her.

Soon she was arching off the table, panting his name, and clutching at his hair with her tight, little fists. He kept right on adoring her with his lips, his teeth, his tongue — a willing supplicant to her delight.

Pamela never would have guessed anything could surpass the pleasure Connor's hands were capable of delivering, but his tender and unholy kiss devastated her every defense. His tongue leisurely swirled over her quivering flesh, bringing her to one shuddering climax after another.

He did not relent, not even when he had driven her half mad with longing. She should have been satisfied. Should have been utterly satiated by the raw pulses of pleasure still cascading through her. But it wasn't enough. She wanted more. She wanted *him*.

"Please, Connor," she moaned. "Make me yours."

She did not have to ask twice.

His shadow covered her a heartbeat before his body did, hiding her nakedness from the face of the moon.

She could feel the back of his hand moving against her in the dark as he unfastened the front placket of his breeches. Then he was there, rubbing his rigid length between her dusky petals, dipping into that aching hollow as if to test the waters.

As he began to gently but relentlessly push his way inside of her, Pamela moaned deep in her throat. There was no comparing the thickness of his finger to *this*. No preparing her untried body for such an extraordinary invasion.

She began to writhe and pant, the cool marble beneath her a stark contrast to the fevered flesh struggling to possess her from above. Bracing his weight on his palms, Connor arched against her, the corded tendons of his throat and the bulging muscles of his forearms betraying the price of his patience, the cost of his control.

There was a sharp stab of pain, as if she was being torn asunder by a blunt club, then Connor slid the rest of the way home.

Pamela clung to him, tears spilling down her cheeks. There was no turning back now. He was buried so deep inside of her that nothing would ever be the same. She would never be the same.

"My Pamela," he whispered, kissing away those tears one by one. "My brave, bonny angel."

His mouth found hers then, giving her a

taste of her own surrender flavored with the salt from her tears. Her sense of helpless wonder grew as he began to move within her. The sharp pain soon became a dull ache that only intensified her awareness of how deep she was taking him, how much of himself he was giving her. From that ache, another sensation blossomed — pleasure, dark and carnal and irresistible.

Connor had feared dealing Pamela a blow that might frighten her off forever. While most women welcomed him *because* of his size, there had been a few who shied away from him, even going so far as to refuse his coins and foist him off on a more "adventurous" companion.

So when Pamela wrapped her legs around him and dug her little heels into the small of his back, urging him on, he was only too happy to oblige. He stopped trying to temper his thrusts with gentleness and drove himself into her again and again — deep and hard and fierce — holding nothing back, including his heart.

Pamela dug her fingernails into Connor's back, forced to hold on for dear life as he used his body to bludgeon her with waves of pleasure. She knew in that moment that this man would not be the first lover of many, but the only lover she would ever want. She was not her mother. If he walked away from her on the morrow, she would never open her heart — or her legs — for another man. She would spend the rest of her life baking shortbread and collecting cats and remembering the moonlit night when a highwayman named Connor Kincaid had stolen both her innocence and her heart.

Then there was no more room for thought, no more room for anything but Connor and the driving rhythm of his thrusts. She had yearned to drive him wild, but he was the one driving her half out of her mind by angling his strokes just enough to strike fresh sparks off of that taut little flint nestled in the crux of her curls. At the precise moment that exquisite friction sent rapture burning through her like wildfire, Connor let out a guttural groan. She felt his powerful body shudder and jerk within hers as he spilled his seed at the very mouth of her womb.

As he collapsed between her splayed thighs, burying his face in her sweat-dampened throat, she gently stroked her hands down his back, welcoming the burden of his weight.

"Och, lass," he finally bit off when his ragged breathing had steadied enough to allow him to speak, "you're so bloody tight."

"I'm sorry," Pamela whispered, frowning in dismay. "I don't mean to be."

Connor lifted his head to give her a disbelieving look. "It wasn't a complaint. What I should have said was that I've never felt anything so fine in all my life."

"Oh! Well, I like that much better." Swamped by relief, she curled her hand around his nape and urged his mouth down to hers.

Their tongues tangled until she felt him begin to stir and swell deep within her, impaling her anew.

She broke off their kiss, her eyes widening with shock. "Why, Mr. Kincaid, have you no shame?"

His mouth curled in a wicked leer. "Haven't you heard that we Scots are a savage lot cursed with insatiable carnal appetites?"

She fluttered her lashes at him. "I suppose a timid little English miss could never hope to satisfy a big strapping Scots lad like you."

"Probably not," he said solemnly. "But I don't think that should stop her from trying, do you? Perhaps if she let him have his way with her at every opportunity, he might even be able to get rid of his sheep."

As he began to move within her, Pamela

sighed against his mouth. "Why do I feel sorry for the poor sheep?"

Crispin slipped through the darkened corridors of Warrick Park as silently as a ghost. There was a time when he would have been terrified to leave his bed once the lamps were extinguished. When his mother had first brought him to live here after his father's death, he had found everything about the immense house foreign and frightening.

They had only been living there for a few short months when his uncle had taken to his chair and never risen again. To a painfully shy, undersized nine-year-old, that chair had seemed like some sort of living monstrosity. He had been haunted by nightmares where he fled down one shadowy corridor after another, unable to escape the shrill creaking of its wheels. If it had ever caught him, he was convinced it would have gobbled him down without leaving so much as a bloodstain on the expensive carpet.

His mother had delivered daily lectures on how he must strive to ingratiate himself to his uncle. She promised him that if he would be a good boy and win the duke's favor, Warrick Park and all of its treasures would someday be his — a prospect that horrified him more than she would ever know. He was plagued by new nightmares then. Nightmares where he was the one imprisoned in that chair for all eternity.

Crispin desperately wanted to please his mother but found it impossible to please the duke. No matter how hard he tried, he could never sit up straight enough or eat neatly enough or answer quickly enough to please his uncle. His every attempt — no matter how earnest — was greeted by a mocking rejoinder or a scathing set-down. That was usually followed by a private scolding from his mother or a stinging slap if she felt he had been particularly clumsy or slow-witted that day.

He had been fourteen when he had finally accepted that he would never win the duke's favor. From that day forward, he had stopped trying. He would greet the man's caustic insults with a sarcastic retort, honing the rapier-sharp edge of his own tongue. He surrounded himself with a circle of acquaintances who believed him to be polished and clever and always ready with a sly quip or a witty *bon mot.* He devoted himself to gambling and drinking and seducing women of easy virtue and any other decadent pleasure that might cast the shadow of scandal over his uncle's good name.

Eventually even his mother had been forced to accept that his uncle would never love him. Crispin might be the man's legal heir, but he would never replace the son he had lost.

The son who had now returned to whisk that inheritance right out from under Crispin's nose.

Crispin's furtive footsteps paused in front of his cousin's bedchamber. He pressed his ear to the door, listening for any hint of movement within.

What he heard instead was a strangled groan, as if someone was in the mortal throes of agony. "Och, Cookie!" a man exclaimed in a Scottish burr so thick it was nearly unintelligible. "It feels like ye're goin' to break me spine in two when ye squeeze me that way. But whatever ye do, don't stop!"

Crispin straightened, wondering if he was losing his mind. He had arrived back at War-rick Park on his horse only a few minutes before the duke's crested carriage had come rolling up the drive. He had cursed his ill timing until he saw both his cousin and Miss Darby disembark from the carriage and head for the Doric temple at the edge of the lake. He had waited until he was sure their moonlight tryst was going to encompass more than just a few chaste kisses before setting off on his own quest. So how had the two of them managed to sneak up the stairs and into the bedchamber without his knowledge?

He pressed his ear to the door again. "Ah, me sweet Cookie," purred that throaty masculine voice, "once yer me bride, we'll play hide-the-sausage-in-the-puddin' every night o' the week."

Crispin straightened more abruptly this time, torn between fascination and horror. Those were hardly the words he'd imagined his stoic cousin using to court the lovely Miss Darby.

His bewilderment was interrupted by a muffled yet rhythmic banging, as if an iron headboard was repeatedly striking the wall. That was when he realized the noises weren't coming from the main bedchamber of the suite but from the connecting dressing room just down the corridor. The dressing room currently occupied by his cousin's hulking valet.

Crispin swore beneath his breath. Those passionate moans and savage grunts might very well mask the sounds of him searching his cousin's bedchamber, but what if they didn't? He certainly couldn't afford to get caught red-handed by the gold-toothed barbarian. Being dragged away from his "pudding" prematurely might put the beefy giant in a very foul temper indeed.

Knowing he had only one course of action left to him, Crispin turned and slipped back into the shadows.

Crispin eased open the door of Miss Darby's suite. There was something both alluring and wicked about sneaking into a lady's bedchamber in the dead of night, even if that lady was not abed. Moonlight bathed the deserted room in a pearly glow. A scent that was mysterious and floral and unmistakably feminine perfumed the air.

He stood with hands on hips, surveying the room for a long moment. In truth, he didn't even know what he was looking for. The best he could hope for was some sort of evidence he could use as a weapon to prove his cousin was not the man his uncle believed him to be. Or the man the guests at Lord Newton's soiree had been fawning over with such disgusting adulation.

Spurred on by that thought, he strode over to the armoire and began rifling briskly through its drawers. He moved on to the dressing table next, but his search yielded nothing of interest or import, unless one could count a handful of hairpins, a half-empty bottle of lilac water and a pair of tortoiseshell combs.

His frustration mounting, he swung around to glare at the bed itself. He couldn't say what instinct drove him there. He only knew that as a boy he had once hidden treasures he knew his mother wouldn't approve of under his pillow — a piece of shiny quartz he'd found in the garden, a robin's tail feather, a book of naughty etchings he'd pilfered from his uncle's library.

He slid his hand beneath the pillows and bolsters piled against the headboard. Nothing. He was withdrawing it when he heard a telltale crackle coming from one of the large feather pillows. He slipped his hand inside its satin cover, his fingers quickly locating a folded piece of paper.

As he unfolded it, a primitive thrill of excitement shot through him.

It was a well-weathered broadsheet — the sort the authorities nailed up on trees and posts when they were searching for someone who had committed a terrible crime. Someone like the nameless highwayman sketched on the page.

A nameless highwayman with a steely gaze and a telltale dimple in his rugged jaw.

A more casual observer might not have recognized the outlaw in the sketch, but Crispin had seen that steely gaze before, had faced it over the length of blade he had believed would end his life.

He returned the pillow to its place, smoothing out its satin cover. If Miss Darby slept with the broadsheet beneath her pillow, she must believe it to be very dear indeed. But it would be even dearer to the Scottish authorities. A bitter smile touched his lips. And dearer yet to him.

"What are you doing here?"

Shoving the broadsheet into his waistcoat, Crispin whirled around to find Miss Darby's maidservant standing in the dressing-room doorway.

CHAPTER 21

Although Crispin would have thought it impossible, the young maidservant looked even more enchanting than she had on the staircase.

Her short, buttery curls were tousled and her dusky blue eyes heavy lidded from sleep. Moonlight sifted through the folds of her nightdress, rendering them translucent and hinting at the svelte curves beneath.

For a moment, Crispin could only stare, struck mute once again by her radiant beauty. He still couldn't shake the sensation that they'd stood gazing at each other in just such a way at some other time, in some other place.

She folded her arms over her chest, giving him a sleepy scowl. "I asked you what you were doing here."

"I came to see you," he said, blurting out the first words that popped into his head.

"Me?"

He nodded, regaining both the use of his tongue and his ability to improvise. "When I saw your mistress at the soiree tonight, I realized you'd be here all alone."

Her face brightened. "You were at the soiree? Oh, tell me all about it, won't you? I was positively sick with disappointment because I didn't get to go. Was there dancing? And French champagne? And little iced cakes shaped like hearts?"

Crispin was puzzled by her reaction. It would have been odd for even the most devoted of maidservants to accompany her mistress to such an event.

He drew nearer to her, unable to resist the temptation. "Had I known you fancied French champagne and iced cakes, I would have smuggled some out of the party for you." He held out a hand to her. "I'm afraid all I have to offer you is a dance."

She warily eyed his extended hand. "How are we to dance when there's no music?"

He cocked his head to the side. "There's always music. Can't you hear it? Why, I hear it every time I look into your eyes."

"Perhaps your ears are still ringing from when we bumped heads on the stairs."

Crispin grinned and withdrew his hand, curiously relieved that she wasn't to be so easily charmed by his flattery. But her next words sobered him abruptly.

"I know why you really came here to-night."

"You do?"

"You came here to seduce me. You thought, 'Oh, the pretty little maid is all alone. Think I'll sneak into her room while her mistress is gone and give her a tumble.' " She arched one silky eyebrow, challenging him to call her a liar. "Am I wrong?"

He slanted her a glance from beneath his lashes, struggling to look abashed. "I'm afraid not. I'm an incorrigible scoundrel and you've no choice but to send me on my way with a scathing rebuke and a hearty slap."

"What about a kiss?"

He jerked up his head, believing he'd heard her wrong. "A . . . a . . . a *what?*"

"A kiss. I've no intention of letting you seduce me, but I might be persuaded to send you on your way with a scathing rebuke and a kiss."

He drew closer to her, his nostrils flaring at her sleepy, feminine scent. "And how might I best persuade you?"

"Well, first I'd have to deliver the rebuke."

He waved a hand at her. "Be my guest."

She rested her hands on her slender hips, glaring daggers at him. "How dare you sneak into my room at such an indecent hour? Just because you're a handsome, wealthy gentleman with women throwing themselves at your feet, that doesn't give you the right to force your attentions on a helpless servant. I may be only a maid, but that doesn't mean I'm not a lady as well and don't deserve to be treated as one!"

"Very impressive," Crispin murmured, still beset by the eerie sense of having played this scene before. "I've never received such a brutal set-down. My ears will be stinging for days!"

"As well they should," she agreed with a feline little smirk.

The wariness returned to her gaze as he reached to cup her cheek in his hand, stroking its downy softness with his thumb. "Perhaps you'll allow me to make amends by proving I can treat you like a lady. By convincing you that I would be satisfied with nothing more than a chaste kiss from your lips."

Crispin was lying through his teeth. He knew such a kiss would only whet his appetite for more. He leaned forward and touched his lips to hers — the broadsheet forgotten, his cousin forgotten, everything forgotten but that tender rose of a mouth blooming so sweetly beneath his.

That chaste kiss soon turned into a lingering caress. By the time Crispin lifted his head, they were both breathing hard.

She backed away from him, an enchanting blush coloring her cheeks. "You'd best go now. If my mistress returns, I can promise you she won't be very happy to find you here. I wouldn't want her to . . . send me packing."

"Nor would I," he confessed, pressing a palm to his chest. "I believe it would break my heart."

She grabbed his elbow and steered him firmly toward the door. "You should be ashamed of yourself! You're doing it again!"

"What?"

"Trying to seduce me! Those flowery words may charm the weak-willed women of your acquaintance, but I should warn you that they have no effect on me."

"Are you so sure about that?" he asked, daring a devilish grin.

Her answer was to throw open the door and shove him backward into the corridor. "Don't bother coming back . . ." She cast a guilty glance over her shoulder, then whispered, ". . . unless you know my mistress is out of the house."

She flashed him a brief, dazzling smile before closing the door in his face. Crispin rested his brow against it, chuckling when he realized he had failed once again to acquire the maddening creature's name.

"What have you done, Crispin?"

His heart lurched as he wheeled around to find his mother standing at the end of the hall like some ghostly white lady from one of his nightmares.

She glided toward him, the hem of her dressing gown rippling behind her. Holding out her hand, she said, "I know why you came here. Did you find what you were looking for?"

The sweet face of Miss Darby's maidservant rose up in his vision. He gazed at his mother's outstretched hand, remembering only too clearly what had happened the last time he had trusted his fate to her hands.

"Nothing. I found nothing."

His mother's hand whipped across his face, delivering a vicious slap. "You're my son," she hissed. "Do you think I don't know when you're lying?"

Something in his eyes made her take a nervous step backward. Her hand darted upward to flutter around her throat like a pale dove. "Forgive me, son. You know I need to keep a better rein on my temper." She blinked a sheen of tears from her dark blue eyes. "It's just when I think about all

I've endured to protect you and ensure your future . . . all I've sacrificed . . ."

Crispin slowly drew the broadsheet from his waistcoat and handed it to her.

She unfolded it and scanned it quickly, her hands beginning to tremble with excitement. When she lifted her head, her eyes were glowing with pride. "Oh, my darling boy, you've done well this time, haven't you? Archibald won't be able to ignore this — or you. He'll have to admit to the world that he's made a terrible mistake and that you are his only true heir. Everything we've ever wanted will finally be within our grasp."

"Everything *we've* wanted, Mother? Or everything *you've* wanted?"

Before she could answer, Crispin sketched her a curt bow and went striding back into the shadows.

Chapter 22

Pamela rested the back of her head against Connor's shoulder, watching the first lavender rays of dawn streak the eastern sky. Connor was sitting with her nestled between his splayed legs, his back propped against one of the temple's columns. A damp chill had come creeping across the grass with the morning mist, but it was impossible for her to feel cold with both Connor's coat and his arms wrapped so tightly around her.

She knew they needed to slip back into the house before some over-industrious servant spotted them. But she didn't want the night to end. If she ever had to sleep again, she wanted it to be in Connor's arms.

It took her several drowsy, delicious moments of watching the wispy clouds melt from lavender to peach to realize Connor was whistling ever so softly in her ear.

A smile touched her lips. "I remember that tune. It's the one you were whistling on the journey to Castle MacFarlane — 'The Maiden and the Highwayman.' I insisted it must be a tragedy since the Scots were such a dour lot, but you said the highwayman seduced the maiden into his bed only to discover she was a lusty wench who couldn't get enough of him."

"Sounds just like someone else I know," he murmured, slipping his hands beneath his coat to fill them with the plump softness of her breasts. Over her husky hum of pleasure, he said, "If you must know, I left off the last verse. The one where he shoots her through the heart because he believes she's been unfaithful and then turns himself in and begs to be sent to the gallows after he learns the lad he saw her kissing was her brother."

"I knew it!" Pamela wiggled around in his arms to give him an accusing glare. "Has there ever been a Scottish ballad that didn't end in tragedy?"

He gently raked a tousled strand of hair from her cheek, the tender glow in his eyes making her heart clutch. "Perhaps you and I can write one together."

"You're just lucky I didn't shoot you when I saw you ogling your sister."

The glow faded from Connor's eyes. "At least you didn't have to worry about her ogling me back."

Pamela sighed. "You can't blame her for not recognizing you. In case you haven't noticed, you're no longer a gangly lad of fifteen. And I seriously doubt she expected to find her long lost brother impersonating a marquess at a soiree in London." She touched a hand to his beard-shadowed jaw. "You saw her last night, Connor. You did the right thing by sending her away. Thanks to you, she's grown into a lovely young woman who's wed to a man who plainly adores her."

Connor snorted. "An *English*man. Apparently sleeping with the enemy has its benefits. The two of them were only visiting London. They're currently living in our ancestral holding of Castle Kincaid, raising a flock of sheep and two wee bairns nearly as bonny as their parents. Most of the clansmen who once rode with me have now turned their hands to honest labor in the service of my sister." He shook his head ruefully. "I spent nearly a decade trying to wrest those lands back from the English and she conquered them without firing a single shot."

Pamela's mouth fell open. "How do you know all that?"

She watched in fascination as the pearly

334

glow of dawn revealed a telltale flush creeping up Connor's throat. "I said she hadn't seen me since the night the redcoats came. I didn't say I hadn't seen her."

"Why, Connor Kincaid, you've been spying on her, haven't you?"

"Only once," he reluctantly confessed. "Two years ago, after I heard she'd married an Englishman, I traveled to Castle Kincaid to kill him."

"You know," she said cautiously, "most people are perfectly content to bring gifts to the newly wed."

He flashed her a sulky look. "I stood outside in the dark and watched them through the dining-room window. I wanted to hate the bastard. But how do you hate a man who looks at your sister as if she was the most priceless treasure in all the world? All I could do was climb back up on my horse and ride away."

"Did you ever think about knocking on the door? That's another skill highly prized by civilized folk."

"What was I supposed to say? — 'Hello, kitten, I'm your big brother. I've a price on my head and bloodstains on my hands and if you give me sanctuary, I'll bring the redcoats right back to your door to destroy everyone and everything you love — just like before.' "

"So you let her go," Pamela said softly, "again." She brightened. "But it's not too late! You could go to her now! Before she and her husband return to the Highlands."

"And what would I tell her? That I've conveniently *borrowed* another man's life? That I'm just as likely to end up dangling at the end of a noose, if only for a different crime?"

For the first time, Pamela felt the dawn chill creep past the warm, cozy circle of his arms and into her heart. "As long as the duke believes you're his son, that will never happen. You'll still have everything I promised you — riches, respect —"

"And all the willing women I care to woo?" he finished lightly.

She inclined her head, stiffening in his arms. "That was part of our bargain. And I intend to honor it."

He brushed the silky curtain of her hair aside, leaving her with no way to hide her taut jaw and the heat she could feel rising to her cheeks. "And what if I only care to woo one woman?"

"Then that's what you should do." Pamela swallowed, his words cutting her heart to the quick. Somehow the idea of Connor courting a wife was much more painful than imagining him with a procession of mistresses. "Once I'm gone, the duke will expect you to find a more suitable bride. From the way the women were eyeing you tonight, I'm sure you'll find no lack of prospects."

"And just who would you deem a suitable bride for a no-count highwayman masquerading as the son of a duke? Because I'm thinking an actress's daughter born on the wrong side of the blankets who can lie to a man's face without batting one of her pretty eyelashes might be just what he deserves."

Pamela jerked her head up, gazing at him in disbelief.

"When he lapses into brooding, as Scots are wont to do, she could give him a sound lashing with her saucy tongue. And when he loses his temper and begins to roar and stomp about like a wounded bear, she could lose her temper and roar right back at him." He stroked his thumb down her cheek, his crooked smile achingly tender. "I guess what I'm trying to say is that I can't think of any more suitable bride for such a man than a hot-tempered, conniving little baggage with more courage than common sense and a touch of larceny in her soul."

His smile faded, leaving her mesmerized by the smoky depths of his eyes. "Stay with me, Pamela. Share this gilded cage with me. Be my marchioness. Be my duchess some-day." Although she would have thought it impossible, the husky timbre of his voice deepened even further. "Be my wife."

Pamela drew in a shuddering breath as Connor's face swam before her eyes, veiled by a mist of tears. She knew in that moment how her mother must have felt when the audience surged to their feet and burst into thunderous applause.

"I don't suppose you've left me any choice," she said, hiding the swell of emotion behind a prim sniff. "After all, you have compromised me. Ruined me for any other man."

"Numerous times," he agreed, not looking the least bit sorry.

"I could hardly go to another man's bed after I let a dirty, thieving Highlander put his hands all over me."

"And in you . . ." he whispered, curling the fingers of one hand around her nape and drawing her mouth to his for a long, lingering kiss while his other hand slipped beneath the coat to have its way with her. By the time he broke away from the kiss, they were both breathless. "Are you sure you won't mind squandering your precious reward on a dowry?"

Pamela slipped one thigh over his, straddling both his lap and his arousal, which was once again straining against the beleaguered seams of his breeches. "Oh, I intend to make you earn every penny. You're not the only one willing to pay for their pleasures."

As her eager hands reached between them, freeing his arousal so it could nudge against the dampness of her curls, Connor groaned. "I was right, wasn't I, lass? Sleeping with the enemy definitely has its benefits."

Pamela rose up to her knees, then slowly sank down, her breath catching on a shuddering whimper as he impaled her inch by glorious inch until she was filled to the brim with his sleek, thick heat.

She cupped his face in her hands, holding herself utterly still so she could exult in the sweet, wild pulse that began to beat where their bodies were joined before whispering, "Why don't we find out?"

Although the sun was peeking over the edge of the horizon and the stables and kitchens were beginning to stir, Pamela managed to slip up the back stairs without being seen. She had only one near miss near the second-story landing, when the muffled thud of footsteps coming down the stairs gave her just enough time to dive into a narrow broom closet.

She emerged with cobwebs in her hair only to recognize the generous backside of the buxom cook who had caught Brodie's fancy descending the stairs. Pamela would have almost sworn the woman was humming a bawdy Scottish ditty beneath her breath.

She climbed the rest of the stairs with a smile flirting with her lips. Once she was safe in her suite, she eased the door shut and collapsed with her back against it, breathing a heartfelt sigh of relief.

Which curdled in her throat when she saw Sophie curled up on the settee in her dressing gown with her legs tucked beneath her. Her sister had a rather peculiar glint in her eye. Pamela usually only saw that look when Sophie had spotted a chocolate confection or a particularly lovely length of ribbon she intended to have, no matter the cost.

Knowing that her sister rarely rose before ten without being cajoled or threatened, Pamela felt her heart sink. "What are you doing up so early?"

Sophie cocked a knowing eyebrow at her. "What are you doing up so late?"

Pamela opened her mouth to invent some story about a drunken coachman or a broken axle on a carriage wheel but closed it just as quickly, knowing it was hopeless to lie to her sister. She and Sophie might bicker like maiden aunts most of the time, but no one knew her better. Even before their mother had died, there had been so many times when it was just the two of them.

Pamela slowly crossed the floor and sank down in the wingback chair by the window, dropping her ruined slippers to the carpet beside the chair. Connor had insisted on carrying her across the grass to protect her from the fresh dew.

She could remember all of the times she'd sat up all night while Sophie slept, waiting for their mother to creep in at dawn — slippers in hand, lips swollen from a stranger's kisses, eyes still so glazed from the pleasures of the night it was as if she could barely see the little girl who had been waiting so patiently for her to come home.

"I suppose there's no help for it then," she said softly. "You must think I'm exactly like Mama."

"I most certainly do."

Pamela bowed her head, Sophie's words stinging even more than she had anticipated.

"You're proud. Passionate. Determined to make your own way in this world without bowing to any man."

Pamela lifted her head as her sister rose and came over to kneel beside her chair. Sophie peered up into her face, her blue eyes wide and guileless. "You share her strengths but not her weaknesses. *Maman* was always thinking of herself, while you think far too little of your own good and far too much of the good of others. You're loyal and kind and generous and the most devoted sister a girl could hope to have."

Pamela gazed down at her sister's beautiful face through a haze of tears.

Sophie squeezed her hand. "She may have been the toast of the London stage and adored by any number of wealthy and powerful men, but I never saw a single man look at *Maman* the way he looks at you."

Grinning through her tears, Pamela tucked a wayward curl behind Sophie's ear. "You know — once I become a marchioness, I do believe I'm going to promote you to housekeeper."

For Pamela the rest of the day passed in an agony of anticipation as she waited for the night to come. While a long, hot bath and an even longer nap soothed away much of the tenderness lingering between her legs, a tantalizing ache remained. An ache she now knew only Connor could ease.

She wasn't sure what was going to be the most difficult — the hours they had to spend apart during the day or the hour spent sitting across from him at supper, playing the role of chaste lady to his courteous gentleman.

The minute she strolled into the dining room that evening and Connor rose to greet her, his smoky eyes aglow with appreciation and a new coat stretched taut over his broad shoulders, she knew the answer.

"My lord," she murmured, bobbing him a demure curtsy when what she really wanted to do was throw herself into his arms and kiss him insensible.

"My lady," he replied stiffly, offering her his arm so he could escort her to her chair.

Even that brief contact was torture. As she slid into her chair, he leaned down and whispered, "I wish you were the main course."

He retreated to the chair directly opposite hers, leaving Pamela with a provocative image of herself laid out naked on that linen-draped table, with Connor free to partake of her at his leisure.

He lifted his wineglass in a silent toast to her while the footmen served the first course and the duke and his sister continued their incessant sniping. It took Pamela several minutes before she realized they were discussing the ball that was to be held in a few days to reintroduce the duke's long lost heir to the *crème de la crème* of London society.

"Now Archibald, you need to stop fussing and fretting, and leave all of the planning to me," Lady Astrid was saying.

The duke shot Connor a mischievous look, resembling a wizened little boy. "That's all well and good, but don't forget that I have a surprise for the lad."

"Don't we all?" Lady Astrid purred like a cat who had stumbled upon a saucer of particularly rich cream. She seemed to be in an unusually fine humor, which set off warning bells in Pamela's head.

Connor rested his glass of wine on the table. "Miss Darby and I have decided the ball would be the perfect time to *officially* announce our engagement."

"Have you finally charmed the chit into wedding you before next December?" the duke asked, spearing a juicy beef olive with his fork.

"I've devoted my every effort to it," Connor assured him solemnly.

Pamela choked on her wine, remembering just how "devoted" some of his efforts had been. She rested the glass back on the table. "I've discovered that your son can be very persuasive when he wants to be."

"A trait he inherited from his father, I assure you," the duke said, winking at her.

She nearly jumped out of her skin when she lowered her glass to find Lady Astrid surveying her from the foot of the table with a benevolent smile. "Just leave everything to me, Miss Darby. I promise you and your fiancé an evening that you — and all of London — will *never* forget."

Pamela paced back and forth in front of the open window in her bedchamber, pausing every fourth or fifth turn to poke her head out the window and glare down at the deserted lawn below.

She hugged herself as a chill breeze drifted through the window, raising the gooseflesh on her arms. What if Connor didn't come to her? What if he had decided to embrace his role as gentleman and was content to bide his time until they were wed?

She sighed and wandered over to the gilt-framed cheval glass sitting next to the dressing table. Her reflection eyed her pensively as she began to tug the pins from her hair. She shook the thick mane loose until it came spilling around her shoulders, then unhooked the bodice of her gown and peeled it away. The sewn-in stays had left pink welts on her tender flesh and it was an immense relief for her heavy breasts to finally spring free.

She untied the ribbons at her waist, letting her skirt and petticoats slide down to pool at her feet, and stood there in front of the mirror, naked except for her silk drawers and stockings.

She had gazed at herself in the mirror a thousand times as she prepared for bed, but tonight she seemed like a new creature. A sloe-eyed stranger — wild and sensual and still desperately hungry despite the many courses served at dinner.

Her dusky nipples were peeping through the glossy tendrils of her hair. She sighed. There were times when she envied Sophie her bobbed curls, but her hair was far too thick and straight to support such a fashionable coif. She reached up to gather the heavy coils at her nape with one hand, exposing her breasts to the caress of the moonlight.

Pamela froze as a sharply indrawn breath warned her that she was no longer alone.

CHAPTER 23

Pamela's breath quickened as the mirror revealed a man standing just behind her — a man dressed all in black, one with the shadows and soon to be one with her.

His eyes met hers in the mirror, the predatory gleam in their silvery depths reminding her just how dangerous he could be. Especially to her yearning heart.

As his gaze drifted downward, some ghost of maidenly shyness brought her hands up to shield her breasts. He simply slid his hands beneath hers so that his big, warm hands were cupping her breasts and her hands were resting lightly on top of his. She closed her eyes and sagged against him as he squeezed ever so gently, claiming them, claiming her.

"My sister is sleeping in the next room," she whispered as he used his thumbs to tease both of her nipples into taut little buds.

He rubbed his lips along the slender

column of her throat, his voice a husky vibration she could feel all the way to her toes. "I'm a thief. I know how to be quiet."

As it turned out, Pamela was the one most at risk for waking Sophie. Connor might not have been able to make her the main course at supper, but he had no qualms about making her his private dessert. Before long she was quaking and shuddering beneath his clever mouth and biting her lip nearly bloody to keep from crying out her ecstasy.

When he bent her over the settee and began to pound into her from behind with driving force, he had no choice but to smother her sharp scream of pleasure with his hand.

And when they finally collapsed on the bed and he made love to her slowly and tenderly — gliding in and out of her as if he had not just all night, but the rest of his life to do so — he was forced to swallow her low moan of rapture with his kiss, while he came without a sound, every muscle in his powerful body surging as he spilled his seed deep within her.

When the strongest of the aftershocks had subsided, Connor threw himself to his back and flung an arm over his eyes, his sweat-sheened chest heaving. "Now I know who's trying to kill me."

Pamela sat up, raking her tangled hair out of her eyes. "Who?"

"You." He lowered his arm to glare at her. "You're an insatiable wench who won't be content until you've milked the last bit of life from my staff, leaving me a hollow shell of the man I once was."

She gave him an impish grin. "It's our new battle strategy for defeating the Scots. It's much quicker and more effective than a parasol." Propping herself up on one elbow, she idly raked her fingers through the crisp whorls of his chest hair. "You know — you really shouldn't tease so when someone might actually be trying to kill you."

He blinked innocently up at her. "So do you think I should have declined Crispin's invitation to archery practice?"

Her eyes widened in horror until she realized he was still teasing her. She gave his chest hair a vicious little tweak to punish him.

He winced. "I did learn something rather interesting yesterday morning at breakfast. It seems that Lady Astrid's dearly departed husband burned to death in his bed."

"Just like my mother," Pamela breathed.

"Astrid blames it on a bottle of brandy and a lit cigar, but who knows?"

Pamela clapped a hand over her mouth as genuine horror washed over her. "Oh, no!"

"What is it?"

"Don't you remember? The first night we met Crispin, I was trying to trick him into revealing something about my mother's death, so I mentioned 'habitual drunkards who leave their cigars lit and burn to death in their beds.' I saw something in his eyes that I thought was guilt but it could have been hurt." She shook her head, shame mingling with her dismay. "He must have believed I already knew about his father's death and that I was being unspeakably cruel."

"It doesn't mean he's innocent, lass," Connor reminded her. "Witnessing such a terrible tragedy can sometimes warp a child's mind."

Remembering all the tragedy that Connor had witnessed, Pamela pressed her cheek to his chest, cherishing the slow, steady beat of his heart. "You won't be truly safe until we find my mother's killer. What if they don't reveal themselves before the wedding?"

"Announcing our engagement at the ball may just force their hand. They can't afford to risk me getting an heir on you."

After all of the decadent pleasures she had enjoyed at his hands in the past few hours,

Pamela was amazed that she could still blush. "That's what Crispin said the first night at dinner. That you should strive to put your babe in me as quickly as possible in case you should meet with an unfortunate accident."

Connor tipped up her chin so he could gaze into her eyes, his solemn tone belied by the depth of his dimple. "In this case, the lad was right. 'Tis my duty."

Pamela gasped as he cupped her rump in his hands and rocked against her, proving he was not only willing, but more than *ready* to discharge his obligations. "I thought you were nothing but a hollow shell of a man."

He shook his head sadly. "I'm afraid your own duty to country and king isn't done yet, lass. If you want to defeat the Scots, you've no choice but to march right back into battle."

She reached down and lightly trailed her fingers over his rigid length. "And just how am I to defeat an enemy armed with such a formidable weapon?"

He arched off the bed and into her hand, clenching his teeth against a guttural groan. "The English have always been very resourceful. I'm sure you'll think of something."

"Oh, I already have." Pamela gave him a

wicked smile, then began to slide down his body, the warm, wet velvet of her mouth working its way down, down, down until he was left with no choice but surrender.

CHAPTER 24

The Duke of Warrick's ball quickly became the most coveted invitation of the year.

Many were desperate for a glimpse of the reclusive nobleman who had once cut such a swaggering path through society. Rumors had swirled around him for years. Some swore a crippling illness had left him a mewling hunchback while others claimed he had only faked his infirmity in order to lure his wife back to his side.

There were those who believed the young duchess had never really run away at all, but that the duke had strangled her in a fit of rage and buried her somewhere on his vast estate. There were even some who whispered that he'd kept her and her babe imprisoned in the attic for all these years to keep them from leaving him.

Although his son's return had laid some of those rumors to rest, others had quickly risen to take their place. Those not fortunate enough to have secured invitations to Lord Newton's soiree had eagerly absorbed the gossip from that affair. The duke's heir was pronounced tremendously pleasing in both face and form, with the sort of towering physique that made women swoon and men grit their teeth in envy. His musical Scots burr was declared something to be emulated, and since that night Burns had become the most requested poet at every reading.

There were still some who refused to believe he had pledged his heart to the gold-digging daughter of an actress. When it was reported that the two of them had quarreled quite passionately right in the middle of Lady Newton's drawing room, it sent several unmarried young women and their ambitious mothers into a tizzy of delight. Perhaps there was still hope he would come to his senses, cast her off and choose a more suitable bride from his own class.

By the time the night of the ball arrived, all of London society was in a frenzy of anticipation.

Especially Pamela.

The rest of her trousseau had been delivered only that morning, freeing her to choose her attire for the evening from a dizzying array of selections. With Sophie's help, she had finally settled on a high-waisted ball dress of airy French gauze draped over a petticoat of ripe mulberry hemmed with not one or two, but *three* flounces that swayed like a bell with each step she took. Her puffed sleeves were gathered just off the shoulders, accentuating the arched wings of her collarbone and the graceful curve of her throat. Her square-cut bodice revealed only a tantalizing hint of her generous cleavage.

Sophie had outdone herself dressing Pamela's hair, coaxing the heavy coils into a profusion of loose curls and securing them atop her head with mother-of-pearl combs in a coif that Sophie assured her was the very height of French fashion.

She looked every inch a lady, which didn't explain how she ended up frozen in the arched doorway of the ballroom, her icy fists clenched inside her silk gloves and her satin slippers rooted to the parquet floor. She'd never seen her mother suffer a single moment of stage fright, but she'd heard sobering tales of other unfortunate actors who had been paralyzed by it.

As her panicked gaze swept the crush of guests crowding the vast ballroom, all of whom would soon be gawking at her, whispering about her and finding her lacking, tiny black dots began to swim before her eyes. She didn't belong on stage. She belonged in the wings, where she could applaud the efforts of others and safely hide from the glare of the footlights.

But then the guests parted to reveal a lone man who towered head and shoulders over most of them. Pamela drew in a deep breath and the dots vanished, leaving her vision crystal clear.

Had he been in attendance, Connor's tailor would have been crushed. Connor had forsaken the elegant evening attire so painstakingly measured and cut for him in favor of the rich woolen folds of his kilt and plaid. Several of the female guests were already stealing peeks at his bare knees from behind their fans and doubtlessly speculating on what he wore beneath the pleated skirt of the kilt. He did the traditional Scots garb such honor that by morning half the gentlemen in London would be frantically summoning their tailors so they could order their own kilts and tartan stockings.

Connor seemed utterly unaware of the stir he was causing. He only had eyes for her.

As their gazes locked, a devilish smile curved the corner of his mouth, reminding her that it had only been a few short hours since he had slipped into her bedchamber and into her. Her fists slowly unclenched.

Her feet began to carry her forward as if they had a will of their own.

A harried footman stepped into her path. "Wait, miss! It's not proper for you to proceed. You must allow me to announce you to the guests."

Recognizing him as the same servant who had tried to refuse her entry on the day they had arrived at Warrick Park, she gave his arm a fond pat. "That's quite all right, Peter. I already know who I am."

As she swerved around him and began to wend her way through the guests, her chin held high and a smile flirting with her lips, she knew exactly who she was.

She was a lady. Connor's lady.

By the time she reached his side, his smile had faded and he was scowling down at her cleavage. Bewildered by his expression, she glanced down at herself but saw nothing amiss. She'd never seen him gaze at her chest with anything but the warmest of admiration.

"You've no jewelry," he finally said, his scowl deepening.

She touched her bare throat self-consciously. "I know it must look a little odd, but I didn't want to spoil my lovely ensemble with a string of paste pearls."

"Don't apologize, lass. 'Tis my fault. I

should have thought to summon a jeweler along with all of those infernal dressmakers." He cast a furtive glance around the room, an avaricious glint lighting his eye when he spotted a sparkling diamond necklace adorning the overripe bosom of a silver-haired matron. "Would you like me to steal something for you to wear?"

Pamela's husky ripple of laughter attracted several curious glances. "Given the way the woman is eyeing you, I'm sure the two of you could work out a trade of some kind."

Connor shuddered. "No, thank you. I have a better idea anyway."

Pamela's laughter died in her throat as he reached back to his own nape, unfastened the delicate gold chain he wore, and drew his mother's locket out of his shirt. She stood utterly still — hardly daring to breathe — as he circled behind her and draped the necklace over her head. The locket, still warm from his skin, nestled against her breastbone as if it had been handcrafted just for her.

She touched her trembling fingertips to the smooth gold, knowing the locket hadn't left his heart since the night his mother had given it to him so that he would never be able to forget who he was.

His hands closed gently over her upper

arms. "Once we're wed," he whispered in her ear, "I'll drape you in a king's ransom of diamonds and rubies and pearls. You can wear them for me when you're wearing nothing else."

She turned to face him, her hand still pressed to the locket. "You can buy me those trinkets if it pleases you," she said softly, "but this will always mean more to me than any king's ransom."

As if on cue, the quartet of musicians seated in the corner struck up the first soaring strains of a Viennese waltz.

Delighted to find an excuse to be in his arms without causing a scandal, Pamela beamed up at him. "Would you care to dance, my lord?"

Folding his brawny arms over his chest, Connor smiled down at her with equal tenderness. "Hell, no."

"They make a striking couple, don't they?" Crispin observed, joining his mother at the railing of the portrait gallery overlooking the ballroom.

She was dressed all in white again. Like a bride. Or a ghost.

"Indeed they do," she agreed in a tone that was surprisingly amiable.

Connor was standing behind Pamela now.

Crispin watched as he gently rubbed her upper arms before bending his lighter head to her darker one and whispering something in her ear.

"What did you do with that broadsheet I found?" Crispin asked his mother.

She shrugged one pale shoulder. "Nothing of import. I simply made a few inquiries."

"And just what did you learn?"

A smile curved her lips. "All in good time, my son. All in good time."

Growing weary of her little games, he shook his head in disgust and turned to go.

She rested her hand lightly on his arm. "Never forget, my darling boy, that everything I've done has been for you. *Everything*," she added, her meaning impossible to miss.

He turned to gaze into her dark blue eyes, chilled anew by the absence of emotion within them. "That's precisely what I've always been afraid of."

Sophie pressed her ear to the bedchamber wall, groaning in frustration as the distant strains of a Viennese waltz came wafting up from belowstairs. If she closed her eyes, she could almost see herself twirling around a candlelit ballroom in Crispin's arms with every admiring eye fixed on them.

She threw herself down on the settee, glaring at the door. There hadn't been a single opportunity for Crispin to pay her another nocturnal visit. Pamela had rarely left her bedchamber in the past week, much less the house. Given the intriguing thumps and muffled moans which emanated from her sister's chamber each night after the candles were extinguished and she believed Sophie was asleep, Sophie wasn't sure she could blame her.

She rose to restlessly pace the room. Pamela had promised her that as soon as she and Connor were safely wed, she would reveal to the duke and the world that Sophie was her sister and not her maid. Sophie hugged herself, smiling to imagine the stunned look on Crispin's face when he discovered she was no lowly maidservant, but . . . but . . . the sister of a marchioness!

Her gaze fell on the rejected gowns still piled haphazardly on the bed. Instead of moping, she supposed she could make better use of her time by hanging them in the dressing room before they wrinkled. She certainly had no intention of pressing them.

Feeling a bit like Cinderella after the wicked stepsisters had gone off to make merry at the prince's ball, she gathered up an armful of the gowns. But when a lustrous pearl-trimmed bodice caught her eye, she let the rest of the gowns slide carelessly to the floor.

The silk of the high-waisted evening dress had been dyed a rich cornflower blue that perfectly matched the shade of her eyes. Unable to resist the temptation, Sophie held the gown up to herself and waltzed over to the cheval glass to admire her reflection. The dress would have been all wrong for Pamela but it was perfect for her. Well, at least it would be if she could find some cotton batting to stuff the bosom.

Humming along with the music drifting up from the ballroom, she swayed back and forth in front of the mirror before finishing her impromptu waltz with a graceful twirl.

When she faced the mirror once again, she was wearing an evil little smirk. "She borrowed my gowns, didn't she?" she reminded her reflection. "Why shouldn't I borrow hers?"

Before she could lose her nerve, she scrambled into the dressing room and tugged one of their old battered valises down from the shelf above the dormer window. The case was stuffed with discarded props they'd filched from the theater over the years, including the music box pistol

Pamela had used to take Connor hostage. It didn't take Sophie long to find *exactly* what she needed to complete her ensemble.

Pamela pursued Connor relentlessly through the crowd, ignoring the avid glances they were getting. "What do you mean you can't dance? I don't understand. I've never seen a man so light and graceful on his feet. Why, you practically dance every time you move. *Every* time you move," she added under her breath, remembering a particularly spectacular motion he had executed in her bed only that morning. He certainly couldn't deny having rhythm.

"My mother tried to teach me to dance when I was a lad. It did *not* go well."

"But any man who can fence and recite poetry as well as you should be able to dance!"

He cast her an arch look over his shoulder, pointing out the illogic of that statement without a word.

Pamela doubled her steps to keep pace with his long strides. "Why didn't you tell the duke? I'm sure he would have engaged a dancing master for you."

"I almost killed the fencing master. Can you imagine what I'd do to a dancing master?" Connor groaned as he veered around a marble column only to find his path cut off by Crispin.

"I need to speak with you," Crispin said, his lean face grim.

Crispin shot the portrait gallery a wary glance, but except for generations of glowering Warricks, it appeared to be deserted.

Connor added his glower to theirs. "So what's it to be this time — a duel of words or swords? I'm afraid I didn't bring my volume of Burns, but I'm sure we could scare up a sword or two if watching you get your fool head cut off will entertain the guests."

"Please." Crispin drew closer to them, his voice low and urgent. "I just need a few minutes of your time."

He opened his mouth, but before he could speak, a collective gasp went up from the crowd.

All three of them turned as one to discover a golden-haired goddess garbed all in blue framed by the arched doorway. The Venetian half mask she wore only added to her irresistible aura of mystery.

As they watched, she rose up on the toes of her dainty little slippers and cupped her hand around the footman's ear to whisper something in it.

The footman cleared his throat uneasily before announcing, "Le Comtesse d'Arby."

CHAPTER 25

"It appears that someone is trying to up-stage you," Connor murmured, chuckling beneath his breath.

Pamela's amber eyes narrowed to dangerous slits. "Someone has been trying to upstage me since the day she was born. Why, the little vixen is wearing my new dress!"

Within seconds everyone was whispering and pointing and gawking at the mysterious beauty who had been bold enough to wear a mask to a ball that didn't require one.

Crispin's jaw had gone slack, along with the jaws of most of the men in the ballroom. He seemed to have forgotten all about his errand and its urgency.

"If you'll excuse me . . ." he murmured, drifting away from them and toward the ravishing creature in the doorway like a man sleepwalking through a beautiful dream.

Pamela started to follow, but Connor

seized her by the elbow and hauled her back. "There's no harm in it. Let the lass have her fun."

A throng of admirers quickly gathered in the middle of the ballroom floor to gape at the new arrival. Before Crispin could even elbow his way through their ranks, rumors had begun to ripple through the crowd.

The mysterious comtesse with the velvet choker fastened around her slender throat was a French orphan whose parents had been taken by the guillotine. She was an infamous courtesan who hoped to secure a position as the marquess's mistress. She was a French spy who had been sent to wrangle secrets from the militia by seducing their commanding officers.

Crispin didn't hear a single person guess that she might be a common maidservant masquerading as a comtesse in her mistress's pilfered clothes.

When an eager young fellow tried to cut in front of him so he could reach her first, Crispin neatly hooked his foot around the man's ankle, sending him sprawling to the parquet floor.

"Forgive my clumsiness. So terribly sorry," he murmured, stepping right over the man without breaking his stride.

She had been expecting him. She didn't even bat an eyelash when he caught her elbow in a possessive grip and urged her into the crush. "So is your mistress going to send you packing for pulling this reckless little stunt?"

She bit her bottom lip, looking more coy than worried. "No, but she might very well spank me."

"She beats you?" Crispin was incredulous. As far as he was concerned, it would be criminal to leave any mark on such exquisite flesh.

"Not even when I deserve it," she admitted with a sigh. "But she has been known to send me to bed without my tea and biscuits when I've been exceptionally naughty."

As several provocative images of her being "exceptionally naughty" in his bed flashed through his mind, Crispin tightened his grip on her elbow, shepherding her into a curtained alcove and away from the prying eyes of his uncle's guests.

"Who are you?" he demanded, urging her around to face him.

Now that they were all alone she didn't seem nearly so bold. As he began to back her toward the wall, the feathers on her mask began to tremble ever so slightly. "You know who I am. I'm Miss Darby's —"

"— maidservant," he finished for her. "And I'm the Prince Regent." He planted his hands against the wall on either side of her head, making it impossible for her to escape his piercing gaze. *"Who are you?"*

"I'm Sophie," she whispered.

"Sophie," he echoed and somehow in that heartbeat of time before his lips descended on hers, it was enough for the both of them.

Crispin felt a surge of triumph when he felt her clutch the back of his coat, not to pull him away but to urge him closer.

"Sophie," he breathed against her parted lips, suddenly finding it the most entrancing name in all the world.

He drew away first, desperate to bring his rioting passions under control before he did something they would both regret.

"How did you recognize me tonight?" She blinked up at him, her sultry blue eyes shadowed by the cat-eye slant of the mask's eyeholes. "How did you know I was the comtesse?"

Unable to keep his hands off of her despite his best intentions, he traced the delicate curve of her jaw with the back of his fingers. "I've been waiting my whole life to find you. I would have known you anywhere. Anytime."

She ducked her head, her unexpected shyness just as entrancing as her boldness had been. "I don't suppose I made a very convincing comtesse."

"On the contrary. I thought it was a remarkable performance. Had I been at the theater I would have leapt to my feet and shouted, 'Bravo!' at the top of my lungs."

She slowly lifted her head, her eyes narrowing. "What did you say?"

"I said I would have leapt to my feet and shouted, 'Bravo' . . ." He trailed off, watching in alarm as the color began to drain from the bottom half of her face. "Sweeting, what is it?"

"You!" she breathed, backing away from him.

He followed her step for step, bewildered by the abrupt change in her demeanor. Before he knew it, they were on the other side of the curtain and beginning to attract a small but fascinated audience.

She pointed a trembling finger at him. It didn't take him more than a glimpse of her stormy eyes to realize it was trembling not with fear, but with rage. "You! I know who you are! You're one of those miserable wretches from the theater who pelted me with rotten vegetables."

She reached up and tore off the mask, baring her face to him and the world. Crispin's heart plummeted toward his shoes as he finally remembered *exactly* where he'd seen that magnificent face before.

It wasn't uncommon for him and a bunch of other rowdy young bucks to terrorize the town on a weekend. Usually their mischief was limited to seeing who could swill the most cheap gin without casting up their accounts on their shoes or tossing unsuspecting passersby into a horse trough. But on one fateful Friday night, when they were already deep in their cups, they had stumbled into a smoky, second-rate theater off Drury Lane.

When Sophie had taken the stage, he had been just as transfixed by her beauty as he was now. Then she had opened her exquisite mouth and ruined everything.

As she had stuttered out her lines in a wooden monotone, the theater had erupted in catcalls and hoots of laughter. Before he knew it, one of his friends had shoved a rotting tomato into his hand. He had tossed it without thinking, then felt worse than rotten when he saw that beautiful face streaked with tomato juice and bits of pulp. She had turned and looked right at him in that moment, her face proud and pale, her blue eyes darkened by accusation just as they were now.

"You threw a tomato at me!"

He raised both hands as if to ward off an attack. "I was foxed out of my head on cheap gin that night! If I hadn't been, I would have remembered it before now."

She snorted. "Ah yes, because you've been waiting your whole life to find me. You would have known me anywhere. Anytime. Except for the night you and your horrid friends bombarded me with rubbish and ran me out of town!"

He shook his head, helpless to defend the indefensible. "Well, you have to admit you were a really awful actress."

She sucked in an outraged breath. "I'd rather be an awful actress than an awful man!" With those words, she snatched a glass of champagne from a footman's tray and tossed its contents right in his face.

She spun around and went storming off, leaving behind a trail of shocked gasps and muffled titters.

"Lovers' quarrel," Crispin muttered to the man nearest to him, earning a knowing and sympathetic nod as he used his cravat to mop his face.

By the time he had swiped all the champagne from his eyes, the exquisite Comtesse d'Arby had vanished as mysteriously as she had appeared.

■ ■ ■ ■

When the musicians struck up yet another infernal Viennese waltz, Connor grabbed Pamela by the hand and began to drag her toward the middle of the floor. He'd had just about enough of watching her wistfully moon over the couples sweeping gracefully around the ballroom. He'd already decided that there would be none of those ridiculous country dances or stately minuets for him. If he was going to make a complete ass of himself in front of half of London, it was going to be with her in his arms.

"Where are we going?" Pamela asked, alarmed by Connor's ferocious scowl. He looked as if he were ready to do murder.

"I'm going to dance with you," he growled. "But if I break your toe as I did my mother's, you have only yourself to blame."

Her heart soared in time to the music as he drew her into his arms, cupping one of her gloved hands in his much larger one and pressing his other hand firmly to the small of her back. As he swept her into the waltz, other couples eager to spy on them rushed to join the dance.

For a dizzying moment it was as if they

were right back in her bed, their gazes locked, their bodies moving in perfect rhythm.

Until his foot came down firmly on her toes.

"Ow!" she exclaimed, making an involuntary little leap of protest.

"Don't say I didn't warn you," Connor said grimly as their next giddy turn nearly bumped a couple right off their feet.

It quickly became apparent that they were posing a danger not only to themselves but to the other dancers as well. Pamela laughed aloud, marveling that a man so graceful both on his feet and off of them could be such a wretched dancer.

She tugged him to a halt. "We can practice later," she told him. "In private."

Her husky promise wiped the scowl right off of his face. Instead of releasing her, he splayed his powerful hand at the small of her back and urged her closer. As he gazed down at her, his eyes going smoky with want, it was as if the two of them were suspended in time while the world continued to spin around them in a whirling kaleidoscope of color and motion.

Pamela would have been content to remain that way forever if the music hadn't lurched to an abrupt halt, leaving the dancers milling about in confusion.

Before they could regain their composure, the footman's resonant voice reverberated from the arched doorway of the ballroom on a note of pure triumph. "His Grace, the Duke of Warrick."

A stunned gasp went up from the crowd as two young, burly footmen appeared in the doorway, bearing the duke's wheeled chair between them as if it were a pasha's litter or the throne of some mighty and ancient king.

"I do believe someone is trying to upstage you," Pamela murmured, shooting Connor a wry glance.

He snorted. "I'm surprised he didn't have heralds dressed as angels announce his arrival with a fanfare of trumpets."

They watched along with the rest of the guests as the footmen carried the chair across the ballroom, then gently lowered it to the floor. Two more footmen followed in their wake, staggering slightly beneath the weight of a tall velvet-draped object. Those in the back of the room were craning their necks to get a better look at the infamous recluse and the footmen's mysterious burden.

The duke's gaunt cheeks were flushed, but it was impossible to tell if his sunken eyes were glittering with fever or excitement. His hair had been neatly combed and lay in a shining curtain over his shoulders. The kiss of hoarfrost at his temples lent him a dignified air. Despite being confined to the chair, he was sitting with his back ramrod straight. His elegant evening clothes masked how wasted his frame had become.

As he surveyed the crowd through his shrewd hazel eyes, Pamela caught a glimpse of the man who must have once commanded every room he entered. The man who had won his duchess's heart, and then been foolish enough to toss it away like so much refuse.

"Most of you already know why you were invited here tonight," he said.

Although an expectant hush had fallen over the crowd, Pamela was still surprised by how well his voice carried.

"After many long years of wandering this world alone, my son — and heir — has finally come home."

That statement produced several surreptitious glances at Connor and a smattering of polite applause.

"At this time I would like to ask him to take his rightful place by my side."

The duke stretched out his hand toward Connor, its palsied trembling betraying the weakness he was trying so hard to hide. Pamela could feel the tension arcing through Connor and knew he would have liked nothing better in that moment than to bolt for the door. But instead, he laced his fingers through hers and started forward, making it clear that this was one ordeal he had no intention of facing alone.

The crowd eagerly parted to clear a path between the two men. As she and Connor approached the duke, Pamela felt a peculiar chill shoot down her spine. She glanced over her shoulder to find Lady Astrid watching them from the gallery, her eyes glowing nearly as feverishly as her brother's.

Pamela frowned, disconcerted by the woman's gloating expression. But there wasn't anything she could do at the moment except obey the duke's summons.

Connor reluctantly surrendered her hand as they approached the wheeled chair. She stepped back a respectful pace, executing a graceful curtsy. Connor bowed as well, but the duke quickly caught him by the hand, urging him to straighten.

Pamela glanced behind them again, sensing movement in the crowd for the first time since the duke had made his grand entrance. There seemed to be several new arrivals slipping past the footmen and into the ballroom. Before she could blink, they had disappeared into the crowd, fanning out in all directions.

Her sense of unease growing, she returned her attention to the duke, praying his speech would be over quickly so she could warn Connor that something might be amiss.

Still gripping Connor's hand, the duke drew him to his side so that they were both facing the crowd. "Ever since the day my son returned to Warrick Park, I've been trying to come up with the perfect gift with which I might welcome him home. As most of you know without my boasting, my fortune is such that I could lay many of the world's greatest treasures at his feet. But by watching him with his lovely fiancée in the past fortnight, I have learned that my son is a much wiser man than I was at his age. He has already come to recognize the value of the dearest treasure of all."

Pamela felt the sting of unexpected tears in her eyes as the duke paused to give her a gracious nod.

As if by prearranged signal, all four footmen moved to station themselves around the object draped by the velvet curtain.

"After searching my heart — or what's left of it — I decided to give my son a gift that would honor not only him, but also the memory of his dear mother."

The duke waved his hand in a dramatic flourish. The footmen tugged a quartet of gold cords and the velvet curtain went rippling to the floor.

An astonished gasp went up from the room as an enormous portrait propped up on a gilded easel was revealed. A portrait of a lady in the first tender bloom of womanhood.

Her hair was piled high on top of her head and lightly powdered in the style of a generation ago, making it impossible to determine its hue. Some might have said it was her striking gray eyes, her ripe lips, or her fine straight nose that made her beauty so uncommon, but Pamela believed it to be the mischievous dimple tucked deep into her right cheek. There was also a beguiling hint of stubbornness to the lift of her jaw, giving the impression that she was not a woman with whom a man would want to trifle. Pamela sighed, thinking how very tragic it was that the duke had learned that lesson too late.

Judging by the tears shining in the man's eyes, he was probably thinking the exact same thing.

Tugging his hand from the duke's, Connor took one step toward the portrait, then another, gazing up at it as if hypnotized. For an elusive moment, Pamela would have almost sworn she saw the glint of tears in his eyes as well.

"That's my mother."

Pamela shot a nervous look at the duke, puzzled by Connor's expression and the lack of color in his face. "Yes, dear, of course it's your mother," she said carefully. "That's why the duke had the portrait put on display. To honor you and her memory."

"No," he replied, his lips barely moving. "You don't understand. That really is my mother."

When she continued to gaze at him as if he'd lost his wits, he swung toward her, the look in his eyes so fierce she took an involuntary step backward. Ignoring her dismayed gasp, he reached down and carelessly snapped the delicate gold chain holding his mother's locket.

He pried open the locket with his thumb and handed it back to her, his expression grim.

Pamela gazed down at the miniature within. The woman in this likeness had light brown hair gathered at the nape in a much simpler coif. Her face was suffused with a glow of happiness. She looked riper, wiser, more at peace with herself and the world.

Different somehow yet still unmistakably the same woman in the duke's portrait.

Pamela lifted her disbelieving eyes to Connor's face, stunned comprehension slowly dawning. If he was this woman's son, then he was also the duke's son . . . and the man's true heir. He was everything he had been pretending to be while she was nothing at all.

Without even realizing it, she began to back away from him.

She had been right all along. She was the one who didn't belong here, the one who would never truly belong here. She might have set this absurd little farce in motion, but hers was a role she was never meant to play. She should have remained backstage, far away from the glare of the footlights and the avid gazes of the audience.

Connor watched her retreat from him, bewilderment darkening his eyes.

By the time Pamela saw the shadows come creeping out of the crowd to surround them, it was too late.

Lady Astrid's shrill voice rang out from the gallery, shattering the reverent hush that had fallen over the ballroom. *"Arrest that man immediately! He's an imposter!"*

CHAPTER 26

The duke sat behind the immense desk in his study in his wheeled throne — judge, jury and executioner all wrapped up in one. The flames leaping on the hearth behind the desk might as well have been springing from the yawning mouth of hell itself.

Not even the constable Astrid had summoned to arrest Connor and Pamela dared to defy his authority, although judging from the disapproving set of the man's thin lips, he would have liked nothing more. He stood stiffly at attention by the door, ready to intervene at the slightest encouragement from the duke.

At the duke's command, the constable's battered and bloodied men had been banished to the corridor, where they were passing the time nursing their bruises and testing for loose teeth.

Connor had not gone down without a fight. Especially not after he had seen the men wrench Pamela's delicate wrists behind her and clap them in irons. It had taken almost a dozen men to subdue him and if one of them hadn't had the foresight to wrest away the loaded pistol he had whipped from his plaid before he could aim and fire, someone would have been carried from the ballroom feet first.

Connor and Pamela were sitting in the leather wingback chairs in front of the desk like a pair of disobedient children awaiting a scolding.

Pamela rubbed her tender wrists, thankful that at least the duke had insisted their irons be removed. Judging by the murderous glances Connor kept throwing the constable, it might not have been his wisest decision.

She was still having difficulty looking at Connor. Still couldn't quite comprehend that he wasn't her highwayman after all, but the heir to a vast empire. How such a thing could have happened was beyond her comprehension. She smoothed her rumpled skirt to give her trembling hands something to occupy them. Her pretty new gown had been torn and stained when the constable's men had dragged her out of the ballroom in front of their shocked guests.

The duke steepled his fingers beneath his

bony chin and gave them both a long, hard look. "Let me make sure I have this perfectly clear. The two of you came here to Warrick Park to deliberately swindle me out of both my fortune and my title. You shamelessly used lies and trickery to gain my trust and affection and to rob my nephew of his rightful inheritance."

"That pretty much sums it up," Connor said, managing to look utterly unrepentant as he leaned back in the chair and folded his brawny arms over his chest.

The duke's shrewd gaze locked on him. "And now that you've been caught with your greedy little hands in the till, you claim to have miraculously discovered that you're exactly who you were pretending to be all along — Percy Ambrose Bartholomew Reginald Cecil Smythe, Marquess of Eddywhistle and heir to the duchy of Warrick."

Connor visibly winced. "Why in the name of God would any man in his right mind name his firstborn son Percy?"

The duke stiffened. "It was my father's name. And I'll have you know that Percy has been a proud name along the northern border of England for generations. Why, the Percys spent years routing the Scots and . . ." He trailed off at the look in Connor's eye.

Connor sat up straight in the chair, gripping its armrests. "I'm not any happier about this than you are." He pointed at the door. "If the woman in that portrait is my mother, then that means you're —"

The duke eyed him coolly, daring him to continue.

Connor swallowed before saying softly, "It means you're the miserable cheating bastard who broke her heart."

"I've never denied that, have I, son?"

"Don't call me that! You haven't the right!"

When the echo of Connor's shout had faded, the duke said quietly, "Well, that remains to be seen, doesn't it?" He turned to Pamela, his voice dispassionate. "I hear that once again it is you, Miss Darby, who will provide me with the proof I need to convince me not to turn the both of you over to the constable for a quick trial and an even quicker hanging."

The constable perked up at the prospect of a hanging, earning a fresh glare from Connor.

"So what's it to be this time, my dear — a letter from the king himself vouching for the lad's parentage or perhaps a wailing visit from the shade of his mother?" The duke snorted bitterly. "God knows the woman has haunted me nearly to my grave in the past twenty-nine years."

Pamela reached into the bodice of her gown. It had been no easy feat hanging on to the locket when the constable's men had seized her. But she had clenched her fist tight and held on for dear life, remembering how his mother had told Connor to guard it with his life.

She rose and moved to the desk. The duke stretched out his hand, but still she hesitated. Once she surrendered the locket into his keeping, there would be no going back. For any of them.

She slowly let the trinket slip through her fingers and into his hand. "I believe this will prove beyond the shadow of a doubt that this man is your son."

She returned to her seat, still avoiding Connor's eyes.

The duke's hands were trembling so badly it took him three tries to pry open the locket. He sat gazing down at the miniature within for several minutes, his expression unchanging.

But when he lifted his eyes to Connor's face, they were burning with an unholy fire. "Where did you get this?"

"My mother gave it to me. Right before she died. My father had it painted when a fair came through our village."

"So she didn't die on the road to the Highlands?"

Connor shook his head. "She didn't die until I was fifteen."

"How?" the duke demanded querulously. "How can any of this be possible?"

"How am I supposed to know?" Connor snapped, his own voice rising. "Perhaps my father found her when she was ill. He had a tender heart and a habit of taking in strays. Perhaps he took her and her babe in as well. All I know is that I never knew the woman in this portrait as anything but my mother and his wife."

"She was *my* wife!" the duke roared, pounding his fist on the desk. "He had no right to her!"

Connor gave him a long level look. "Apparently, neither did you."

The duke seized the iron wheels of his chair and wrenched the chair to the side, as if he could no longer bear to look upon any of them. His hair fell in a lank curtain around his face. "So you came here to swindle an old fool out of his fortune only to discover that you were exactly who you were pretending to be."

"Aye," Connor confessed. "That seems to be the way of it."

The constable stepped forward, hat in hand. "You've suffered enough of this pair's nonsense, your grace. Why don't you allow me to summon my men and have them locked up until you can determine what should be —"

The duke lifted his hand, stifling the man in mid-sentence. His shoulders began to shake. A strangled sound emerged from his throat, launching him into one of his more terrible coughing fits. Pamela inched to the edge of her chair, fearing he was going to expire right before their eyes, making Connor the duke.

But when he rolled his chair back around to face him, she realized he wasn't coughing, but laughing. Laughing without a trace of bitterness. Laughing so hard that tears were streaming down his haggard cheeks.

Struggling to catch his breath, he pointed a palsied finger at Connor. "Such ingenuity! Such gall! There's no denying that you're my son now, is there? But the joke's on you, isn't it, lad? And I'll wager you haven't even thought about the worst of it yet. If I'm your father, then that means that Astrid is your aunt and Crispin is truly your —"

"— cousin," Connor finished, dropping his head into his hands with a groan.

"Your grace," the constable snapped,

striding toward the desk. "Surely you're not going to just let them get away with such a nefarious scheme!" He drew a piece of paper from his coat and shook it at the duke. "What about this broadsheet? It all but proves this man is guilty of any number of crimes against the crown."

The duke took the broadsheet from the man's hand and gave it a cursory glance. "This proves nothing. There may be a slight resemblance, but the man in this sketch is wearing a mask. He could be anyone." He wadded the broadsheet into a ball and tossed it over his shoulder into the fire.

The constable began to sputter. "Wh— Wh— What about this woman then? Surely you're going to allow me to arrest her. Why, she's nothing but a common criminal!"

Connor tensed and started to rise, but the duke waved him back down before crooking a finger at Pamela.

She reluctantly rose and moved to stand before the desk like a recalcitrant schoolgirl, her hands clasped in front of her.

"What do you have to say for yourself, girl?"

She lifted her head to look him boldly in the eye, much as she had done that first day in the solarium. "We haven't been completely truthful, your grace."

He began to chortle anew. "Now there's a shock, isn't it?"

"I didn't come here just to bilk you out of your fortune. I came here to find my mother's murderer. I have every reason to believe the fire that killed her was no accident. That someone set it in order to destroy your duchess's letter. Someone very close to you who wanted to make sure your true heir was never found."

The duke's smile faded, leaving him looking troubled — almost pensive.

"I was the one who convinced Connor" — Pamela cleared her throat with some difficulty — "*his lordship* to help me by appealing to his sense of chivalry."

Connor sprang to his feet. "The lass is lying! She appealed to my greed and to my lust for revenge against the English. She's the innocent one. I was only in it for the money."

The duke eyed Pamela with a shrewd eye. "Oh, I think you were in it for much more than that." He shook his head. "Clever, resourceful girl. I liked you the moment I saw you."

Shock rippled through her. "You called me a bold and reckless girl. And a cheeky chit."

"And have you done anything to disprove

that estimation?"

She inclined her head. "I suppose not."

"Very well, then. You're dismissed."

The constable went red, then purple. "But your grace —"

The duke sighed. "If this man is really my son and this girl brought us together just as she promised to do, then what crime has she committed?"

The constable opened and closed his mouth several times before snapping it shut. "What about the girl's preposterous claim that someone may have murdered her mother?"

"Oh, I believe I can take care of that situation. You'll simply have to trust me." He included Connor and Pamela in his sweeping gaze before saying pointedly, "All of you."

The constable slammed on his hat, bristling with disapproval.

"I do have one task you could perform before you leave," the duke said.

The man brightened, plainly hoping there was still someone lurking about the mansion who needed to be hanged. "How can I be of service, your grace?"

The feverish glow had left the duke's eyes, leaving them as cold as the glitter of freshly cut diamonds. "On your way out, you can tell the butler to ring for my sister."

Astrid slipped into the study, struggling to look sympathetic and demure instead of wildly triumphant. Her brother sat all alone behind his desk, studying the face of what appeared to be a gold pocket watch. The flames dancing on the hearth behind him cast his face in shadow.

She dropped gracefully into one of the wingback chairs in front of the desk, already anticipating how graciously she would respond when he began to congratulate her on her cleverness. "I saw the constable and his men leaving the grounds. May I assume those dreadful miscreants are now in their custody and on the way to Newgate?"

Her brother snapped the watch shut and slipped it into the pocket of his waistcoat. "You may assume whatever you like. But I'd appreciate it if you didn't call my son a miscreant."

"Your son?" Despite the cozy warmth of the room, Astrid felt a chill tickle her spine. "Surely you don't mean that imposter? He's not your son. That broadsheet I turned over to the authorities proved he's nothing but an incorrigible criminal who's escaped the hangman's noose for the last time. Please tell me you haven't deluded yourself yet again!"

The look he gave her was pitying, but without a trace of mercy. "I'm not the one who has deluded myself, Astrid. Did you really think you could make me believe that boy didn't belong to me? To *her?* The first time I looked into his eyes and saw his mother looking back at me, I knew who he was. I never doubted it for a minute, not even when you were howling for his blood and the constable was clapping him in irons."

Astrid bit her bottom lip to still its sudden trembling, tasting the salty warmth of her own blood on her tongue. "I was only trying to protect you. I've always tried to look after you, you know," she told him, despising the whining note in her voice.

"Indeed you have. But I made a very curious discovery in the past week. Whenever I don't drink the tea you prepare for me, I don't cough — or sleep — nearly as much. As a matter of fact, I've felt myself growing a little stronger each day."

Astrid gasped in shock as he gripped the edge of the desk and slowly inched his way upward until he was standing on his feet like a haggard ghost of the man he had once been.

She clutched at her throat. "What are you trying to imply?"

"That I think it's time you packed your bags and left this house," he said gently. "Don't worry. I'll see to it that you lack for nothing. I've already rented a cottage and hired a private nurse. I'll provide a generous allowance for you until the day you die."

"What about my son?" she hissed. "Are you going to cast your nephew into the streets as well?"

"I believe I'll leave that decision up to *my* son. If Percy — if *Connor* wants him to stay, I'll allow it."

She straightened until her spine was as stiff as an iron poker, standing face to face with her brother for the first time in years. "How very benevolent of you," she said with a sneer. "You're no different from Father, are you? He couldn't wait to be rid of me either." As if watching someone else from a great distance, she could hear her voice rising on a shrill note. Could see the ugly beads of spittle flying from her lips. "Father never even saw me. He would look right through me as if I wasn't even there. He married me off to a drunken sot and I had to endure the lout's crude fumblings night after night until he got his whelp on me. I wrote Father dozens of letters begging him to let me come home. But he never even took the time to answer one of them. He never cared about me. All he ever cared about was you — his precious heir!"

"You should go, Astrid. Before I'm forced to call back the constable and ask him to investigate the tragic death of Marianne Darby."

Astrid felt an icy shroud of calm descending over her. "You'll be sorry, Archie. I promise you that you'll rue the day you cast me out of your life!" With those words, she turned on her heel and stalked toward the door.

It wasn't until the door had slammed behind her that her brother sank back into his chair, running a weary hand over his face. "I already do, Astrid," he whispered. "I already do."

Pamela perched on the edge of Sophie's dressing room cot, watching her sister sleep. Judging by the grimy tear tracks staining Sophie's fair cheeks and the wrinkled blue gown tossed carelessly over the back of a chair, it didn't appear that her sister's masquerade had ended any more successfully than her own.

She brushed a curl from Sophie's cheek, thinking how heartbroken the girl was going to be when she discovered she'd missed one of the scandals of the century. The gossipmongers and scandal sheets would no doubt be abuzz with the news for weeks to come. After all, it wasn't every day that a marquess and his fiancée were hauled out of a ball hosted in their honor in irons.

She gently tucked the blanket around Sophie's shoulders. She might as well let her sleep for now. She would have to wake her soon enough.

Pamela returned to her bedchamber and the task at hand, making a concerted effort not to look at the tightly latched window. But it wasn't so easy to steer clear of her bed where Connor had held her tenderly in his arms until the wee hours of the morning. Or the cheval glass she had stood in front of while he wrapped his arms around her from behind and encouraged her to watch their entwined reflections while he pleasured her. Or the settee where he had —

Pamela squeezed her eyes shut, a blade of fresh pain lancing through her heart. She could leave the lamps lit and latch the window, but there was nothing she could do to bar the doors of her heart. No way to stop the memories from stealing past her defenses and wreaking havoc on her fragile determination.

She dropped her burdens on the bed and drifted toward the window. The night beyond seemed darker than ever before, the moonlight paler and more brittle. The somber-eyed woman gazing back at her from the wavy glass bore little resemblance to anyone she knew. She rested her brow against the cool glass and closed her eyes, feeling a hot tear trickle down her cheek.

She was reaching up to dash it away before it could be joined by others when her bedchamber door flew open. Clapping a hand to her pounding heart, she whirled around to find one very large, very angry Scotsman standing in the doorway.

Chapter 27

If Connor were dressed all in black and gripping a pistol, he would have looked exactly as he had on that moonlit road in the Highlands on the night they had met. "Did you really think latching the window was going to keep me out?"

She stiffened. "You'll be the master of this house someday. I suppose you can go wherever you like."

He started forward and she took a wary step backward. He stopped, eyeing her incredulously. "What do you think I'm going to do, lass? Lift my hand to you?"

She couldn't tell him that she was more afraid of him putting his hands on her. She knew just how persuasive and irresistible those hands could be.

Resting them on his hips, he surveyed the untidy room, taking in the open trunk sitting on the floor, the battered valise perched on the settee, the gowns and shoes scattered across the bed. His gaze finally returned to her. She wasn't wearing her elegant ball dress or her nightdress, but a simple copper merino gown with frayed seams and a high neck that had been out of fashion for at least three seasons.

The sight obviously did not improve his temper.

He shook his head. "I should have known it would come to this. It's just like the English to cut and run at the first sign of a battle."

She sucked in a sharp breath. "And I should have remembered that the Scots are notorious for not fighting fairly. In case you didn't notice, the battle has been won. The duke's beloved son has been restored to the bosom of his family. He's now free to take his rightful place in society."

"Free?" Connor shook his head in disgust. "I'll never be free again. I'll spend the rest of my life behind bars — imprisoned in this gilded cage."

She drew closer to him, unable to help herself. "That's not true, Connor. You'll be truly free now. Free to travel the world. Free to study. Free to move through society without always looking over your shoulder because the hangman might be one step behind you." She inclined her head, adding softly, "Free to choose a bride who will do honor to your station in life."

"I already have."

She lifted her head. Whatever he saw in her eyes made him close the distance between them in two strides. His fingers dug into her upper arms, giving her a rough little shake. "Dammit, Pamela, I'm still the same man! The man you took to your bed only last night. The man who had to put his hand over your mouth to keep you from waking the entire household when he —"

"No, you're not!" she cried, the words pouring straight out of her lacerated heart. "You're not the same man at all. That man was a rogue — an imposter, just as I was. You're a marquess. And someday soon you'll be a duke, while I'll never be anything more than the bastard daughter of an actress. You've had two fathers now. I'll never even have one!"

Connor released her and moved back a step to put some space between them. Pamela eyed him warily, unnerved by his quick surrender and the dangerous gleam in his eye.

He folded his arms over his chest, the motion accentuating the natural arrogance she had noted in his bearing upon their very first meeting. "If you no longer fancy yourself fine enough to be my bride, then you can be my mistress." His smoky gaze drifted lazily down her, then back up again, heating everything it touched. "You've already proved you have the skills to please me."

She gasped, unprepared for such a blow.

He lifted one shoulder in a careless shrug. "You needn't look so shocked. It would hardly be unheard of for the daughter of an actress to warm a marquess's bed. I'll be well equipped to provide for you and Sophie. I can buy you a modest house somewhere, some bonny jewels, perhaps even a wee dog to help you pass the time when I'm too busy with my duties — or my wife — to pay a visit to your bed."

She lifted her chin. "And just what would I be expected to offer in exchange for the privilege of becoming your mistress?"

"Whatever I wanted." He leaned down to bring his mouth close to her ear, his husky whisper sending a shiver of longing through her soul. "Whenever I wanted it."

"Very well," she said coolly. "I accept your offer. I couldn't have become your bride tonight, but there's nothing to stop me from becoming your mistress."

He straightened, his face going so still it could have been carved from granite. "There isn't?"

"Of course not. All you have to do is tell me what pleases you." She tossed her head, with a low, throaty laugh. "Don't worry. I know how to play the role of strumpet. I saw my mother do it often enough — both on the stage and off of it. Shall I lie down on the bed and lift my skirts? Or should I bend over the settee?"

"Stop it," Connor growled.

"Would you prefer to have me on my back?" She slanted him a provocative glance. "Or my knees?"

"Stop it, Pamela. Now!"

"I was only trying to please you."

He seized her face in his hands, his gaze as raw as his voice. "If you want to please me, lass, then stop all this nonsense and marry me."

Connor's fierce tenderness was far more difficult to bear than his cruelty or his mockery. Pamela inclined her head, not wanting him to see the tears welling up in her eyes. "I am afraid I can't do that, my lord. I have no choice but to set you free from any promise you made to me before we knew the full circumstances of your birth, any obligation that might prevent you from assuming your title and all of the privileges and duties that go with it, includ- ing the duty of finding a suitable bride and producing an heir of your own."

As Connor withdrew his hands from her, she could do nothing to stop the tears from spilling down her cheeks.

His laugh was short and rueful. "This was our plan from the beginning, wasn't it? That you would beg off our engagement and break my heart. I'm sure I'll cut quite the tragic figure in the eyes of society. There will probably be no shortage of sympathetic women eager to console me."

His words cut to the heart, but Pamela knew she had no right to rebuke him. He wasn't being cruel now, only honest.

"You're still entitled to the reward, you know," he said.

She drew in a shuddering breath, forcing herself to lift her head and meet his gaze. "I don't want it."

His eyes were as silvery and distant as the moon. "You may not want it, but Sophie deserves it. Why don't you just consider it payment for services rendered?"

As Connor turned and walked out of the room, gently closing the door behind him, she collapsed to her knees beside the settee, burying her face in the cushions to muffle her sobs.

Pamela had been crying for a long time

when she became aware that someone was softly stroking her hair. She jerked up her head, her heart leaping with a wild and undeserved hope.

Sophie was curled up on the settee next to where she'd been resting her head, her golden curls rumpled and her eyes puffy from sleep.

Her sister touched a hand to her tear-ravaged cheek. "What ever is the matter, Pammie? I've never seen you cry like this. Not even when *Maman* died."

"I couldn't," Pamela confessed, croaking out a hiccup. "I had to be strong for you."

"There, there, dear," Sophie crooned, giving her hair another tender stroke. "Why don't you let me be strong for a little while?"

Although she would have sworn she didn't have a single tear left to weep, her sister's compassion opened a brand new floodgate. The whole story came spilling out of her then — between sobs and snuffles and hiccups and several brief pauses to honk loudly into the worn handkerchief Sophie held up to her nose.

By the time she was done, her eyes were nearly swollen shut and she was too exhausted from weeping to lift her head from her sister's lap.

"Let me see if I have this straight," Sophie

murmured, gently raking her fingers through Pamela's disheveled hair. "As long as Connor was a dangerous ruffian with a price on his head who was highly likely to get you both hanged before all was said and done, you were willing to marry him. But now that you've discovered he's a wildly wealthy nobleman who can give you everything you've ever dreamed of, you've tossed him aside like an old boot."

Without lifting her head, Pamela nodded, then shook her head, then nodded again.

"And all because you're so desperately noble and unselfish that you're determined to throw away your happiness — and his — just to prove it."

Pamela slowly lifted her head to look at her sister.

Sophie wrinkled her pert little nose at her. "Don't you see, Pamela? Connor is the best thing that ever happened to you. He makes you greedy. And selfish. And willing to do whatever it takes to get what you want. And judging by the noises that have been creeping beneath my door every night for the past week, I'd say that what you want is him."

"Of course I want him! I want him more than life itself! But I'm hardly duchess material."

"Oh, please! The man clearly adores you.

He doesn't care if you're a princess or a milkmaid. And besides," she added firmly, "if you won't marry him, I will." A vengeful little smile curved her lips. "And wouldn't that just serve his miserable cousin right!"

She rose, stretching and yawning like a graceful little cat, and padded back toward the dressing room. "If you manage to lure him back to your bed after you've told him what an idiot you've been, try to keep it down, won't you? I need my beauty sleep."

When her sister was gone, Pamela scrambled to her feet, joy surging in her heart. Suddenly, she felt deliciously greedy. And wildly selfish. And willing to do whatever it took — no matter how devious or wicked — to get what she wanted. And what she wanted was Connor. In her arms. In her bed. And in her life for every day — and night — that remained of it.

She started for the door, then stopped dead, letting out a terrible shriek when she came face to face with her own reflection in the cheval glass.

Somehow Connor knew he wouldn't find the ballroom deserted. Yet he ended up there anyway, traversing the alternating squares of moonlight and shadow until he stood before the portrait of the elegant young duchess he had known only as "Mother."

The duke wasn't gazing up at the portrait but down at the open locket in his hand. "I wish I could have known this woman," he said softly. "She looks so peaceful. As if she'd finally stopped striving for all the things she could never have."

"Like your fidelity?"

The duke snapped the locket closed. "She probably paid that old crone in Strathspey to tell everyone she was dead. She was a clever girl." A wistful smile touched his lips. "Too clever for the likes of me. After all — what better way for her to disappear and to protect you than to create another life for herself? With another name. Another family. Another man . . ."

"A good man," Connor assured him. "They had a daughter together. My sister Catriona."

The duke squinted up at him. "Was she happy then? Truly happy?"

Connor nodded. "I rarely saw her without a song or a smile on her lips."

"I'm glad for that. I wanted her to be happy. I'm only sorry I wasn't the man who could . . ." The duke trailed off, rubbing his thumb gently over the front of the locket. "She did love me, you know. Once."

"Of course she did. If she hadn't, you wouldn't have been able to break her heart."

"Did she . . . die well?"

Connor briefly squeezed his eyes shut, seeing that last tearful smile his mother had given the man she loved, hearing the distant echo of a pistol shot in his memory. "She would say so. And in the end, I suppose that's all that matters."

The two men gazed up at the lovely young woman in the portrait who had shaped both their lives — first by her presence, then by her absence.

It was Connor who finally broke the silence. "You should be amused. It turns out that I'm my father's son after all. Pamela is leaving me."

The duke's face crumpled in genuine dismay. "Oh, no, lad! You mustn't let her do that!"

"And just how am I to stop her?" Connor raked a hand through his hair, his frustration finally erupting in a bitter oath. "If we were back in Scotland, I could just kidnap her and force her to marry me at gunpoint, then keep her chained to my bed until I could persuade her that she belonged there. But what the hell am I supposed to do here among you *civilized* folk? Browbeat her? Threaten to sue her for breaching our betrothal contract?"

The duke grasped both arms of his chair and slowly leveraged himself to his feet. Connor watched in amazement as he took one unsteady step toward him, then another, finally drawing close enough to clap a hand firmly on his shoulder.

The man's shrewd hazel eyes were glittering with emotion. "Don't make the same mistake I did, son. Don't let pride stand in your way. Don't browbeat her. Don't threaten her. Love her. Simply love her."

Pamela sat on the stool in front of the dressing table, muttering to herself and frantically daubing rice powder on her nose with a hare's foot. She'd never been a pretty crier like Sophie, and her protracted episode of weeping had left her both swollen and splotchy.

She'd been trying to repair her face for nearly half an hour with indifferent results. She leaned back on the stool with a sigh, tossing the hare's foot back in the dish of powder. There was simply no help for it. If Connor was going to love her, he was going to have to love her even when she looked like a puffy-eyed lobster.

With any luck he would have already extinguished the candles in his bedchamber. She hugged back a delicious little shiver of anticipation, smiling to imagine his surprise when she slipped into his room and into his bed. She could only hope he wouldn't shoot her. Although given how much of a dunderhead she'd been earlier, she probably wouldn't blame him if he did.

She was rising from the stool when she heard a peculiar scritching noise coming from behind her. Her heart leaped with joy when she realized the sound was coming from the window.

She should have known a stubborn Scotsman like Connor wouldn't surrender that easily. Especially not to an equally stubborn English lass.

She flew over to unlatch the window and drag up the sash with eager hands. "Get in here this minute, you fool Highlander, before one of the footmen sees you and you ruin my reputation. Of course my reputation is probably in tatters anyway, after half of London watched me being hauled off in irons, so you might as well finish making a social pariah of me."

She backed away from the window, grinning in anticipation, as a figure garbed all in black climbed through it.

But when he straightened, her smile faded. The intruder was a good half foot shorter than Connor. And squatter — broad in both the shoulders and hips. He wore a crude burlap mask draped over his head with jagged slits for eyeholes.

He lunged for her, clapping a hand roughly over her mouth and cutting off her scream before even Sophie could hear it.

Connor stood outside of Pamela's door, gazing down at the crystal knob in his hand in disbelief. He gave it another experimental twist, followed by a violent jiggle. Nothing happened. This time the stubborn little minx had not only locked the window, but the door as well.

Connor sagged against the door, heaving a sigh. When he was handing out his sage advice, the duke might have warned him he was going to be reduced to begging outside a locked door. The old man had probably had ample experience at it.

"Pamela?" he said softly, trying to keep his voice low so that every nosy servant in the house wouldn't hear him. "I know you can hear me, so there's no point in pretending you can't."

Silence greeted his words.

"I know you've somehow gotten it into your bonny head that you're not good enough for the likes of me. But the truth is

I'm not fit to polish your boots. Being born a nobleman doesn't make me a noble man. You can call me your lord all you like, but I'm still that same thieving, no-count Highlander who stole your drawers.

"I'll never be worthy of a woman like you, but if you'll let me, I'd like to spend the remainder of my days striving to be." Remembering the duke's admonition not to let pride stand in his way, he rested his brow against the door. "I'm not my father. I love you, lass, and I've no intention of going through the rest of my life being the man who was fool enough to lose you."

He held his breath to listen, but didn't hear so much as a whisper of sound coming from within the room. He lifted his head to scowl at the door. He'd never judged Pamela to be so heartless.

He could feel his temper rising. "Damn it all, woman, I'm a marquess and I'm going to be a duke someday. This is *my* house and I order you to open this door at once and bloody well marry me!"

Reaching the limits of his rather limited patience, Connor lifted his foot and kicked the door open, sending it crashing against the wall on its broken hinges.

The room was deserted. For a staggering shard of time, Connor thought Pamela was already gone. But her trunk was still sitting open on the floor; the bed was still littered with dresses and shoes. Before he could go striding over to the dressing room door to demand some answers from her sister, it came flying open.

A bleary-eyed Sophie was jerking a knot in the sash of her dressing gown, her motions brisk and furious. "Just because you two lovebirds have better things to do than sleep, that doesn't mean the rest of us poor lonely souls don't need to . . ." She trailed off as she spotted Connor standing there all alone. A bewildered frown creased her brow. "Where's Pamela?"

"That's what I'd like to know," he said grimly. "Her door was locked. From the inside."

Sophie gazed up at him, a gentle breeze ruffling her hair.

Connor slowly turned, a chill of foreboding coursing down his spine. The window, which had been so carefully latched earlier, was standing wide open.

CHAPTER 28

When Crispin opened his eyes to find Sophie hovering over him like a celestial angel in a filmy white gown, he knew he must still be dreaming. Her blue eyes were quizzical and a gentle glow haloed her short golden curls.

Grinning sleepily, he reached up to draw her into his arms, eager to travel wherever this dream might take him.

A pair of hard hands jerked him out of the bed and slammed him against the nearest wall. His cousin's face loomed in his vision, its rugged features set in ruthless lines. "Where is she?"

Crispin blinked frantically, trying to figure out how his beautiful dream could have turned into a nightmare with such bewildering speed. He was still half drunk from sleep and all the champagne he'd imbibed after Sophie had doused him in the stuff. Shortly after she'd stormed out, he'd left the ballroom with a full bottle in each hand. He had made short work of them in the solarium, then stumbled off to his chamber to fall into bed with his clothes still on.

He was still incapable of forming a coherent thought — much less a word — when Connor slammed him into the wall a second time, making his already pounding head pound even louder.

"Where is she?"

Crispin gave Sophie a perplexed glance. "Why, she's right there beside you. Can't you see her?"

"I'm not talking about Sophie," Connor snarled. "I'm talking about Pamela. Where in the bloody hell is she?"

"How in the bloody hell am I supposed to know? She's *your* fiancée, isn't she?"

Crispin's nightmare worsened when a hulking figure separated itself from the shadows. He was wearing a long nightshirt and a tasseled nightcap. Copper braids poked out from beneath the nightcap like a writhing horde of Medusa's snakes. A gold tooth winked from the front of his mouth.

He leered at Crispin, cracking his massive knuckles as if he wished they were Crispin's spine. "Give me ten minutes alone with the lad and I'll make him talk."

Flummoxed anew, Crispin clutched at the

front of Connor's shirt. "Isn't that your valet?"

Sophie blew out a sigh. "You two are hopeless. Why don't you let me talk to him?"

She was forced to edge under Connor's arm when he refused to relinquish his grip on Crispin's cravat. Despite his befuddled state, Crispin had no trouble focusing on her lovely face.

"My sister Pamela is missing," she said, enunciating each word as if speaking to a child. "We have reason to believe she may have been taken against her will."

"Your sister? Ah ha! I knew you weren't her maid!"

"Yes, I'm afraid that was a bold-faced lie. Now we were hoping that you — or perhaps your mother — might have some information as to her whereabouts. Unfortunately, we can't question your mother because her bed is empty."

A helpless giggle escaped Crispin as he imagined them bursting into his mother's bedchamber and manhandling her in such a manner.

Connor shook him until his teeth rattled, forcing Sophie to beat a hasty retreat. "If you can't tell us where to find Pamela, then I'd strongly suggest you tell us where to find your mother."

Crispin snorted with laughter. "She's probably out collecting eye of newt or skinning some kittens to make a new pair of gloves."

Growling beneath his breath, Connor lifted him clean off his feet. For a dizzying moment, Crispin feared he was about to go sailing through the nearest window — without the benefit of having it opened first. But Connor simply tossed him back onto the bed before raking a hand through his hair in disgust.

Crispin's dream grew even stranger when a breathless footman in full livery came charging into the room. "There you are, my lord," he said, sketching Connor a hasty bow. "We've been searching the entire estate for you. This missive just arrived. The man who delivered it claimed it was urgent — a matter of life and death."

Connor snatched the folded piece of vellum from the servant's hand. While he scanned the lines scrawled on the paper, the footman eyed their odd little party with some trepidation. Connor's valet winked at him, which only seemed to worsen his agitation.

Sophie stood on tiptoe to peer over Connor's shoulder, a frown clouding her pretty brow. "I know this address. It's the Crown

Theatre on Drury Lane. The one where *Maman* died."

Ignoring the throbbing protest of his head, Crispin sat straight up in the bed. "I know that address as well. I took my mother there once so she could see Marianne Darby on the stage. Mother went to take tea with her a few times after that. I believe she saw her last on the very day she died."

Crispin finished his cheerful recitation to discover they were all looking at him as if he'd sprouted a second aching head.

Even after all these months, the smell of char and ruin still lingered in the air. Connor stepped over a crumbling timber, marveling that such a wasteland could have once been a thriving theater. The roof had collapsed in the flames that had devoured the building, leaving three towering walls still open to the sky.

Dawn would be coming soon, but judging from the dark bellies of the clouds brooding over the theater, it would bring with it not sunlight but rain.

Connor edged his way around a blackened column to find himself staring into the hollow eyes of a plaster cherub, its once elegant gilt veneer now blistered and peeling.

From behind him, Brodie let out a low

whistle. "If e'er there was a place for ghosts, laddie, this is it."

Connor glanced back at the cloaked girl gingerly picking her way after them, knowing she had more reason to fear the ghosts that haunted this place than they did. He'd brought Sophie along against all of his best instincts. The note he'd received had warned that Pamela's life would be forfeit if he notified the duke or the authorities that she was missing and Sophie had threatened to throw the tantrum of all tantrums if left behind. He could only pray that Pamela would have a chance to yell at him for letting himself be bullied by such a spoiled slip of a girl.

A footfall sounded to the left of them. Connor swung around, drawing his pistol.

Crispin slowly emerged from the morning mist that was creeping through the shattered beams of the collapsed galleries. He lifted his hands in the air, looking sober in more ways than one.

"What are you doing here?" Connor asked without lowering the pistol.

"I want to help. She's my mother. I might be able to reason with her." When Connor cocked a skeptical eyebrow, he added, "There's always a first time."

"Are you armed?"

Crispin nodded, opening his coat to reveal

a rapier and two dueling pistols.

Sophie sniffed. "What? Was the greengrocer all out of rotten cabbages?"

Disregarding Connor and the threat of his loaded pistol, Crispin lowered his hands to glare at her. "So you're willing to overlook the fact that my mother may very well have burned your mother to death in her bed, but you won't allow me to forget that bloody turnip, will you?"

"It was a *tomato*." Folding her arms over her chest, Sophie presented her back to him, her slender shoulders stiff.

Connor slid his pistol back into his belt with a sigh. "You can stay. But I'll expect you to do as I say." He nodded toward Sophie. "And if you get in my way, I'll let her shoot you."

Crispin nodded grimly, then fell into step behind them. When he tried to help Sophie over a splintered board, she jerked her elbow out of his reach.

As they ventured deeper into the blackened heart of the theater, measuring each step as if it would be their last, Connor could feel his own heart begin to pound in a painful rhythm. Since watching his parents die, he hadn't known a moment's fear over his own well-being — not even when the hangman had slipped that shoddily knotted noose over his head. No matter how desperate the situation, his hands had always been steady, his aim ever keen. But now there was something more precious at stake. Something he valued far beyond his own misbegotten life.

They were nearing the front of the theater when Sophie gasped as if she'd just seen the shade of her dead mother. Connor and Brodie instinctively drew their pistols.

It was no wraith that had materialized on the stage in front of them, but Lady Astrid. She no longer looked like the perfect lady. Her hair was as wild as her eyes and her white dress was rumpled and stained. Connor could only pray the stains were soot and not blood.

"Lady Astrid," he said coolly. "Or would it be Lady Macbeth?"

She lifted her chin to give him a smile that was almost flirtatious. "I believe it was Shakespeare who said, 'All the world's a stage and all the men and women merely players.' I'm guessing that would include you and your pretty little whore."

His finger twitched on the trigger. "Where is my fiancée?"

She crooked a pale finger toward stage left and a squat man wearing a crude burlap mask came shuffling onto the stage, shoving

421

Pamela in front of him. Her hands were bound behind her and a man's cravat had been used to gag her beautiful lips. When Connor saw the ugly bruise marring her creamy cheek, it was all he could do not to shoot Lady Astrid and her henchman dead right then and there.

But he couldn't take the risk because Pamela's captor had his burly arm locked beneath her breasts and the mouth of his own weapon rammed against the tender underside of her jaw. It was a delicate one-shot pistol — nearly identical to the one Pamela had used to take him hostage. Judging from the terrified glint in her eye, this one was no toy.

Connor had expected her eyes to light up with hope when she saw him, but instead they darkened with dread. She shook her head frantically, moaning around the gag.

Crispin stepped out of the shadows, his own pistol held at the ready and his face taut with revulsion. "What have you done now, Mother?"

Lady Astrid looked briefly surprised to see her son, but she recovered quickly. "What I've always had to do, my dear boy. Look after your best interests."

"My interests? Or yours? You know damn well I never gave a flying fig for Uncle's title or his fortune. I would have gladly traded them both for an approving pat on the head every now and then."

Her lips twisted in a sneer. "Then you're every bit as witless as your father was, aren't you? He hadn't a drop of ambition in his entire body. But he had an ample supply of brandy flowing through his veins, didn't he? I've always wondered if it made him burn faster when I left that cigar smoldering in his bed."

Sophie blanched but Crispin didn't even flinch. Connor knew in that moment that Crispin had been hiding his mother's terrible secret for most of his young life. That she must have somehow convinced a petrified young boy that he had to keep his silence because she had done it all for him. That he was to blame for his father's death.

Sophie edged nearer to Crispin, reaching out to gently touch his arm as he gazed up at his mother and said softly,

"Even as a boy I never knew whether to pray that you weren't mad or to hope that you were."

"We'll have plenty of time to sort out whether she belongs in Bedlam or Newgate *after* she frees Pamela," Connor said grimly. "What do you want from me?" he asked her.

Lady Astrid's voice was deadly calm.

"You're a Highlander. You should understand barter. The equation is simple. Her life for yours."

Connor snorted. "What are you going to do, woman? Shoot me dead in front of all these witnesses, including your own son? That's not really your style, is it? You don't usually like to dirty your lily-white hands."

"Nor will I have to."

Pamela began to struggle even more frantically, her tear-filled eyes silently pleading with him.

"I know just how squeamish the London authorities can be, especially when under the thumb of a man like my brother," Lady Astrid said. "Anticipating that tonight might not go as planned, I took the liberty of contacting an old family friend — a man who has always respected the letter of the law and the responsibility bestowed upon him by the Crown."

Connor's hand tensed on his pistol as two dozen English soldiers came melting out of the ruins, muskets at the ready. Before long, he and his party were surrounded on all sides by those hateful red coats. Their ranks parted just long enough to let their commanding officer through.

"I'm sure you remember Colonel Munroe," Lady Astrid said as if she were introducing the two of them at a tea party. "From what I understand, you made quite an impression on him at your last meeting."

As Connor eyed the gloating officer, he remembered standing in a sunlit meadow with Pamela by his side. Remembered how she had boldly defied the colonel and passionately defended him, even though he'd done nothing to deserve it.

The colonel locked his hands at the small of his back, taking up his familiar bowlegged stance. "I must say it's a pleasure to see you again."

Connor bared his teeth at the man. "I'm afraid I can't say the same."

Lady Astrid beamed at them both. "Colonel Munroe has graciously agreed to escort you back to Scotland, where you will stand trial for your many crimes."

Brodie growled beneath his breath.

"And if I were you," she added, "I wouldn't expect my brother to save you. Even *his* arm can't reach as far as the Highlands. But don't worry — I'll make sure your little strumpet gets the reward she was promised. I'm sure she earned every halfpenny of it on her back."

Connor turned in a broad circle, sweeping his gaze and the mouth of his pistol over the steely-eyed redcoats who surrounded them — weighing his options, weighing the odds.

"Oh, you can fight if you like," Astrid assured him with an airy wave of her hand. "But I should remind you how easy it will be for your poor fiancée to get caught in the crossfire."

Connor knew there would be no crossfire. Just Lady Astrid's henchman pulling the trigger of his pistol and blowing Pamela's brave and bonny head clean off.

By the time his gaze returned to Pamela, there was no Munroe. No redcoats. No Lady Astrid. There were only the two of them.

Connor smiled at her the same way his mother had smiled at Davey Kincaid in the moment before she'd pulled the trigger that had ended her life. With all his heart, with all his soul, and with every expectation that someday they would be together again — if not in this life, then in the next.

Pamela was keening low in her throat now, tears streaming down her cheeks to soak the gag. She shook her head and strained against her captor's grip, silently begging Connor not to do what he was about to do.

He heard Brodie groan and Sophie gasp as he laid down his pistol and slowly raised his hands. The redcoats swarmed around him, wrenching his powerful arms behind his back and clapping them in irons.

He did not look at Pamela again but simply stared straight ahead as they marched him from the theater and out of her life.

CHAPTER 29

Catriona Wescott gazed down at the letter in her hand through a shimmering haze of tears. A footman had delivered it only moments ago, interrupting the nap she and her husband were about to take with their two wee poppets. The children were still curled up in the blankets of their bed, fast asleep and blissfully unaware of their mother's agitation.

"What is it, darling?" Simon asked. He was standing beside the bed, his green eyes darkened with concern.

She glanced up at him, eager to show him that her face was alight with joy, not sorrow. "It's from my brother. It's from Connor. He's alive!"

Simon leaned over the bed, giving her shoulder a tender squeeze as she tore open the letter with shaking hands. Connor had disappeared from her life more than fourteen years ago and from his own life more than five years ago. She'd been searching for him ever since returning to the Highlands to claim Castle Kincaid, but to no avail. The clansmen who had ridden by his side for more than a decade and who now served her had all warned her that if Connor Kincaid didn't want to be found, he wouldn't be.

She tore open the letter with shaking hands, fresh tears springing to her eyes when she saw the familiar scrawl inside.

My wee kitten,

Since I have no way of knowing if you ever received the letters I sent all those years ago when you were just a girl, I realize this missive may come as something of a shock.

They are going to hang me for my crimes and when I'm gone, there will be some who will tell you I was a bad man. But I'm here to tell you that the love of a good woman made something better of me, if only for a short while.

It might also be a shock to learn that I have seen the woman you have become and that it made my heart sing with pride. Tell that handsome Englishman of yours that if he doesn't treat you well, I will return from beyond the grave to haunt him. As for those two bonny wee bairns of yours, never let them forget that they are not only Wescotts, but Kincaids.

After I am gone you may hear things about our mother as well, but all you need to remember is that you have every reason to be proud of her. She was a true lady in every sense of the word, just as you are. Godspeed, my dear kitten. I will ever be . . .

Your devoted brother,
Connor

Catriona lifted her stricken eyes to her husband's face. "Oh, Simon, we have to do something! He's writing to say good-bye. They're going to hang him!"

As they clapped the irons on his wrists and led him from the jail, Connor squinted up at the stark silhouette of the gallows. They were as familiar to him as a dear friend or an old lover. Even during those brief stolen moments of joy he had found in Pamela's arms, somehow he'd always known they'd be waiting for him at the end of his journey.

This was one dance to which he knew all the steps.

He marched between two redcoats, a

balmy breeze ruffling his hair. It was a glorious Highland afternoon, with fluffy white clouds drifting across the crisp blue canopy of the sky. A lark was trilling somewhere in the distance and the rich smell of Caledonian pine scented every breath.

Connor drew a breath deep into his lungs, knowing it would be one of his last. He scowled, haunted by a faint whiff of lilac that seemed to be dancing on the wind. His final regret in a lifetime of many was that he would never again inhale that intoxicating scent from Pamela's hair, never know another taste of her sweet lips.

He'd never even told her how much he loved her. He'd told her bedchamber door, but somehow he didn't think that counted for much when all was said and done.

He and his stony-faced escorts reached the foot of the gallows far too soon. Connor's gaze traveled up the broad wooden steps to find the masked hangman waiting for him at the top of the platform, his patience enduring but not inexhaustible. Connor closed his eyes briefly, hearing once again the creaking of the rope as his father's body swayed against the night sky. He was forced to open them when one of the soldiers gave him a harsh shove.

As Connor began to climb the steps, the

hangman folded his arms over his chest, his sleeveless vest showing off his bulging muscles to their most intimidating advantage.

Connor had nearly reached the top of the platform when he heard a burst of merry chatter and a ripple of feminine laughter. He turned to find scores of well-dressed gawkers pouring onto the lawn that surrounded the gallows, parasols and picnic baskets in hand. All of the women wore bonnets and the men wore hats to shade their fair skin from the afternoon sun, leaving their faces in shadow.

Connor snorted. He should have known the English would come to watch him hang. As far as they were concerned, there was no finer entertainment than watching a Scotsman's neck snap at the end of a rope. Not even fox hunting or horse racing could compare.

He shook his head in wry disbelief as they spread out their lap rugs and settled down to unpack their afternoon tea. If he wasn't fortunate enough to break his neck in the initial fall, they could savor the added delight of watching him gasp and twitch and kick his last while they sipped their wine or nibbled a freshly baked biscuit.

He glanced at the man calmly watching

the proceedings from the balcony of the jail, knowing that Colonel Munroe would be delighted to have an audience for their little farce. Perhaps he could even use it to wrangle a promotion from his superiors.

The soldiers guided him to the trap door while the hangman took up his position at the lever, his eyes glittering through the eyeholes of the dark sack covering his head.

When they offered Connor a similar mask, he shook his head. After watching his parents die, he wasn't about to hide from his own death. He would leave this life as he'd lived it — with eyes wide open and fixed on the freedom promised by the sky.

One of the soldiers was draping the noose over his neck when a disturbance broke out below.

Connor squinted against the sun to find a slender woman shoving her way through the crowd of gawkers. She wore a long black hooded cloak as if she was already in mourning.

She ran up to the soldiers stationed at the foot of the platform and caught one of them by the front of his scarlet coat, her voice rising on a note of hysteria. "You have to let me see him! He's my brother and I haven't seen him in nearly fifteen years." Her voice caught on a heartrending sob. "Oh, please, you have to let me say good-bye!"

Connor felt as if his own heart was being rent in two. He'd had no way of knowing if his letter would reach Catriona before he was gone. As he witnessed her anguish, he was almost sorry it had.

When the young soldier firmly detached her hands from the front of his coat, shooting the other soldier a disgusted look, she dropped to her knees and threw her arms around his thighs. "Please, sir, I beg you! If you've an ounce of Christian mercy in your soul, you'll at least let me give him a kiss of farewell."

"Let the poor chit say good-bye!" someone called out from the crowd.

"One kiss won't hurt," a man shouted. "After all, 'twill be his last."

A chorus of catcalls quickly rose from their audience as the woman's piteous pleas shifted the mood in Connor's favor.

"Colonel?" The young soldier looked to his commanding officer, his face flushed with uncertainty.

Both Connor and Munroe knew exactly what harm it might do to the colonel's reputation should word get out that he had denied a condemned man's sister her last chance to say good-bye. "Oh, very well," Munroe snapped. "But tell her to make it quick. Kincaid has wasted enough of my time already."

The crowd fell into a respectful silence as Catriona slowly climbed the steps with her head bowed and the hood still shielding her face. Connor hadn't wanted his sister's last memory of him to be with his wrists in irons and his neck in a noose, but there wasn't much he could do about that now.

He stiffened as she slipped her slender arms around his waist, filling his nostrils with the impossible fragrance of lilac water. She tipped her head back, revealing an impish smile and a pair of sparkling amber eyes.

"Hello, brother dear," she said in a husky murmur. "Miss me?"

CHAPTER 30

For an agonizing moment Connor thought his heart was going to stop, sparing the redcoats the bother of hanging him. He strained against the irons, desperate to wrap his arms around Pamela, even though he knew he ought to be shaking her insensible for taking such a terrible risk.

He lowered his mouth to her ear, his own voice a frantic whisper. "Have you lost your wits, lass? If Munroe recognizes you, he'll have no qualms about hanging you right alongside me."

Her lips moved against his throat, their irresistible softness caressing the old rope scars they found there. "Which is exactly where I'd want to be . . . *if* you were going to hang." She let out a muffled sob for the benefit of the soldiers, tightening her grip on his waist and burying her face in his chest.

Connor nearly laughed aloud. Here he

was standing at the very gates of hell itself and she still had the power to arouse him. Never more so than when she slipped the key to the irons she had pilfered from the hapless soldier at the bottom of the steps into his hand.

He clenched his fist around it, shielding it from the soldiers' eyes. "And just what am I supposed to do now?"

"Wait," she whispered. She tipped her head back again, eyeing him with open longing. "What about that kiss I was promised?"

Connor knew he should brush her cheek with a brotherly peck. That's what everyone would expect of him. But he'd spent too many long days since the redcoats had dragged him away from her dreaming of this moment. Too many lonely nights dreaming of other moments he'd spent in her arms . . . and her bed. If this was to be their last kiss, he had every intention of making it one she would remember for the rest of her life.

Knowing he was risking everything, he leaned down and brushed his lips against hers, coaxing her to open for him so he could drink deeply of her sweetness. She kissed him back with a tender fierceness that tasted of love and hope and all the dreams he'd surrendered on the night his parents had died.

As the crowd on the lawn hooted and whistled, one of the soldiers on the platform nudged his wide-eyed companion. "Two of them must have been close."

"That's enough," Munroe shouted in disgust. "Remove the woman at once. It's savage rabble like this who give decent, God-fearing Scots a bad name."

Before the soldiers could lay their hands on her to drag her away, Pamela separated herself from Connor. With the dignity befitting a soon-to-be-bereaved sister, she adjusted the hood of her cloak, bowed her head and retreated down the stairs.

She melted back into the crowd without a backward glance. If not for the icy metal of the key burning a hole in his fist, Connor might have believed he'd imagined her. That the hangman had already pulled the lever, leaving his air-starved brain to conjure up one last beautiful, feverish dream.

"Let's have done with this!" Munroe shouted, flexing his hands on the balcony rail. "My tea is cooling."

The soldiers retreated to either side of the platform. The hangman rested his hand on the lever. For the first time, Connor saw the familiar tattoo of a serpent writhing on the bulging muscles of his upper arm. Hope surged in his heart, forcing him to bite back a grin.

That grin faded with the first ugly call of "Hang the bastard!"

"Stretch his miserable neck!"

"Hang him! Hang him!" the onlookers began to shout in unison, the virulence of their rising chant making even the soldiers look uneasy.

Connor watched as one of the gawkers reached into his picnic basket and retrieved a shiny red tomato. As it came sailing through the air, he braced himself, helpless to avoid its impact.

But the tomato hit the soldier closest to him square in the face, eliciting a startled yelp. The man was still swiping pulp from his eyes when a fat cabbage flew past Connor, striking the second soldier so hard it knocked him clean off the platform. Suddenly the air was full of flying produce, all of it aimed at the hapless redcoats. Before long, they were all staggering about, half blind and cursing.

That quickly, Connor had the irons unlocked. As the chains clanked to the platform, Brodie jerked off his hangman's hood and tossed him a pistol, his gold tooth winking in the middle of his familiar grin.

Connor watched in amazement as the

crowd took advantage of the chaos they had created. They dropped their parasols and whipped off their hats and bonnets in one smooth motion to reveal that most of them were men. This time when they reached into the picnic baskets, their hands didn't emerge with produce but with pistols. Pistols they quickly trained on the English soldiers.

Connor swung his own pistol toward the balcony only to find it deserted. Munroe had always been a coward when not backed by a battalion of soldiers. When Connor saw a single horse with a lone red-coated rider go thundering down the road in a cloud of dust, he knew that the colonel had beat a wise and hasty retreat, preferring to run so he could live to fight another day.

As Connor and Brodie descended the steps, the redcoats reluctantly tossed down their weapons, realizing they were both outnumbered and out-armed. After that, it only took a handful of men to round them up and herd them toward the gatehouse, where they could be safely secured before they had time to gather their wits and decide to hang the whole lot of them.

As Connor tucked his pistol in the waistband of his breeches, a woman appeared at the bottom of the hill. Throwing off her cumbersome black cloak, she came sprinting up the hill and into his arms, her face alight with joy.

Connor lifted her clean off the ground, crushing her to his chest while sweeping her in a wide circle. "You wee fool! I always said you had more courage than common sense and now you've gone and proved it."

She beamed up at him as he reluctantly set her on her feet. "We didn't have any choice. The duke is on his way here with a full pardon from the king, but we knew he wouldn't arrive in time to save you. We had to do something."

He glowered at her. "So you decided to just rush in and rescue me all on your own."

"Well, not exactly . . ."

She stepped aside, giving him a clear view of the rest of his rescuers for the first time. He spotted Crispin first, surrounded by a dozen or more cocky young bucks, most of them still grinning with delight.

Crispin sauntered forward, jerking a thumb at his friends. "Most of them were bored with the brothels and the gambling tables and wanted a more scintillating challenge than just dunking some hapless stranger in a horse trough."

"And what about you?" Connor asked. "Were you bored as well?"

Crispin shrugged, keeping his face carefully bland. "I figured it was the least I could do after what my mother did to you."

"We won't have to worry about Lady Astrid anymore," Pamela assured him, shooting Crispin an awkward glance. "When the duke found out what she did, he had her committed to Bedlam. She has private quarters with a private nurse. He believed it would be kinder than Newgate."

Connor studied the fresh tomato spattered across Crispin's cheek and down the front of his shirt. "Did you suffer from friendly fire, lad?"

"I wouldn't exactly call it friendly." Crispin's eyes narrowed. "I'm afraid some of us don't have very good aim."

"On the contrary," Sophie said, twirling her ruffled parasol as she sashayed forward. "Some of us have perfect aim."

"Does this make us even then?" Crispin asked her, swiping tomato pulp from his cheek.

"I should say not. You still called me an awful actress."

"Well, you called me an awful man."

"You *are* an awful man."

"I'm a better man than you are an actress."

Biting off a strangled shriek of rage, Sophie spun around and went storming off, with Crispin fast on her heels.

Pamela sighed. "Do you think she'll ever forgive him?"

"Not if she's smart," Connor replied with a knowing smirk. "Although maybe we should have warned him about the parasol."

His smile faded as a second group approached and he began to recognize many of his own clansmen. They were men he had ridden with for years before becoming a highwayman. Young Callum, no longer a gangly boy, but a man. Handsome Donel, whose sly tongue was always getting him into trouble. Cocky, rawboned Kieran — the dearest friend he'd ever had. And a host of others who had once been as close to him as brothers.

"How?" he whispered hoarsely. "How did you come to be here?"

Pamela stepped aside as the men parted to reveal a woman in a stylish pink bonnet. She shyly came forward, followed by a tall, broad-shouldered, golden-haired man who was eyeing Connor with more than a hint of wariness.

Connor's breath caught in his throat as the woman lifted her chin, revealing the face beneath the bonnet. He had once known her as a freckled moppet with a wild tangle of strawberry curls. Now she was a striking young woman with an adoring husband and two freckled moppets of her own.

"My wee kitten," he whispered, touching a trembling hand to her cheek.

"You're the only one I've ever allowed to call me that, you know," Catriona said, tears shining in her misty gray eyes. "I thought I was going mad when I saw you in London. I thought I'd conjured you up out of thin air because I still missed you so badly. But when we ran into Pamela and her men when we were on the way here to try to stop them from hanging you, I discovered that you had been real all along."

Her pretty face crumpled as she threw her arms around his neck just as she used to do when she was a little girl. Connor squeezed his eyes shut and crushed her against him. The last time he'd held her like this, they had been two terrified children with only each other to cling to in a world gone mad. Now when they stepped out of each other's embrace, there would be other arms waiting to enfold them.

Connor reluctantly surrendered her to her husband, watching as the handsome Englishman whisked a perfectly starched handkerchief from his waistcoat pocket and handed it to her.

The two men sized each other up for several minutes before Simon finally said,

"I'm relieved to know I won't have to worry about you returning from beyond the grave to haunt me."

Connor studied him through narrowed eyes. "If you ever treat her badly, I can haunt you even more easily from this side of the grave."

Simon gave him a lazy grin. "You know — I can't wait for you to meet your namesake. Our own little Connor can scowl just as fiercely when we make him wash behind his ears."

Still chuckling, he led his wife to the shade of a nearby elm, leaving Connor standing there with his mouth hanging open.

When Pamela slipped her arm through his, he said, "They have a lad named Connor. Did you know that?"

"I did. And a little girl named Francesca," she gently informed him.

"Francesca," he whispered.

It was the name he and Catriona had known their mother by. She had kept her secrets close to her heart, preventing him from knowing her as well as he would have liked. And she had died far too young, preventing him from knowing her as long as he would have liked. But to have known her at all had been a great privilege.

He turned to Pamela as something occurred to him. "If Catriona was here the whole time, then why did you pretend to be my sister?"

"Oh, please! I knew I could play the role of your sister far more convincingly than she could."

"Ah, yes, that kiss was *very* convincing."

She rested her hands on her hips. "You were the one who kissed me."

"Only after you begged. And I should point out that you kissed me back. With a great deal of *sisterly* enthusiasm."

"Well, I have always wanted a brother," she admitted.

He cupped her cheek in his hand, stroking his thumb over the softness of her lips. "What about a husband? Would you care to have one of those instead?"

"Hmmmm . . . I'm not sure. Since your father is doing so well and has even abandoned his chair for a walking stick, you may not be able to make me a duchess for quite some time." She sighed. "I'm just not sure I could settle for being a mere marchioness."

Connor tugged her into his arms with a growl. "Have you forgotten that we're back in the Highlands, you wicked lass? If you refuse my suit this time, I'll just get Brodie to help me kidnap you and force you to marry me at gunpoint. Then I'll keep you chained to my bed until I can persuade you that you belong there."

"Which, if memory serves me correctly," Pamela replied breathlessly, "would probably take about three minutes." She lowered her eyes shyly. "If you must know, I was thinking that we should probably stop at Gretna Green on the way back to England and let one of those blacksmiths marry us. I wouldn't want our first babe to be born on the wrong side of the blanket."

"Our first babe?" Connor scowled down at her until comprehension slowly dawned, leaving him slack-jawed with astonishment.

He nudged her chin up with his finger and Pamela nodded, joyful tears shimmering in those extraordinary eyes of hers. "I'm afraid your devoted efforts to get an heir on me as quickly as possible have met with success."

He reached down to cup a reverent hand over her belly, marveling that the child they had made could be growing inside her slender body.

She grinned up at him through her tears. "If it's a boy, do you think your father is going to insist that we call him Percy?"

"If he does, I'm afraid I'll have to shoot him."

Pamela laughed aloud as he swept her into a dizzying embrace, raining kisses down on her upturned face.

A disgusted voice interrupted their joyful reunion. "Now, there's somethin' I never thought I'd live to see."

Connor reluctantly lifted his head. "And what's that, Brodie?"

The Highlander shook his head, his braids waggling in mock disapproval. "Connor Kincaid surrenderin' to the English without even puttin' up a fight."

"Oh, he put up quite a fight," Pamela assured him, patting Connor's chest.

"I most certainly did," Connor said. "But even the bravest and boldest warrior knows when it's time to lay down his arms."

Ignoring Brodie's snort, Connor crushed Pamela's lips beneath his in a tender and fierce kiss, joyfully surrendering his freedom and his future to the bonny English lass who had captured his heart.

EPILOGUE

As Pamela carried a piping hot tray of short-bread onto the terrace, a plump yellow kitten darted between her ankles, nearly sending her sprawling. While she regained her balance, swearing softly beneath her breath, the cat retreated to lick its front paw and give her an offended look — making her feel as if she had deliberately set out to crush a kitten or two beneath her heel before the morning was done.

The kitten and its four siblings delighted in frolicking beneath their feet at every opportunity. Even the shortest stroll or jaunt down the stairs had become an exercise in survival. At least the mother cat was content to spend her days stretched out on the low stone wall surrounding the terrace, basking in the warm September sun.

Pamela might not have been so clumsy if she hadn't felt so ungainly. But the babe inside of her seemed to be growing as fast as the kittens.

As she approached the wrought-iron table where Connor was jotting down figures in a set of leather ledgers, she held the pan out in front of her, displaying it proudly. "Look, darling. I baked you some more short-bread."

Connor groaned. "Oh, dear Lord, not again."

Pushing the ledgers aside, she set the pan on the table. "I do believe it's my best effort yet."

"Well, I can't argue with that," he said, tentatively poking the smoldering lump of dough with his finger. "You know — I don't understand why you don't just let Cookie make the shortbread. After all, the duke did send her all the way from London to be our cook."

"And when would she have time? Ever since she and Brodie eloped, I can't get either one of them out of bed."

Connor slipped an arm around her waist, drawing her into his lap and nuzzling her neck. "Perhaps we should follow their example."

Pamela wrapped her arms around his neck, shivering with delight. Connor had loved her body when it was new to him and he loved it even more now that it was ripe with his child. She knew at least one Scot who did have insatiable carnal appetites and she took great delight in satisfying them at every opportunity.

She rested her head on his shoulder, feeling as warm and content as the mama cat as she gazed out over the breathtaking vista before her.

She had finally gotten her cottage by the sea. Who knew that one of the duke's largest holdings was on the east coast of Scotland? The stone manor house perched on the majestic cliffs overlooking the North Sea was so vast and sprawling that she and Connor still both got lost occasionally and had to find their way back to each other.

For a semi-reformed highwayman, Connor had settled quite comfortably into the role of lord of the manor. He'd spent the last few months welcoming the Scottish tenants back to the land and teaching them how to manage the sheep that had displaced them. Swayed by his influence, several of the local English landowners had begun to do the same.

"I got a letter from Sophie today," Pamela informed him. "She's coming for Christmas."

"Uh-oh," he said. "I got a letter from Crispin today. He's coming for Christmas too."

"Don't worry. I won't tell her. We'll let it be a surprise," Pamela said, already gleefully anticipating her sister's reaction. "I'm afraid Crispin is going to be quite distraught when he discovers she's cajoled the duke into sending her to Paris to study acting as soon as the war is officially over."

Connor snorted. "If she takes to the stage again, Crispin won't be the only one distraught. They might just decide to bring back the guillotine."

Pamela began to count potential guests on her fingers. "So if Sophie and Crispin and Catriona and Simon and their brood and your clansmen and their families and the duke all come for Christmas, we're going to have quite a houseful."

Connor gently rested his hand on the impressive mound of her belly. "With any luck we'll be able to add one more to the guest list before Christmas Day arrives."

"Ah, yes, wee Percy!"

He gave her a look that made her glad he no longer carried a loaded pistol. At least not all the time.

She offered him a tender kiss to soften his scowl. "If it's a boy, we'll call him David — Davey for short, just like your da," she said, referring to the man who had finally given his mother a future — and a love — she could believe in.

"And if it's a girl," Connor assured her, "we'll call her Marianne, after your mother."

She rested her cheek against his, gazing out over the tumultuous sea. "Are you ever bored, my love? Do you ever miss being a highwayman?"

"Are you joking? Between those blood-thirsty kittens and your shortbread, every day is a new adventure. I was more afraid this life would be too tame for a lass like you. A lass accustomed to swindling men out of their inheritances . . . and their hearts."

"Well, I might be a wee bit bored at this very minute," she confessed, giving his ear a teasing nibble. "Perhaps I just need some big, strong highwayman to carry me off and have his way with me."

"Well, you don't have to ask twice, lass."

She squealed as Connor swept her up in his arms and started across the terrace, his effortless strength making her feel as if she wasn't the size of a small cow.

"Look out!" she shrieked as one of the kittens darted into their path.

He stepped over it without breaking his stride, as eager as she was to embark upon their next grand adventure.